One Fell Sweep

One Fell Sweep

Innkeeper Chronicles

Ilona Andrews

This ebook is licensed to you for your personal enjoyment only.

This ebook may not be sold, shared, or given away.

This is a work of fiction. Names, characters, places, and incidents are either products of the writer's imagination or are used fictitiously and are not to be construed as real. Any resemblance to actual events, locales, organizations, or persons, living or dead, is entirely coincidental.

One Fell Sweep
Copyright © 2016 by Ilona Andrews
ISBN: 9781540857217
Edited by Lora Gasway

ALL RIGHTS RESERVED.

No part of this work may be used, reproduced, or transmitted in any form or by any means, electronic or mechanical, without prior permission in writing from the publisher, except in the case of brief quotations embodied in critical articles or reviews.

NYLA Publishing
350 7th Avenue, Suite 2003, NY 10001, New York.
http://www.nyliterary.com

To Lora Gasway
Thank you for everything. We miss you and deeply regret your passing.

Chapter 1

A faint chime tugged me out of sleep. I opened my eyes and blinked. I'd dreamt of a desert, a vast endless sea of shifting yellow sand under a white sun. I had wandered through it, ankle-deep and barefoot, feeling the grains of sand slide under my toes with each sinking step, trying to find something or someone. I had looked for hours, but found only more sand. The soothing ceiling of my dark bedroom was too much of a shock after the sunlit dunes, and for a confusing moment, I didn't know where I was.

Magic chimed in my head again, brushing against my senses, feather-light and quick, but insistent. Someone had skimmed the boundary of the inn.

I swung my feet to the wooden floor, picked up my broom, and went down the shadowy hallway. Beast, my tiny Shih Tzu, darted from under the bed and trailed me, ready to attack unknown invaders. It was five days before Christmas, and I wasn't expecting guests, especially not at two o'clock in the morning. But then, of course, when Gertrude Hunt Bed and Breakfast did receive guests, they were never the usual kind and they rarely announced themselves.

The hallway ended in a door. I swiped the knitted cardigan hanging on the hook to the right of the door, wrapped myself in it, and slid my feet into a pair of slippers. This

December started with a flood and then turned unseasonably cold. At night, the temperature got down into the low thirties, which in Texas terms meant the apocalypse had to be nigh. Going outside was like stepping into a freezer, while the inside of the inn was warm and toasty, so I bundled up when I went out, then shed sweatshirts and cardigans at random doorways when I came back in.

The door swung open in front of me and I stepped out onto the balcony.

The cold air hit me. Wow.

The moon shone brightly, spilling silver light through the gauzy shreds of night clouds. My apple orchard stretched to the left. Directly in front of me a huge old oak tree spread its branches over the lawn, limbs nearly touching the balcony. To the right, Park Street ran parallel to the inn. Exactly opposite Gertrude Hunt, Camelot Road shot off Park Street, leading deep into the Avalon subdivision, filled with the usual two-story Texas houses with old trees on the trimmed lawns and dark vehicles parked in the driveways.

All was quiet.

I probed the night with my senses. The inn and I were bound so tightly that I could feel every inch of the grounds, if I chose. The intruder had touched the boundary but hadn't entered, and now he or she hid.

I waited, trying to keep my teeth from chattering. My breath made tiny clouds that melted into the night.

Silence.

Someone was out there, watching me. I could feel the weight of their gaze. Shivers of fear or cold ran down my spine. Probably both.

"I know you're there. Come out."

Silence.

I peered into the night, scrutinizing the familiar landscape. The row of hedges separating Park Street from my lawn appeared undisturbed. No strange footprints crossed the lawn. Nothing hid in the oak tree, nothing rustled the bushes behind it, nothing troubled the cedar twenty feet behind the bushes...

Two amber eyes stared at me from the shadows under the cedar. I almost jumped.

"Sean!" He nearly gave me a heart attack.

Sean Evans didn't move, a darker shadow in the deep night. Several months ago, we'd met just like this, except that time he was marking his territory on my apple trees. Now he just waited, silent, respecting the boundaries of the inn.

"Come closer," I called, keeping my voice low. No need to wake up the entire neighborhood. "I don't want to shout."

He moved, a blur, ran up to the oak, leapt, bounced, and landed on the branch near the balcony. Déjà vu.

Beast woofed once, quietly, just to let him know she was there in case he decided to try anything.

"Is something wrong?"

I scrutinized his face. When Sean first moved into the Avalon subdivision, he'd caused a mild epidemic of swooning. If someone looked up "ex-military badass" in the dictionary, they would find his picture. He was closing on thirty, with a handsome face he kept clean-shaven, russet-brown hair cut short, and an athletic, powerful body. He was strong and fast, and crossing him was a dumb idea. He was also a werewolf without a planet, something the overwhelming majority of people on Earth had no idea existed. Several months ago, while Sean helped me defend the Avalon subdivision from an interstellar assassin, he'd learned about his origins and then left to find himself. He ended up being trapped in an interstellar war in a place called Nexus, and it took all my resources to break him free of it.

The war took a toll. A long scar now marked his face. The pre-Nexus Sean had been arrogant and aggressive. This new Sean was quiet and patient, and if you peered into his clear amber eyes, you would find a steel hardness. Sometimes you would see nothing at all, as if you were gazing into the eyes of a tiger. No hunger, no rage, just an inscrutable watchfulness. Sean and I had gone to the movies three nights ago, and a drunk guy tried to pick a fight with us outside the theater after the show. Sean looked at him, and whatever that man saw in Sean's eyes must've cut right through the alcohol haze, because the drunk turned around without a word and walked away.

I could handle the arrogance and the anger, but that watchful nothing alarmed me. He hid it well enough. I saw him have conversations with people around the neighborhood, and none of them ran away screaming. But the nothing was still there. He didn't say more than two words to me through the whole evening. With his other neighbors, he took pains to pretend to be normal, but I knew exactly what he went through. With me he was himself, and that Sean held the door open for me, offered me his jacket when he thought I was cold, and put himself between me and the drunk, but he wasn't talking. Whatever he had lived through on Nexus had pushed him outside the normal human life and I wasn't sure I could pull him back into the light.

"How did you know?" he asked. "I stayed off the inn grounds."

"The peace summit gave the inn a boost. Gertrude Hunt is spreading its roots and you skimmed the zone of the new growth." I pushed slightly. The boundary of the inn glowed with pale green for a second and faded again. "That's the new boundary."

"Sorry," he said. "I'll keep it in mind. I didn't mean to wake you."

"Couldn't sleep?" I pulled the cardigan tighter around myself.

"Just have a feeling, that's all."

"What kind of feeling?"

"Like something is going to happen."

"If something is going to happen, we might as well wait inside."

And I just invited him in. In the middle of the night. While wearing a cardigan and a Hello Kitty sleeping T-shirt that barely came to my mid-thigh. What exactly was I doing?

"Do you want to come in?" My mouth just kept going. "I'll make you a cup of tea."

Brilliant.

An amber sheen rolled over his eyes. "At two o'clock in the morning real men drink coffee. Black."

He took his coffee with cream. Was that a joke? Please be a joke.

"Aha. And do they wait to drink it until it's old and bitter and then compare the chest hair growth it produced?"

"Possibly."

Definitely a joke. Hope sparked inside me. It was tiny, but it was so much better than nothing.

"Well, if any men here would dare to drink a cup of sissy hazelnut coffee with lots of cream, they are welcome to come inside."

He leaned a little closer. "Are you inviting me in?" His voice held just a touch of suggestion to it.

Suddenly I wasn't so cold anymore. "Well, you're already here, it's freezing, and we can't just stand here on the balcony and talk. Someone might see us and get the wrong idea."

Actually, nobody would see us, because it was the middle of the night and if we got in trouble, the inn would screen us from the street.

He leapt off the branch and landed softly next to me. He was so very... tall. And standing too close. And looking at me.

"Wouldn't people get the wrong idea if they see me sneaking into your house in the middle of the night?"

I opened my mouth, trying to think of something clever to say.

The sky above Park Street split in an electric explosion of yellow lightning and spat a boost bike.

Sean whipped around.

The needle-shaped aboveground craft tore down the road a foot above the payment, its engine roaring loud enough to wake the dead. The windows in the inn vibrated. Car alarms blared down the street.

Oh no.

The deafening blast of sound receded and came back, growing louder. The idiot had turned around and was coming back this way. Sean took off, leaping over the balcony.

"Smother cannon," I barked.

The roof of the inn split open, the shingles flowing like melted wax, and a three-foot-long cannon barrel slid out.

The boost bike thundered, engine roaring.

Lights came on in the two closest houses. Damn it.

The boost bike shot into my view.

"Fire."

The cannon made a metallic *ting*. The lights in the Ramirez residence went out. The lamp post turned dark. The engine of the boost bike died like someone had thrown a switch.

An electromagnetic pulse is a terribly useful thing.

The bike spun, rotating wildly, crashed into a lamppost and bounced off, landing on the pavement, and skidding to a stop. Twenty feet from the inn's boundary. Crap.

In a moment Mr. Ramirez would realize his lights refused to come on and he would do exactly what most men did in this situation. He'd come outside to check if the rest of the neighborhood had lost power. He would see us and the boost bike that clearly didn't look like it belonged on Earth.

I leapt over the balcony. A massive root snaked out of the ground, catching me, and set me gently on the grass. I dashed to the street, the broom in my hand splitting to reveal its glowing blue insides and flowing into a spear with a hook on the end.

Sean darted to the bike, grabbed the small passenger, and threw him backward toward the inn. Roots snatched him out of the air, the lawn yawned, and they dragged him under. I hooked the boost bike with my spear. Sean grasped the other edge, strained, and we half-dragged, half-carried it to the inn's boundary.

Behind me a door swung open. Sean grunted, I cried out, and we heaved the bike and my broom over the hedge. I spun around and faced the street.

Mr. Ramirez walked out, his Rhodesian Ridgeback, Asad, trailing him.

"Dina," Mr. Ramirez said. "Are you okay?"

No, I'm not okay. "Some dimwit just drove his bike up and down the street!"

I didn't even have to manufacture the outrage in my voice. I had outrage to spare. All visitors to Earth had to follow one rule: never let themselves be discovered. That was the entire purpose of the inns. I'd had too many close calls already and as soon as I got inside, the rider of the boost bike would deeply regret it.

"We're fine," Sean said.

"This is completely ridiculous." I waved my arm and pulled the cardigan tighter around myself. "People have to be able to sleep."

"People have no sense," Mr. Ramirez said. "My power went out."

"Looks like he hit a lamppost. Might've damaged the power lines," Sean offered.

Mr. Ramirez frowned. "You might be right." His eyes narrowed. "Wait. Isn't your house all the way down the street? What are you doing here?"

"Couldn't sleep," Sean said. "I went jogging."

Asad sniffed the metal skid marks on the pavement with obvious suspicion.

"Jogging, huh." Mr. Ramirez looked at him, then at me, taking in my cardigan and T-shirt, then at Sean again. "At two o'clock in the morning?"

I wished very hard to be invisible.

"Best time to jog," Sean said. "Nobody bothers me."

Asad pondered the marks and let out a single loud bark.

"Hey!" Mr. Ramirez turned to him. "What is it, boy?"

It smelled like something inhuman had landed on the pavement, that's what.

The huge dog put himself between Mr. Ramirez and the marks and broke into a cacophony of barks.

"Hmm. He barely ever barks. I better get him inside. I'm going to file a police report in the morning." Mr. Ramirez looked at Sean and me one last time and smiled. "Good luck with your jogging."

No. He didn't just wish Sean and I happy jogging.

"Come, Asad."

I shut my eyes tight for a second.

"You okay?" Sean asked.

"Jogging?" I squeezed through clenched teeth. "That's the best you could come up with?"

"What else was I supposed to tell him? He isn't going to believe that I woke up out of a dead sleep, got dressed, and ran four hundred yards here in the time it took him to go downstairs and open the door."

"He thinks we're sleeping together."

"So what if we are? We're adults last time I checked."

"Tomorrow he'll talk to Margaret and by afternoon the whole subdivision will be talking about our 'jogging'. I'll be fielding rumors and questions for a week. I don't like attention, Sean. It's bad for my business."

Sean smiled.

Ugh. I turned around. "Come inside."

"You sure?" He was grinning now. "People might get the wrong idea."

"Just come inside," I growled.

He followed me in.

Inside my front room, the long flexible roots of the inn pinned a creature to the wall. He was about the size of a ten-year-old human child, four-limbed, and wearing a pocketed leather harness from which hung a wide brown cape. A beautiful crest of emerald-green, yellow, and crimson feathers crowned his head. Earth's evolutionary theory said that feathers evolved from scales and therefore were unlikely to ever appear on the same creature. Nobody mentioned it to the biker, because the rest of him was covered in beautiful green scales, darkening to hunter green on his back and lightening to cream on his throat and chest. A male Ku. I should've known.

The Ku were actually reptilian and had more in common with dinosaurs than birds. They lived in tribes and stumbled onto the greater galaxy by accident while they were still in the hunter-gatherer stage. They'd never moved past it. On Earth, climate change combined with the rising population created starvation, which became the catalyst for the development of horticulture, which in turn eventually led to agricultural society and feudalism. The Ku faced no such pressures. They didn't try to understand the galaxy and the complicated technology of other species. They simply accepted it and learned to use it. Talking rules to a Ku was like reading a modern law brief to a toddler. This one, apparently, decided it would be a great idea to bring his boost bike to our planet and drive up and down Park Street.

"Have you lost your mind?"

The Ku looked at me with round golden eyes.

"This is Earth. You can't make noise. You can't ride boost bikes. Humans can't know. You almost got all of us into big trouble."

The Ku blinked. His eyes were clear like the summer sky: no thought clouded their depths. I sighed. I wanted to yell at him some more, but it would accomplish nothing.

"Well? What do you have to say for yourself?"

He opened his mouth, showing sharp teeth. "Message!"

"Do you have a message for me?"

"Yes!"

Who in all the worlds would send a message by a Ku? Might as well shove it into a bottle and toss it into the ocean. It had about the same chances of reaching its recipient. I held out my hand. The roots released the Ku just enough for his arms to move. He reached into a pocket on his harness, pulled something out, and dropped it into my palm.

A silver necklace with a dolphin pendant. I went cold.

"And this!" The Ku dropped a grimy clump of paper into my hand.

Gingerly I pulled it open. A string of coordinates written in hurried cursive and five words.

In trouble. Come get me.

"Dina?" Sean loomed next to me. "You've gone pale."

"I need a ship."

"Why?"

"I have to go to Karhari."

His eyebrows furrowed. "That's deep in Holy Anocracy territory. What's on Karhari?"

Karhari was a closed planet. I had no way to access it from the inn, which meant I had to get there the conventional way. I'd have to buy passage from Baha-char. Applying for permits would take forever and they probably wouldn't be granted, which meant a smuggler and I couldn't even begin to guess how much time that would cost me...

Sean thrust himself into my view and gently touched my shoulder. I looked up at him.

"Talk to me. What's on Karhari?"

"My sister."

Chapter 2

I stood in my kitchen and tapped my foot. On the wall the communication screen remained dark with a faint blue ring pulsing every few seconds. Last night I had dug into the available information on Karhari. Things were worse than I thought. Karhari wasn't just closed. It was under a Holy Anocracy restricted travel seal. The Holy Anocracy consisted of aristocratic clans called Houses, each with their separate domain, and only a handful of Houses were permitted to enter Karhari's atmosphere. Anyone without an appropriate House crest would be shot down. There wouldn't be time to explain, bribe, or offer apologies. A quick check of my contacts at Baha-char, the galactic bazaar, told me that the entirety of my savings couldn't buy me entrance. I was reduced to begging.

Maud wouldn't have asked for my help unless she was in imminent danger. I would beg, offer favors, and promise the moon and sky to save my sister. After I got the Ku settled last night, I had placed a message to Arland of House Krahr. It was late morning now. He hadn't responded.

Arland and I had a history. He had helped Sean and me to track down the alien assassin, or rather we helped him, since the assassin was here because of the internal politics of House Krahr in the first place. He had also participated in the peace summit, which turned out very well for the

Holy Anocracy, in no small part because of me. Technically, I could claim he owed me a favor. Practically, he was the Marshal of a powerful vampire House, who had plenty of responsibilities and probably couldn't drop them on the spur of the moment.

The waiting for a response was nerve-racking.

A seven-foot-tall darkness loomed next to me. Orro thrust a small plate in front of my nose. I looked down at a small bagel covered with purple jam.

"Eat!"

"Thank you, I'm not hungry."

Orro's foot-long spikes rose. He growled. Given that Quillonians resembled terrifying monsters who stood upright, had hands armed with savage claws, muzzles filled with fangs, and backs covered with foot-long black quills, the effect would give any sane human a lifetime of nightmares. I was past caring.

"Eat!"

He wouldn't give up until I did. I grabbed the bagel and bit into it. Like everything Orro cooked, it tasted like pure heaven. Orro muttered under his breath, waited until I finished the whole bagel, and stalked away.

As a Red Cleaver chef, he should've been cooking banquets at the best gourmet restaurants in the galaxy. But an unfortunate poisoning accident left him disgraced. I found him at Baha-char, when he was at the end of his rope, and although his contract with me was finished, he refused to leave. Gertrude Hunt was now his home.

The communication screen was still blinking.

I paced back and forth. Arland was my best bet. If I couldn't get him to help me, I had no idea where to go next.

Pacing back and forth wasn't going to get Arland to answer any faster. I stopped and forced myself to turn away. Through the kitchen window, I could see the backyard. The boost bike lay opened on the back patio. Sean was elbow deep in it, while the Ku, whose name was Wing, of all things, pranced around him. Beast cavorted around them, gathering sticks and spitting them at Sean's feet.

I waved my hand and the inn opened the window, letting the cold air in.

"...Of course the stabilizer failed."

Sean plucked a weird looking gadget from a tool chest. He'd asked if I had tools and I gave him access to the repair garage. He saw the rows of shelves filled with an assortment of mechanical wonders, swore in appreciation, and then picked out a tool chest.

He reached into the guts of the boost bike, plucked something out, and tossed it on the grass. "That's what you get for buying spare parts from an Alkonian chop shop."

"Cheap parts!" Wing volunteered.

"Look, it can be fast, good, or cheap. You can have any two but never all three."

"Why?"

"It's the law of the universe."

When did he learn to fix boost bikes?

Something clicked within the engine. Blue lights ignited on the bike's dashboard.

Wing raised his hands and emitted a piercing screech. Discretion wasn't even in his vocabulary.

Behind me the communication screen chimed. I jumped.

"Accept the call."

Arland's face filled the screen. Handsome, with a mane of golden hair framing a powerful masculine face and penetrating blue eyes, Arland would've stopped traffic at any major intersection. Women would get out of their cars to take a closer look, until he smiled, and then they'd see his fangs and run away screaming.

The Marshal of House Krahr looked splendid in full armor, a deep black shot through with blood-red.

"Lady Dina," he boomed. "I'm at your command."

And he'd lost none of his flair for the dramatic. "Are you going to war, Lord Marshal?" Please don't be going to war.

"No, I was attending a formal dinner." He grimaced. "They make us wear armor to these things so we don't stab ourselves out of sheer boredom. How might I be of service?"

"I have to go to Karhari. The matter is urgent and I desperately need your help."

Sean came in and washed his hands at the sink.

"Karhari is the anus of the galaxy." Arland frowned. "What could you possibly want there?"

"My sister."

His blond eyebrows crept up. "You have a sister?"

"Yes."

"What is she doing at Karhari?"

"I don't know."

The last time I had heard from Maud was over three years ago, and at the time she was on Noceen, one of the more prosperous of the Holy Anocracy's planets. Klaus and I had gone to see her when we were searching for Mom and Dad. It was a short visit. Finding out that Mom and Dad had disappeared nearly broke her. She would talk with Mom all the time while my parents' inn was active, so when communication abruptly ceased, she'd had no idea what had happened. She tried to get passage back to Earth, but her husband was involved in some sort of complicated vampire politics and she couldn't go. During that meeting, I got a feeling that everything wasn't going well, but she wouldn't say what the problem was.

Caldenia entered the kitchen, wearing a beautiful pink robe, and took a seat at the kitchen table. Orro swept by and a plate with a bagel and jam landed in front of Her Grace.

She picked the bagel up, biting into the dough with her unnaturally sharp teeth. When most people bit a bagel, we clamped it down and pulled, tearing it. When Caldenia bit a bagel, there was no clamping down and pulling. Her teeth simply sheared it, as if the dough had been cut with big heavy scissors.

"Lord Arland, my sister sent a message to me asking for help. She isn't the sort of person to ask for assistance." In fact, Maud would rather die than ask for help, but she wasn't willing to gamble with little Helen's life.

"It's very important I get to Karhari as soon as possible. Is there any way you could expedite my application for a permit?"

"I'm afraid that's not possible."

My heart sank.

"There are no permits being issued for travel to Karhari. As I've said, it's a pit of a planet. Most of it consists of boring plains with large herds of massive herbivores wandering aimlessly through them. There are no good hunting grounds, no great mineral wealth, so it offers very little in the way of value. It was colonized early in the history of the Anocracy and then we lost touch with it for almost five hundred years. The descendants of the original settlers have been cut off for so long that even though the planet was brought back into the Anocracy's loving embrace a hundred years ago, the rule of law is barely recognized there. It's the place we send our criminals, exiles, and heretics."

My sister was stuck in eighteenth century vampire Australia.

"Is there anything that can be done? Anything at all?"

"There is only one thing to do." He hit me with a dazzling smile, displaying his sharp fangs. "I'll take you there personally."

"What?"

"My uncle's cousin was granted holdings on Karhari, so House Krahr has a presence there. As Marshal, I can travel there any time I wish."

I almost jumped up and down. Still, my history with House Krahr had been complicated already. And Arland had developed a somewhat seasonal infatuation with me. "Are you sure? The fuel expense must be significant..."

He leaned closer to the screen. "The expense will be minimal. We'll use the Earth jump gate, bounce off the net here, and will be in Karhari by tomorrow morning. Besides, thanks to you, House Krahr has found itself in a very advantageous position on Nexus. Our profits have soared. I can bounce back and forth between here and Karhari thirty times before the House Steward will gently chide me to keep an eye on the budget. Family is all any of us have. It is decided. Will you be ready in an hour?"

Just like that. "Yes!"

"I shall be in orbit in a few minutes. Is it only you or are you bringing anyone with you?"

"She's bringing me," Sean said, stepping next to me.

Arland's upper lip trembled. He killed it before it became a snarl and peered at Sean. "What happened to your face? Never mind, not important. Your presence isn't necessary. Lady Dina will have sufficient protection."

"Is the Marshal threatened by my presence?" Sean asked, his voice calm.

"Hardly."

"Then I see no reason why I can't come along."

"Karhari isn't Earth, werewolf. You've never fought a vampire in open combat. You aren't ready for a planet full of us."

What?

Sean's face was calm. "As you said, the rule of law is barely recognized on Karhari. I should be right at home."

Arland struggled with it for a moment. "Fine. I'm not one to keep a man away from a funeral pyre when he's jumping over obstacles to get to it. We shall meet in an hour."

The screen went black.

Never fought a vampire… That made no sense. When Sean led the Merchants' defense on Nexus, he slaughtered enough vampires for several lifetimes. That's what the peace summit was about. The Holy Anocracy, the Hope-Crushing Horde, and the Merchants of Baha-Char had fought over rights to Nexus, a mineral rich planet. Sean had led the Merchants' forces as Turan Adin, an immortal general in dark armor. It turned out that Turan Adin was very much mortal. The Merchants had been going through mercenaries, and every time one died, they picked out his replacement and put him back in the armor. Sean turned out to be the last and the best. He lasted longer than anyone would have expected, but the war on Nexus was killing him from the inside out. To save him and convince the three factions to agree to peace, I had linked them all, Sean and myself included, to the inn. We had shared memories. Arland was there.

"Arland doesn't know. How can he not know you were Turan Adin? You shared Nexus memories with the rest of us."

Sean frowned. "When I think back to it, I don't know which memories were his. I don't think he knows which ones were mine. When you linked us, you asked only about things that happened on Nexus. I was always Turan Adin on Nexus. The armor never came off. I thought of myself as Turan Adin. I left Sean here on Earth with you."

The werewolves of Auul were poets. Sometimes I forgot that, and then he said something like that.

"Will you tell him?"

Sean shook his head. "If I do, he'll try to kill me."

"Why?"

"We met in battle once. I had a chance to kill him, and I didn't. He knows that."

Arland was a proud man. Sean was right; he wouldn't be able to handle it. Then again, having Sean near Arland wouldn't be doing wonders for Sean's recovery either.

"Are you sure you want to come?"

He looked at me for a minute. "I'm going to pick up some equipment. Don't leave without me."

"And if I do?"

"I'll have to chase you in my ship and blow the galaxy's existence wide open. Please don't leave without me."

He headed out the door.

I crossed my arms and looked at Caldenia. "Does everyone have an interstellar ship except us?"

"You should get one." She licked the jam from the corner of her mouth. "We do have to keep up with the Joneses, my dear."

⚜ ⚜ ⚜

Being catapulted into orbit by the summoning gate was about as fun as riding one of those towering carnival rides without restraints. It made you want to vomit and you were one hundred percent certain that you were going to die. Logic said that only three seconds passed from the point Sean and I stepped into the blood-red glow until the moment we landed in the transport bay of Arland's ship, but it felt like much longer. I blinked, adjusting my backpack on my shoulders. Arland estimated that the entire trip would only take two days, and I had packed light.

Sean had packed heavy. A large military-style duffel bag, packed to the breaking point, rested on his back. He carried a smaller duffel. I had a feeling that the smaller duffel was the one with his clothes. He scanned our surroundings like we were in enemy territory.

I looked around, too. Gray square stones lined the floor under my feet. Similar stones climbed the hundred-foot-tall bulkhead of the huge chamber around us. Long vines with narrow pale green leaves dripped from the stones, their delicate pink flowers spicing the air with a gentle aroma. The crimson banners of House Krahr stretched over the walls. In the middle of the chamber a beautiful old tree with black bark spread its massive branches with wide green leaves and crimson blossoms. A stream rushed through an artificial river bed, falling in an artful cascade of small waterfalls and winding under the arches of the tree's roots. The illusion of standing in the courtyard of a vampire castle was so complete, I could barely believe we were on a spaceship.

I glanced at Sean. "Extravagant."

He shrugged. "It's space. No friction means little need for aerodynamics."

"But mass is still a factor." The heavier the ship, the longer it took to accelerate and decelerate and the more fuel it required.

"Vampires," Sean said, the way parents usually said "teenagers" when their children were out of earshot.

A door slid open in the far wall and Arland appeared, in full armor, moving briskly toward us. The sight of a vampire in syn-armor was impressive. Arland had taken it up a notch. He didn't walk, he strode, like a tiger within his domain.

"Look," Sean said under his breath. "He's making an entrance."

Keeping the two of them civil would prove a challenge. "He's doing me a big favor. Do you think you could refrain from baiting him for the duration of this trip?"

"I'll try. But it's going to be difficult."

A female vampire, also in full armor, ran up to Arland and thrust some high tech tablet under his face. Arland waved her off and marched on.

"Very difficult," Sean said.

"Try harder," I murmured, trying to keep a friendly expression on my face. "I'm sure you can do it."

"My deepest apologies." Arland hit me with a dazzling smile. "I was held up by the petty minutia of House matters."

"No apologies necessary," I told him. "Thank you so much for your help. I'm deeply grateful."

Arland turned to Sean and narrowed his eyes. "That's a lot of hardware."

They must've scanned Sean's big duffel.

"Better to be prepared."

"Where did you get the weapons?"

"I have my ways," Sean said.

"I'm watching you," Arland told him.

"I'll keep that in mind."

And that's just about enough. "Lord Arland, it's so kind of you to lend us your ship."

He smiled. "It's my pleasure. Please, this way, Lady Dina."

Arland held out his arm bent at the elbow. I was on the grounds of House Krahr. When in a vampire ship... I rested my hand on his forearm just below his wrist. He didn't shoot Sean a triumphant glance but his expression told me he wanted to. We strolled down the path around the tree to the exit.

"I must ask your forgiveness. While this is my personal vessel, humble as it may be, it is still of military purpose and by necessity of function is spartan in appearance."

I caught a glimpse of Sean's face. His expression was completely neutral.

"It's very beautiful, my lord."

"It pleases me immensely that you like it. It is home away from home, so to speak."

We passed through the doors into the hallway.

"I'm curious, how will the inn fare without you?" Arland asked.

I had avoided thinking about the inn for almost three minutes. He had just broken my winning streak.

"My sister provided me with exact coordinates. With luck, she will be waiting for us, so we should only be gone for a short while. The inn can take care of itself." Assuming Officer Marais didn't come snooping, Caldenia didn't murder anyone because she found them appetizing, Orro didn't have a nervous breakdown because he couldn't buy groceries for two days, and if all of them plus Beast managed to keep their cool, the inn should be fine. I hoped. At least Wing had checked out before I left. He asked for the nearest inn, and I sent him to Brian

Rodriguez near Dallas with strict instructions to not take any detours.

Mr. Rodriquez ran Casa Feliz, one of the largest, best known inns in the entire southwest. He used to be friends with my parents. We, the innkeepers, were a reclusive, paranoid lot. Interactions between us were rare, unless two inns happened to be close together and the innkeepers were friends. Most of our business ran on a handshake and communications took place in person or via encrypted channels. In a show of great trust, Mr. Rodriguez had given me his personal cell phone number and I had used it a couple of times to ask him for advice. He was the reason Orro huffed and puffed in the kitchen. His staff would be able to handle a Ku without any issues.

"I have looked at the coordinates you've given me," Arland said. "According to our records, this place is a Road Lodge, a tavern and an inn in the middle of nowhere where travelers stay for a night or two before continuing on their way elsewhere. The type of hovel that attracts convoy raiders, bandits, and other characters of ill repute."

Maud knew how to blend in.

"As unpleasant as this possibility might be, I must ask what will happen if your sister isn't there."

"She will be there."

"Your faith in your family is to be commended," he said. "We may encounter resistance." He said that the way most people would say, "We may encounter chocolate cake. With frosting!"

"I'm sure we will." If there was no resistance, Maud wouldn't be hiding in some hellhole.

"In the event of such an occurrence, I once again offer you my full support. Allow me to be your shield, Lady Dina. For you and your sister."

"Thank you, Lord Arland."

I had no idea how Maud's husband would react to that. Melizard was the second son of the Marshal of House Ervan. Here is hoping no ancient feuds existed between House Ervan and House Krahr or things would get awkward.

The door in front of us opened and we walked into an observation room. Two hundred and seventy degrees of transparent glass beyond which the galaxy stretched in all its glory, the distant nebulae in a hundred colors swirling among the stars. Tables and booths dotted the floor. Arland turned and led me up a staircase to the balcony, where a long table waited for us, filled to the brim with food, most of which seemed to be various cuts of meat.

"Of course, the skills of my chef cannot match your Quillonian, but I don't believe you'll be disappointed." Arland pulled out my chair. "Please."

I took it. A gentle melody, at once soothing and haunting, floated down to us from some invisible speakers. To my left Sean rolled his eyes.

This was going to be an interesting trip.

⚜ ⚜ ⚜

Arland was right. Karhari truly was the anus of the galaxy and I was getting an eyeful of it from my seat in Arland's landing shuttle. Flat, dry, ugly, the planet stretched for miles without any reprieve for the eye. Its soil was brown, the plants that grew on it were greenish-brown, and the bur, the giant herbivores that moved through the plains like shaggy boulders, were also brown. I'd shoot myself within two days of living here.

Arland's family crest granted him the right to enter Karhari airspace, but the Road Lodge sat far outside of his relative's lands. Technically it was within a different House's territory, a local House. Arland had planned to land with a squad of his soldiers, but the local House shot that idea down. Words like "invasion", "provocation", and "armed excursion" were thrown around. After tense negotiations, Arland won the right to bring a single shuttle and two people. I had to be one of them, because Maud wouldn't trust anyone but me, and I had insisted that Sean was the other.

Back when we met, during his first trip to Baha-char, Sean had found a shop run by a veteran werewolf. The shop had contained a special armor made specifically for an alpha-strain werewolf like him. When he put it on, the armor became a part of his body. Normally he kept it relegated into tattoos just under his skin, but right now it was out, sheathing his body like a black jumpsuit. I caught a glimpse of it under the collar of his loose T-shirt when he'd climbed into the flier.

The agreement Arland made specified that none of us could carry ranged combat weapons. The list of what we couldn't bring was quite long and axed most of everything Sean had in his duffel. Sean and Arland had a long conversation about it and the vampire House politics, at the end of which they concluded that we were being set up but that they had it handled.

The bleak terrain rolled outside the shuttle's window. Why, Maud? Why Karhari? What happened to the castle? Was little Helen with her or did she somehow get here by herself? The more I thought about it, the more uneasy I became. Neither Arland nor Sean asked me why my sister might be in this hellhole, and for that I was grateful.

"There it is." Arland pointed to a dark rectangular structure.

Put together from prefab hard plastic and studded with five-foot spikes, the Road Lodge looked about as hospitable as the raider fortress from Mad Max. I pulled my gray travel robe tighter around myself. So far from the inn my power was much weaker, so I brought something from the days Klaus and I had zigzagged across the galaxy trying to find my parents.

I hadn't heard from Klaus for so long. I didn't even know where my brother was.

"You sure you don't want a knife?" Sean asked. He'd offered me one twice already.

"No, thank you."

"Lady Dina will be perfectly safe in my presence," Arland said.

Sean gave him a cold stare and settled back into his seat.

Lady Dina would be safe in her own presence. I checked the glove on my left hand. It was more of a gauntlet than a glove and it looked like several layers of latex gloves were fused together with superglue and then dipped in wax. It was made to the mold of my hand from the hardened spit of a rare alien animal. Despite its thickness, it was surprisingly flexible, but I wanted it off all the same. It wasn't the glove. It was the memories of what I did when I wore the glove and the anticipation of what I might have to do that made my skin crawl.

Hopefully, we would just get there, pick up Maud and whoever was with her, and get out, quick and quiet. Quick and quiet.

I swallowed. My heart was speeding up and I needed to calm down fast. Vampires were like cats; if it moved, they swatted it and if I walked into that place agitated, they would zero in on me. I didn't want to attract attention.

"What could the locals gain by setting you up?" I asked Arland.

"A war with House Krahr on this planet. Since they're a local House they likely have no idea of our capabilities. They probably want my uncle's cousin's land. Or perhaps they want to claim that I attacked them, so that they can demand financial compensation." He grinned at me. "Either way, it will be exciting."

The Road Lodge grew as we neared it. Sean pulled on a dark gray windbreaker and pulled the hood over his face.

Arland circled the Lodge and landed on a landing strip, next to a couple dozen different vehicles. The shuttle's door swung open and I climbed out into the dirt.

Hold on, Maud. I'm almost there.

Sean landed next to me. Arland was last. He'd put on a dark cloak with a deep hood. The draped fabric hid most of him, but did nothing to obscure the fact that he was wearing armor. He tossed something into the air. With a quiet whir, a small gray sphere the size of a pecan hovered above us.

"What is that?" I asked.

"Insurance," Arland said. "It projects a feed to the shuttle. Whatever happens, I require a record of it. Follow me."

He headed for the entrance. We followed.

The door slid open at our approach and we stepped inside. A purple light slid over us - a weapon scan. Arland's camera passed through it without setting off any alarms and rose toward the ceiling.

A cavernous room spread before us with a long bar counter on the right side and a mass of tables and booths on the left. A big metal cage on the left, just by the door, held an assortment of firearms secured by a metal lock. Judging by the ring of dead insects near it, it was electrified. Right. A leave your gun at the door kind of place.

A staircase in the middle of the dining area led upstairs, probably to the guest rooms. Big shaggy heads of bur bulls, horned and tusked, decorated the walls. Vampires of every age and size occupied the booths and the chairs, most cloaked and all armored. Here and there an odd alien nursed some weird drink, watching the other patrons with wary eyes. The scent of mint and the deep, nutty odor of caffeine-laden vampire liquor hung in the air.

Not a single banner. Dust on the floor, grime on the tables. The contrast between the pristine beauty of Arland's vessel and this place was startling. The Holy Anocracy, with its laws and rules, was very far away.

Nobody turned and looked at us as we came in, but they watched us, the weight of their gazes cold and pressing down right between my shoulders blades. None of the people looked like Maud.

I sat at the bar. A vampire woman, her armor dented and having seen much better days, stopped by me. "What will it be?"

"Mint tea." I dropped credit chips on the counter. My mother always told me to keep common currency on hand, even if only a small amount, and I had raided my stash for this trip.

She swiped the chips off the bar and looked at the two men next to me.

"I'll have what she is having," Sean said.

"None for me."

The cloak's hood hid most of Arland's face, but judging by the curve of his mouth, he could barely contain his disgust.

The tea arrived in semi-clean cups. I sipped the tea and took my hood down. *Here I am.*

Nothing. If Maud was here, she was waiting. I kept drinking my tea.

"Big guy on the left," Sean said quietly into his cup.

"I see him," Arland said.

A huge vampire, his face cleaved by a ragged scar, rose from one of the tables on the left and started toward us. He was older than Arland by at least a couple of decades. A mane of dark hair hung loose down his back, and judging by the greasy look of it, if his hair had ever known what shampoo was, it had surely forgotten by now. Scuffs, dents, and gouges marked his armor, its original black luster lost beyond repair. A sword hung from his waist, not the typical blood weapon of the Anocracy's warriors, but a savage-looking hacking blade.

He stopped a few feet from Arland. "You're not from around here."

"Such keen powers of observation," Arland said.

"Your armor is clean. Pretty. Do you know what we do to pretty boys like you here?"

"Is there a script?" Arland asked him. "Do you give the speech to all who enter here, because if so, I suggest we skip the talking."

The vampire roared, baring his fangs.

"A challenge." Arland smiled. "I love challenges."

The bigger vampire went for his sword. Arland punched him in the jaw. The other vampire flew a few feet and crashed into a booth that conveniently broke his fall.

He jumped to his feet and charged, sword in hand. Arland ducked under his swing and hammered a short brutal punch to the vampire's ribs. A loud crack sounded, like a dozen firecrackers going off at once, as the armor split along some invisible seam. Arland grasped the protruding edge of the breastplate and jerked it up. The armor crunched on itself, collapsing. The older vampire tumbled to the ground, his right arm immobilized, his left bare.

"Nice," Sean said.

"If one is going to wear armor, one must properly maintain it," Arland said.

The older vampire tried to rise. Arland waited until he got halfway up and kneed him in the face. Blood poured from the vampire's face. Arland kicked him. The attacker collapsed and lay still.

"Anyone else?" Arland asked.

Seven vampires rose at once.

"Couldn't leave well enough alone, could you?" Sean said, pulling a large knife with a dark green curved blade from the sheath on his waist.

"Might as well get it over with." Arland ripped off his cloak and tossed it aside. His face wrinkled in an ugly snarl, showing his fangs.

Five more vampires stood up. This wouldn't end well.

"Stay behind me," Sean told me.

A figure in a tattered brown cloak jumped onto the table behind the vampires, jerked a blood sword and a dagger out, dashed to the nearest standing vampire, and sliced his head off.

The vampires roared.

The swordsman sprinted through the room, running on the tables, slicing and cutting like a whirlwind. Everyone moved at once. People screamed, pulling weapons, and overturning tables. Some ran to the back, others charged us. Sean sprinted forward, carving his way through the attackers.

A vampire grabbed the swordsman's tattered cloak and jerked at it. The cloak came free, revealing Maud in syn-armor, her short blue-black hair flying. She dropped to her knees on the table and buried her dagger in his throat. Blood sprayed her face. She pulled the dagger out with a short jerk, rolled on the table, just as another vampire shattered it with a blow of his blood mace, and sliced across his face with her sword.

Next to me Arland stood frozen.

I reached over and pushed his mouth shut. "Arland!"

He stared at me, as if waking up from a dream.

I pointed at Maud. "Help my sister!"

For a stunned half-second he stared at me, and then he pulled out his blood mace, roared, and tore into the mass of bodies like a raging bull.

I slipped the handle of the energy whip into my right hand and squeezed it. A thin flexible filament slid from it, dripping to the floor. There was Maud. There was Sean and Arland. Where was little Helen?

I moved forward, picking my way through the fight to where Maud had originally jumped. A female vampire charged at me, her mouth opened, her hammer raised for the kill.

Sean hurled his attacker aside and turned toward me.

I flicked my wrist. The filament ignited with bright yellow and the energy whip sliced at the oncoming vampire. She howled, the deep gash that nearly sliced her chest in two instantly cauterized. I flicked the whip again - she wouldn't recover from this injury anyway - and her head rolled off. That was the problem with an energy whip. A wound to the torso almost always meant a slow and painful death.

I kept moving.

A chair flew at me. I ducked and ran straight into a male vampire. He grabbed me, jerking my neck to his mouth. I grasped the end of the whip with my left hand - the glove was the only thing it wouldn't cut - and pushed the stretched whip through the vampire's face. It cut straight through the helmet and bone, and the top half of the vampire's skull slid to the floor. The body crashed, with me on top of it. I rolled to the side, under a table, scrambled on my hands and knees and saw a small shape under another table in the distance.

"Helen!"

The small creature under the table turned toward me. *Found you.*

I crawled from under the table. In front of me vampires clashed, all local - whenever there was a big fight, people settled personal scores. I flicked my whip, lengthening it. It made a sharp electric crack. Once you heard it, you never forgot it. Suddenly the floor before me was clear. I ran through the opening, dropped to my knees, and pulled Helen from under the table. She clutched at me, a five-year-old girl with pale hair and the round green eyes of a vampire.

"Aunt Dina!"

She remembered me! "I've got you."

I scrambled up, supporting her weight with my left arm. A vampire rushed us. Helen hissed, pulled out a knife, and swiped at him. He leaned out of the way, his axe swinging toward us. Sean thrust himself in front of me, catching the axe in mid blow. The vampire strained. Sean sliced at him, the green blade cutting through armor like a sharp knife through a pear.

"Follow me."

I chased him through the slaughter. Midway to the door Maud appeared next to me, her blades bloody.

"Arland!" Sean roared, his voice covering the din of fighting.

I turned and saw the Marshal, covered in blood, bellowing like a bull, as his mace reduced armors and bones to a bloody pulp.

"Arland!" Sean yelled again.

The Marshal saw us and turned, following. We tore out of the front door and ran to the slick black shuttle. The doors swung open - Arland must've activated the remote - and Sean leaped into the pilot seat and started flipping switches.

Maud climbed into the passenger seat and I handed Helen to her.

A clump of vampires pushed out the door. It fell apart, revealing Arland snarling, fangs bared. He swung his mace and cracked one attacker's skull, grabbed another by his throat with his left hand, snapped his neck, and threw him aside like a rag doll. Maud's eyebrows crept up. She paused for a second, while sliding Helen into the seat restraints. "Who the hell is that?"

"The Lord Marshal of House Krahr."

I landed into the seat next to her.

Arland brained the last attacker, ran to the shuttle, and jumped into the seat next to Sean. The tiny camera zipped into the cabin behind him.

A screaming crowd exploded out of the doors and ran for the shuttle.

"Do you even know how to fly, werewolf?" Arland barked.

"Buckle up." Sean pulled a lever.

The shuttle streaked into the sky.

My sister hugged her daughter to her.

"What happened? Where is Melizard? Where is your husband?"

"Melizard is dead," Maud said, her eyes haunted. "He led a revolt against his House. They stripped him of all titles and possessions and sent us to Karhari. Eight months ago he crossed the wrong local and the raiders killed him."

"We killed them back," Helen told me.

"Yes, my flower." Maud petted her daughter's hair, an eerie smile on her lips. "Yes, we did."

Chapter 3

The shuttle docked. Arland paused in the seat, scrutinizing Sean.

"Where did you learn to fly the Holy Anocracy's shuttles?"

"Wilmos," Sean said. "An old werewolf at Baha-char. I owed him for some armor he sold me, so I did some mercenary work. He gave me a crash course."

Arland made a short noise that was the vampire equivalent of a harrumph and sounded a lot like a deep-throat snarl.

The doors of the shuttle swung open. Three vampires stood, waiting, two men and a woman. One of them, an older male, carried a stack of thin towels. Arland stepped out, grabbed one of the towels, and wiped his face. The towel came away bloody.

"Get us out of here before I succumb to temptation and initiate the kinetic bombardment of this dump," Arland growled.

The female vampire bowed and took off, issuing commands into her communicator.

The other male vampire checked his tablet. "My lord, your injuries…"

"Do you require medical attention?" Arland asked us.

"No," Maud and I said at the same time.

Arland glanced at Sean. Sean shook his head.

"Lady Dina, if I might have a moment?" Arland asked.

Maud was on my right and I caught a flicker of panic in her eyes. It was very brief but it made my stomach turn. My childhood had few unshakeable truths, but one of them was that my older sister was afraid of nothing. Maud never backed down and never asked for help. When I was a child and someone was mean to me, I went and got Maud, because after she talked to them, they would never be mean to me again.

The vampire with the tablet tried again. "Your injuries..."

"Are minor," Arland said. "Lady Dina?"

"Of course."

We walked away a few dozen feet. I glanced at Maud. Helen was standing next to her, hugging her leg. My sister looked ready to pull her sword out at any moment.

"You didn't tell me that your sister was married to a knight of the Holy Anocracy."

"I'm sorry. I was focused on rescuing her and my niece."

"I'm not upset," Arland said, glancing back at Maud and frowning. "But I do not like to be misled."

"It wasn't my intention to mislead you." Yes, it was. A lie by omission was still a lie. I would've told him anything to get Maud and Helen out of there and I didn't want to risk vampire politics interfering with that. "I wasn't certain of my sister's status. I'm sorry if this will cause issues between House Krahr and House Ervan..."

"What?" Arland drew back. "No. I don't care what House Ervan thinks. If I field a quarter of our fleet, it will still be three times as much as the entirety of what House Ervan can scrape together. I'm not talking about that. I'm talking about…" He waved his hand, trying to find the right words.

"Lord Arland, sometimes it helps to speak plainly."

"Sword," he said. "She has a blood sword."

"Yes, she does." Where was he going with this?

"She killed four vampires and maimed another two."

I nodded. "Yes, she did." And he had been counting, apparently.

"She's wearing syn-armor. It's been custom fitted and the patch seam on her left side is recent. When one seals a gash in one's armor while it is still on their body, one moves the sealing tool from the outside in, creating the raised pattern pointing toward the center of the body, as is seen on your sister's armor. It feels more natural this way and lets one gauge the risk of structural collapse if the nano threads within the armor are compromised. When one seals the armor after taking it off, the pattern is reversed, because when we face the armor suit, we tend to repair it by moving the tool from center of the body out."

"Okay?"

"She repaired her own armor. She didn't feel it was safe to take it off, so she did it while she was wearing it. That requires skill and experience. One wrong move, and you can critically injure yourself."

Oh, Maud. "I fail to see the significance of this."

Arland dragged his hand through his hair, exasperated. "From my interactions with my cousin's wife, I understand the women of Earth to be delicate creatures, powerful in their own right, but not on par with females of the Holy Anocracy when it comes to martial prowess. My cousin's wife does not wear syn-armor or carry blood weapons."

I made a mental note to introduce him to a female MMA championship match the next time he stopped at the inn. "Lord Marshal, I have no idea what kind of woman your cousin's wife is. Human women, like vampire women, come in all varieties. For example, I don't like violence, but I will kill to protect my family and my guests."

"Yes, but I believed you to be an exception due to your unique position."

"I'm not an exception. Most Earth women would do whatever they had to do to protect their loved ones, and while our culture is less martial than yours, human female warriors exist. Maud was always very good with weapons and never hesitated to use them. I'm sure being married into a Holy Anocracy House meant she had to fight for the honor of the House more than once. Being exiled to Karhari, where she had to defend herself and my niece, only sharpened her skills, so if you don't mind some advice, treat her as you would treat any skilled female vampire fighter. It will be safer for everyone involved."

Arland looked at me as if seeing me for the first time. Yes, the princess you were expecting put on her armor and left to kill the dragon. So sorry.

"Lord Arland, my niece is covered in blood. If you don't mind, I would like to get her to my cabin where she can shower."

"Of course," he said.

We walked back to Maud, Sean, and Helen. My sister searched my face, waiting. Beneath our feet the floor shuddered slightly as the massive ship accelerated toward the gate that would catapult it countless billions of miles across the galaxy.

"Come on," I told her. "Lord Arland has most graciously provided me with a very large cabin. Let's get cleaned up."

⚜ ⚜ ⚜

The cabin Arland assigned me wasn't just spacious, it was luxurious and decorated in a beautiful teal-gray, blue, and pink color scheme, which I would shamelessly copy the next time a vampire came to stay at the inn. The door behind us slid shut.

I turned around and hugged Maud. She hugged me back.

Helen pulled on my robe. "Hugs."

"Hugs." I let go of Maud and picked her up. "How do you even remember me? The last time I saw you, you were this tiny." I held my thumb and index finger about an inch apart.

Helen giggled, showing her fangs. "Mommy showed me pictures. She said if she died you would take care of me."

All the fun went out of me.

"I'll take care of you," I said. "Always. And we'll start with a bath."

"With water?"

I didn't even want to know why she asked that.

"With all the water," Maud said. "All the water ever."

I carried her into the bathroom. A massive tub rested in the middle of the room, sunken low into the floor so it could be sealed when the ship maneuvered. I turned on the water. Helen pulled off her clothes. The dust and blood had combined into a sort of paste that saturated the fabric beyond the point of return.

"Dina," Maud said.

"I think her clothes are a lost cause," I said.

Helen jumped into the bath and splashed. Dark swirls spread from her through the water. Maud had the strangest look on her face, half-pain, half-happiness.

"Wash your hair, baby," my sister said, grabbed my arm, and pulled me out of the bathroom.

"What is it?"

"Dina, I don't want to make trouble for you. You can drop us off anywhere outside of Holy Anocracy territory."

"What are you talking about?"

Her voice was quiet and urgent. "Melizard dishonored his House. They didn't just exile him, they removed all traces of his existence from the family tree. It's like he never was born, I was never his wife, and Helen was never his daughter or a child of House Ervan. Two thirds of exiles sent to Karhari die within the first three years. Before they sent us, I begged—", her voice broke, and she swallowed, "—I begged his mother on my knees to take Helen so she wouldn't have to go into exile with us. That bitch looked me straight in the eye and told her guards to remove the strangers from her house. I can't go back to the Holy Anocracy."

"We're not going back to the Holy Anocracy."

"I don't want to make trouble between you and your vampire. I've put you into a bad position and I'm so sorry. House Krahr is one of the most powerful Houses." She raised her hands. "Look at this ship. I don't want to ruin it for you."

"It's not a problem."

In the bath Helen dived and surfaced, laughing.

"Dina, I saw his face when the two of you were talking."

"You threw him off his stride. His cousin is married to a human and he has an odd fascination with Earth women. He just didn't realize not all of us are shrinking violets. He was explaining to me how you sealed your armor while wearing it and how it didn't compute in his head."

Maud frowned. "The two of you aren't together?"

"No."

"Then how?" she raised her arms, encompassing the ship.

"I asked him for a favor. He offered, actually."

"The Marshal of House Krahr just offered to take his destroyer and come rescue me because you asked him?"

"Yes."

She stared at me. "Why?"

"He's a frequent guest at the inn and he felt obligated to help because the inn hosted a peace summit that saved a lot of vampire lives and resulted in his House making a lot of money. Also, he's a kind man."

"The inn? You found Mom and Dad?"

Pain stabbed me straight through the heart. "No. My inn. Gertrude Hunt."

She looked at me, her face blank.

"I'm an innkeeper," I told her. "We're not going to the Holy Anocracy. We're going to Earth, to my inn. We're going home."

All the blood drained from Maud's face. She looked at me as if she didn't understand, then her lip quivered and my sister cried.

※ ※ ※

It's amazing how much dirt could come off one little girl. When we finally extracted Helen from the bath, the water had turned a muddy brown. We toweled her dry and put her into one of my T-shirts. She yawned, curled up on the soft covers, and held out her hands. "Fangs."

Maud handed her two daggers in dark sheaths. Helen hugged the daggers and fell asleep. Maud gently covered her with a blanket.

I pulled a T-shirt and a pair of jeans from my backpack. Maud was taller than me by two inches and shaped differently. We both had Mom's butt and her hips, but Maud's legs were always more muscular and her shoulders broader. I offered the clothes to her.

"I had to guestimate the size. Go clean up." I told her. "I'll watch her."

Maud touched the place where a crest would've sat on her armor and grimaced. "Old habits."

They had stripped the crest from her when they threw her and her husband out of House Ervan.

She bent her left arm, slid aside a bulky looking chunk of armor at least two shades lighter than the rest of the charcoal-colored armor plates, and typed in the code. If Arland ever saw that, he would have a heart attack from the sheer inefficiency of it. It was like trying to type commands into a computer except instead of the keyboard, you had an old, rickety typewriter with half the letters missing.

A few seconds passed. Maud bared her teeth. "Work, damn you." She slammed her arm into the bulkhead. With a faint whisper, the syn-armor came apart, separating into individual pieces. Maud shed the breastplate, the wrist guards, the shoulder pads, the sleeves, one by one adding them to a pile against the wall, until she stood in a dark blue jumpsuit. The jumpsuit had seen better days - the elbows were threadbare. The smell of sweat, blood, and human body that hadn't been washed for far too long spread through the room. I wrinkled my nose.

"Do I stink?" she asked.

"No. You smell like a fresh lily in the middle of a crystal-clear pond."

She stuck her tongue out at me, took the clothes, and disappeared into the bathroom.

Someone knocked on the door, gently, almost apologetic.

"Open," I said. The cabin's door slid upward, revealing a vampire man carrying a black round case about two feet tall and three feet wide.

"With compliments from the Lord Marshal," he said and departed.

It seemed like forever before Maud finally emerged from the bathroom. The clothes fit her well enough, and if I ignored the look in her eyes that said she'd seen too many ugly things, I could almost pretend that she was the old Maud, before my parents disappeared and Klaus vanished into the starry vastness of the Cosmos. Except for her hair. The last time we met, she'd had a long waterfall of hair all the way down to her waist, like most vampire women. She loved her hair.

Maud saw the container.

"Arland sent you an armor repair kit," I told her.

"How considerate." Her voice had a touch of ice to it. She peered at it and smiled.

"What?"

"I just realized I don't have to wear the armor ever again." She paused. "I should probably repair it anyhow. You never know."

She sat cross-legged on the floor in front of the kit and touched its polished surface. The container split into petals curving from the center, lit from within by a soft peach glow. The kit opened like a flower, its center slid upward, turning and opening into a tower of shelves containing small intricate tools and several crystal vials filled with colored liquids: red, black, pearlescent, and peach.

Maud pulled her breastplate close, took a cloth from one of the shelves, sprayed some pearlescent solution on it, and rubbed the armor. Dirt and dust dissolved almost instantly, revealing the black material of the armor underneath. There was a kind of hypnotic rhythm to it. Swipe, wait a moment as the solution evaporated, swipe again.

"What happened to your hair?"

"I chopped it the day they dropped us off on Karhari. It was too hard to keep clean. Water is precious on Karhari. There is almost none on the surface. It rains a decent amount during the rainy season, but the upper crust of the planet is porous rock. All the rain water seeps through and accumulates in underground rivers. They drill for it, the way we drill for oil. As the water passes through the rock, it picks up some nasty salts and must be purified... Long story short, water was expensive."

That explained it.

"We always made enough money to keep us hydrated," she said. "And the meat was easy to come by. The bur are violent once riled up, but pretty stupid."

"How did you live?"

"We hired out."

She finished wiping the armor down, took a scanner from the shelf, and passed it over the breastplate. It made a soft musical chime. She put it back, selected a thin, needle-like instrument from the shelf, and carefully touched it to the largest dent. Thin filaments glowing with peach color peeled from the needle's tip and danced across the dent, pulling the substance of the armor apart.

"Exile or no exile, Melizard was still a Marshal's son. All that training and experience were worth something, and they didn't take our armor, our weapons, or our skills. So we traveled from House to House, Lodge to Lodge, and picked up whatever work was available. Usually convoy guard jobs or private security force openings. We were with a mercenary company for a while and it was almost okay." Maud glanced at me. "It was still horrible, but they had a walled-in base, we had our own room, and we could leave for a job knowing Helen would be safe. We were well liked and the money was decent by Karhari's standards."

"What happened?" I had a strong suspicion I knew the answer.

"What always happened." She sounded bitter and tired. "Melizard."

Maud typed a code into a small terminal within the kit. The filaments turned pale green and knitted the armor back, this time without the dent.

"He waited about six months until he thought he had built up enough support and started rocking the boat. He didn't like the jobs we were getting, and if he were in charge, he would get us better jobs, and everyone would be swimming in water, and things would be fair. That was his favorite word. Fair. It wasn't enough to be respected and earn a decent living. He had to run things and he didn't want to wait for it."

"They threw you out?" I guessed.

"They threw him out. They told me Helen and I could stay."

"But you didn't."

She glanced at me for a second. "No. I didn't."

The Melizard I knew was the perfect younger child: blindingly handsome, witty, charismatic, with a bright smile, the kind that told you right away that you could trust him because he was a good guy, even if he was up to no good once in a while. He was the son of the Marshal of House Ervan, handsome, rich, a legend on the battlefield by the time he met Maud, and the kind of catch young vampire girls dreamed of. Maud fell for him hard, but she stuck to her guns. I was sixteen when they met. He worked on her for two years. Maud was like a swan. It took a lot to earn her loyalty but once she gave it, she gave it for life.

"Is that what happened with House Ervan?"

She nodded. "Something like that. After we got thrown out of the camp, I told him it was the last time. That he didn't care about me or Helen and all he had were these idiotic ambitions that landed us in the middle of a damned wasteland again and again. If he pulled that crap one more time, he was on his own. He swore to me that he would put everything right. He did everything he could: he promised, he begged, he smiled that charming smile, except I was over it."

"Then why did you stay with him?"

She glanced at Helen sleeping under the covers. And instantly I knew. Helen must've adored her father with all her little heart. Melizard was so lovable, handsome, and funny. It would take her years to figure out that he was a terrible parent.

Maud inspected the repair. It was like the dent was never there. She chewed on her lower lip, turning the armor under the light this way and that, and moved on to the next dent.

"After that, House Kor hired him," she said. "To be their sergeant. They were in a land dispute with another House, and it was getting ugly. They didn't want me, they just wanted him. They needed someone skilled in tactics, with some name recognition, and they needed him fast, because the other House was going on the offensive. Melizard agreed to take the job. He trained their soldiers, he overhauled their entire force, and he did what he always did when you put him on the battlefield: he tore through his enemies. The other House realized that they had to take him out."

"Did they kill him?"

"No." Maud paused and looked at me. "They offered him twice as much money. They didn't want him to fight for them. They just wanted him to not show up."

"He told them to shove it, right?"

"No. The moron took the money."

"Are you serious?"

"It's like the planet was slowly driving him mad, eroding his soul piece by piece. I didn't even recognize him anymore. He took that blood money and he had the audacity to tell me he was doing it for me and Helen. That I, horrible witch that I am, accused him of not caring for his wife and daughter and when he took the money, he was thinking of us and where we would be if he died in battle."

I tried to reconcile the Melizard I remembered with that and couldn't.

"According to him, House Kor was too weak to win anyway and all their victories were temporary. But he'd trained them too well. They won and after they figured out what happened, they hired a gang of raiders and tracked us down in another province. They arranged for a local House to offer a lucrative job and when Melizard took the bait, they killed him. I watched it happen."

Her voice lost all emotion, as if she were talking about something completely unimportant.

"I was supposed to come with him but at the last minute he told me to stay back, almost like he had a premonition. Helen and I were laying on a nearby hill when they cut him to pieces while he was still alive and then burned his body. They put his head on a stake and stuck it on the House wall."

"Did Helen see?"

"No. I covered her eyes. But she saw the head. There was no way around that."

Maud glanced at her. "She surprises me. She's my daughter. She came out of me; I was there. But there are times she does weird things and I don't know if it's human weird or vampire weird. This was one of those times. You'd think a child that young wouldn't be able to understand death, but somehow she figured out that her father wouldn't be coming back and that a blood debt had to be paid. I thought she would be heartbroken, and she was for a few days, then she bounced back like it never happened. Maybe it's because Melizard spent so little time with her in the past two years. We were either on the job together or he was on the job on his own. She got used to him leaving. I don't know."

Neither did I. I was the youngest child. No baby brothers or sisters and a five-year-old was brand new territory. "What happened after he died?"

"Then a blood debt needed to be paid. So I found them, one by one, and I killed them all. Took me most of these last eight months."

That was my sister. She watched her husband murdered and then hunted his killers against impossible odds, all the while trying to protect their daughter, and she summed it up like she was describing going to a grocery store on Tuesday.

"By the time I was done, I had a list of relatives howling for vengeance a mile long and two offers of marriage." Maud took another cloth from the kit, sprayed some black liquid on it and polished the breastplate.

"Didn't take them up on it?" I winked at her.

"I'm done with vampires. Hell will freeze over before I let another one anywhere near me or Helen. They're all the same. Anyway, there is no future on Karhari. You were my last hope."

"Why send a message with a Ku?" I asked.

"Well, I didn't have a lot of choices," she said. "And this Ku was hitching a ride on an Arbitrator's ship."

"Really?" Why did I have an odd feeling about this?

"An Arbitrator stopped at a Lodge where Helen and I were hiding."

"What?" It couldn't be.

"No idea what he was doing on Karhari. I've never seen one up close before. Beautiful man, golden blond hair. Walked with a cane."

George. Just like I thought. The man who'd orchestrated the peace summit.

"Anyway, he paused by my table and said that I looked like someone from Earth and how odd it was to see someone like me and Helen in that wretched place. And I said that I was from Earth and still had family on the planet. He told me that he wouldn't be going to Earth for a while, but that he would be stopping in the vicinity to drop off some clients and that a Ku in his party liked delivery jobs, so if I were to write a message, he would see that it reached my family. It was a shot in the dark. I never thought it would work."

George knew exactly who she was. Of course he did. He probably wanted something in return, if not now, then later. That man never did anything without calculating all the variables. And I didn't care. From now on he would stay free in the inn as long as he lived.

"Thank you for coming to get me." She reached out to me and I hugged her.

"It will be okay," I told her the way our mother used to tell me when everything was bleak and all I could do was cry about it.

"It will be okay," my sister echoed and hugged me back.

Chapter 4

I paced back and forth before the circular summoning gate. We were due to arrive in range of Earth at any moment. When we did, the empty space defined by the gate would become blood-red, I'd step into it, and then I would be home. If home was still standing.

Maud and Helen went to the stream to look at the colorful fish, but not before Maud told me I had turned into our mom and then laughed. At least she could still laugh.

"If you keep pacing, your shoes will start smoking from the friction," Sean said.

I almost jumped. I hadn't heard him come up behind me. I turned around and there he was, dressed in his usual jeans and a T-shirt, clean-shaven. His hair was still slightly damp. He must've recently taken a shower. The heavy duffel rested on his back, the small duffel was in his hands. The subcutaneous armor he had gotten from Wilmos had shrunk into swirls of tattoos and their dark edges peeked out from under his sleeves and above his collar.

"Hi."

"Hi," he said.

I realized that I hadn't even thanked him yesterday. I'd just grabbed Maud and walked away and then didn't leave the suite for the entirety of the trip back. Not that it was very long - about twelve hours or so - but still.

"Thank you for coming to rescue my sister."

"You're welcome."

It would help if I stopped staring at him like a fool.

"How is she?"

"Maud?" Yes, who else would he be asking about? Ugh. "She's resilient."

"Look at the way she stands," Sean murmured.

When you picked up a child and held her, it was natural to pop a hip out and sit her on it. I'd seen Mom do it in the pictures where she held me or Maud. When I picked up Helen, I had unconsciously done the same thing. Maud was holding Helen so she could see the fish better, but her hips were perfectly straight. She supported her daughter's entire weight with her arms and Helen wasn't light. I had no idea what the average weight for a five-year-old girl was, but Helen was probably forty, maybe forty-five pounds.

It's hard to pop the hip out while wearing armor. Maud stood like a vampire.

"It will wear off," I said. I sounded like I wanted to convince myself.

Sean didn't say anything.

"Are you going to stick around?" And why did I just say that?

"Where would I go?" he asked.

I was making a spectacular idiot out of myself today. I had to get to the inn. Worrying about it was driving me crazy.

"I don't know," I said. "The galaxy is a big place. A certain werewolf once told me that he wanted to open his eyes and see it."

"I saw it."

"Learn anything interesting?"

Sean's eyes flashed with amber. "I learned that sometimes what you go looking for isn't as important as what you leave behind."

My face felt hot. Did I just blush? I hoped not. "What did you leave behind?" Oh, I was such an idiot.

He opened his mouth.

The doors in the far wall opened and Arland marched out. He was in full armor. His blood mace hung at his waist. He carried a large, black bag slung across his shoulders and an equally large bag in his right hand. Another male vampire, russet-haired and a few years younger, followed him, distress plain on his face.

Arland stopped by me. He didn't look at Maud. Maud pretended she didn't see him.

"Lady Dina."

"Lord Arland. Thank you again for rescuing my sister and for letting us ride in this amazing ship."

"It was a small matter," he said. "I wanted to speak to you concerning a promise you made to me."

What promise, when, where? "Yes?"

"You once told me that I would always find myself welcome at your inn."

Oh, that. "Of course."

Arland smiled, baring the edge of his fangs. "I find myself... stressed."

"Stressed, my lord?"

"Stressed by the burdens of House matters. I find myself bending under the weight of overwhelming responsibility."

Sean chuckled. "You live for that shit."

Arland valiantly ignored him. "I desire a sojourn. A brief respite from the many matters requiring my attention. I do believe I've earned it."

The russet-haired vampire stepped forward. "Lord Marshal, your uncle was most specific—"

Arland bared his fangs a little more. "My uncle is, of course, concerned for my well-being."

The male vampire looked like someone had slapped his face with a fish.

"He knows the many pressures I face and he would be delighted to know I've taken steps to remedy my condition, isn't that so, Knight Ruin?"

"Yes, my lord," the russet-haired vampire said, resigned. "Lord Soren will be delighted."

Lord Soren popped into my head in all his burly, grim-faced, older vampire glory. "I didn't know the Knight Sergeant knew the meaning of the word."

"His grizzled exterior hides a gentle heart."

Knight Ruin nearly choked on air.

"You're welcome to spend as much time at Gertrude Hunt as you need, my lord. We are honored by your presence."

"It's decided, then."

The summoning gate turned crimson.

"And we're here. How fortuitous." Arland stepped into the red light. Sean laughed under his breath and followed him in.

Maud approached, leading Helen by the hand. "You're letting him stay at the inn?"

"Of course." Considering that he just flew his destroyer halfway across the galaxy for her sake, it was the least I could do.

Maud said nothing, but I could see the sigh on her face.

"It's a big inn," I told her. "You will hardly see him."

She grinned at me. "I was right. You did turn into Mom."

"Please." I rolled my eyes.

She grabbed her bag, squeezed Helen's hand, and stepped into the crimson glow.

I followed her.

Vertigo squeezed me. A strange sensation of flying but without moving rolled through me, rearranging all my organs, and then I landed on the grass in the orchard. Early morning colored the sky a pale pink. Against the light backdrop, Gertrude Hunt stood out, with all her endearing Victorian oddities: the balconies protruding in strange places, the tower, the sunroom, the eaves, the spindle work, the overly ornate windows, and I loved every inch of it.

The trees shivered, greeting me. Magic pulsed from me through the house to the very edges of the property and the house creaked, reconnecting. If Gertrude Hunt were a cat, it would've arched its back and rubbed against my feet, purring.

Still standing. Nothing out of place. I took a mental tally of the beings inside. Caldenia, Orro, Beast, and the nameless cat. Everyone is present and accounted for. Oh phew. Phew.

Maud bent over, squeezing her eyes shut for a second. "I hate those things."

Next to her Arland stood straight, like an immovable mountain of vampire awesomeness immune to silly things like nausea. Sadly for him, my sister completely ignored him and his iron stomach. She shook her head, probably trying to shake the last echoes of the summoning gate out, straightened, and saw Gertrude Hunt.

"Dina, this is lovely."

Helen gaped at the orchard.

The back door burst open and Beast exploded onto the lawn, black and white fur flying.

Helen's eyes went wide and she hid behind Maud. Beast jumped into my arms, licked my face, wiggled free, and dashed around in a circle, unable to contain her canine glee.

"It's a dog," Maud said. "Remember the pictures?"

"Her name is Beast," I told her. "She's nice. If you make friends, she will guard you and keep you safe."

The ground by me parted and my robe surfaced, the plain gray one. The inn was trying to make sure I didn't leave again. I picked it up and slipped it on over my clothes. *See? It's okay. I'm home.*

"Your face is different," Helen said, looking up at me.

"It's because she's an innkeeper," Maud said. "This house is magic and she rules it. She is very powerful within the inn."

"You're part innkeeper, too," I told her. "Does it make you feel a little funny being here?"

Helen nodded.

"That's because you're my niece. The inn will listen to you, if you're kind to it."

Helen turned and hid her face in Maud's jeans.

"Too much," my sister said and ruffled her hair. "It's okay, little flower. It will be okay. We're home."

Sean was walking away with his bags.

"Sean," I called.

He turned around and kept walking backward.

"Come have breakfast with us."

"When?"

"At seven." Orro always served breakfast at seven. The least I could do was feed Sean.

"I'll be there."

He turned around and kept walking. He never told me what he left behind.

I watched him stride away for another breath and turned to Gertrude Hunt. The back door opened.

"Gertrude Hunt welcomes you, Lord Arland," I said. "Please follow me to your rooms."

⁂

Maud crossed her arms and examined the bedroom. The floor and walls were a pale cream stone. A shaggy rug, a deep comforting brown with reddish streaks, stretched by the bed. A large floor-to-ceiling window opened onto the orchard. Lamps of frosted glass shaped like inverted tulips dotted the walls. A plain bed protruded from the wall, furnished with white linens and fluffy pillows.

Maud's bedroom in our parents' inn was a dark place, filled with books, weapons, and oddities we all collected either from excursions to Baha-char or from regulars who occasionally brought us gifts. Dad used to joke that Maud never grew out of the cave phase. The bedroom she just made could've belonged in any of the vampire castles. She did add some human touches to it - the lines were softer and less geometric - but overall, if we had large delegations of vampires coming in, I'd make her fix up their quarters.

"Told you," I said. "Like riding a bicycle."

She frowned. "I'm rusty."

She was a little rusty. It took her nearly half an hour to figure out what she wanted and when she pushed the inn to do it, it moved sluggishly. Maud wasn't one hundred percent connecting to Gertrude Hunt. That was okay. It would come with time.

"Mama?" Helen stuck her head through the doorway. "I made my room."

I'd formed adjoining rooms for them.

"I can't wait. Let me see." Maud hurried over.

I followed and stopped in the doorway. Helen had made a pond. The entire room was lined with stone and filled with about a foot of water. A stone pathway led to the middle of the pond, where a large simulated tree bent to form a crescent shaped structure, a backward C. A small bed rested in the lower curve of the crescent, black sheets, black pillows, and a fuzzy pink blanket. Small, narrow windows punctured the dark walls, showing a glimpse of the orchard on all three sides. Helen must've wanted to see the orchard on every side, so she bent physics without realizing it. Dad always said that it was much easier to teach a child to be an innkeeper than an adult, because a child had no preconceived notions about what was possible. She'd kept the windows small, though. Trees were still a little scary.

"I can't make the fishes." Helen's face looked mournful.

"The inn can't make the fish," I told her. "But we'll go out and buy some, okay?"

"Okay."

Magic chimed in my head. "Time for breakfast."

I led them down the stairs. In the kitchen Orro dashed about. Helen had already seen him and didn't bat an eye. For some reason, trees were scary but a seven-foot-tall monster hedgehog with foot-long needles and sharp claws was totally okay.

Caldenia was already seated. Her platinum-gray hair was impeccable, as was her makeup, and her sea-foam gown. She looked every inch a galactic tyrant ready for her morning meal.

"Is that who I think it is?" Maud murmured next to me.

"It is. She has a lifetime membership."

"I remember when we went to camp and you wouldn't go past your waist into the lake because you were convinced there were brain-eating amoebas in there. It's like I don't even know you anymore. When did you lose your mind?"

"When Mom and Dad disappeared. You were married and far away. Klaus wanted to keep searching. I had nothing and then the Assembly gave me this inn. It had been dormant for a very long time and it needed guests."

"I'm so sorry," Maud said.

"I'm a Demille." I smiled at her. "We always manage. By the way, I didn't forget that you dunked me into that lake. Payback is coming."

"Bring it on."

"Arland is coming down the stairs," I warned her. I'd reopened the vampire wing I had built during the peace summit. The inn hadn't absorbed it yet, so Arland had the entire palatial suite to himself.

She turned subtly.

I tracked Arland with my magic as he descended the stairs, walked through the hallway hidden from us by the wall, emerged into the front room, and finally entered the kitchen. He was out of his armor, the sign of highest trust from a vampire knight. He wore loose fitting black pants and a textured brown tunic pulled up on his forearms. His blond hair was carelessly pulled back into a ponytail at the nape of his neck. Arland wasn't just handsome, he was striking and when he smiled, it was the kind of smile that could launch a vampire armada. He was also built like a superhero: massive shoulders, defined arms, and a powerful chest, slimming down to a narrow, flat waist and long legs. Watching him walk toward us was an experience.

I glanced at my sister. Nothing. Cold as an iceberg.

"Mom!" an urgent whisper said behind us.

I turned. Helen was holding the nameless cat. The huge Maine Coon I had rescued from a glass prison in PetSmart stared at me with slightly freaked out eyes, clearly not understanding how this small human creature dared to grab him.

"He has fangs," Helen said.

"That's a kitty," Maud said. "Be careful. They have sharp claws."

"What's his name?"

"He doesn't have one," I told her. I hadn't gotten around to it. "I tell you what, you can name him."

Helen's eyes got almost as big as the cat's. "I can?"

"Yes."

"I'm going to name him Olasard, after he who hunts the evildoers and rips out their souls."

The Ripper of Souls gave me a befuddled look.

I looked at Maud.

"There weren't a lot of kids' books," she said. "Melizard used to recite the heroic sagas for her."

A gentle magic tug told me Sean was coming to the door. I went into the front room and opened it for him. Sean hadn't bothered changing. Still jeans and a T-shirt. For some reason, I liked him just like this.

"Hi again," I said, feeling awkward for no reason. "Come inside. We have food."

"Thanks for inviting me."

We went to the kitchen. Normally Caldenia, Orro, and I took our meals together at a breakfast table, but given the larger company, I extended the kitchen to accommodate the big heavy table the inn pulled out of storage. Rustic, made of an ancient scarred door that must've at one point graced a mission or an old Texas hacienda, it was sealed with several coats of resin until it shone.

We took our seats at the table. Orro had gone the traditional American Breakfast route: stacks of light as a feather pancakes with butter melting at the top; paper-thin crepes filled with strawberries; tiny, muffin-sized apple pies with delicate dough lattices on top; hash browns; heaps of bacon and sausage; and three types of eggs, over easy, sunny side up, and scrambled. He swept by giving me the Look of Death, and retreated into the kitchen. Later I would get a lecture about not letting him know in advance that extra guests would be arriving.

"Her Grace, Caldenia ka ret Magren," I said. "My sister Maud and her daughter Helen."

"*Letere Olivione.*" My sister inclined her head. "We're honored by your presence."

"Honored is such a serious word, my dear." Caldenia flashed her sharp teeth. "I'm but a quiet, country recluse now, no one important."

Maud put eggs, a crepe, a sausage link, and a piece of bacon on Helen's plate.

"Your regal presence elevates all surroundings with its magnificence," Arland said. "A diamond in the rough shines ever brighter."

"My dear boy, I did miss you." Caldenia sipped her tea.

Helen bit a piece of bacon. Her eyes got big again and she scarfed it down and reached for the platter. Arland had reached for the bacon at the same time. They stared at each other across the table. A vampire standoff.

Helen wrinkled her face, showing him her tiny fangs.

Arland bared his scary fangs, his eyes laughing.

A low, tiny sound came from my niece. "*Awrawrrawrawr.*"

"Helen!" Maud turned to her. "Don't growl at the table."

Arland leaned back, pretending to be scared. "So fierce."

Helen laughed, her giggles bubbling up. "*Awrawrawr.*"

Arland shuddered.

Helen giggled again, grabbed her mug, and hurled it at the wall. The mug shattered. I looked back. Helen's seat was empty. The platter of bacon had vanished.

Sean lost it and laughed.

"What a delightful little girl," Caldenia said, her eyes sparkling.

Maud looked lost. "I... She never... "

"The child has an inborn grasp of tactics." Arland grinned.

Magic chimed, announcing a visitor. Hmm. In broad daylight? Coming in from the northwest, not the street. I'd have to meet them in the stables. I hadn't yet collapsed the inn structure left over from the summit, mostly because I was so damn tired. It had taken so much energy to put everything where it needed to go so it would be invisible from the street, and packing it back in would take time and effort. Short term, the maintenance took less energy since everything was already formed and there. I was going to wait until after Christmas.

"Excuse me." I picked up Helen's plate, added one of the small apple pies to it, went into the front room, and lifted the green cloth on the side table. Three sets of eyes stared at me: one canine, one feline, and one half-human. I held the plate out. It was snatched from my hands. I dropped the cloth back down and headed to the stables through the hallway.

Sean stepped out of the kitchen and quietly followed me. I let him catch up.

"Problems?"

"Visitors," I said.

We made our way to the stable gates.

In the field, beyond the small area of Otrokar holy ground, a green spiral sliced through the fabric of existence, unwinding from a single point into a funnel. Darkness puffed into the mouth of the funnel and withdrew, taking the spiral with it. An odd creature landed on the grass. Five feet tall, it stood on two grimy metal legs ending in metal hooves. The legs were a mess of old dented metal, gears, tiny lights, and thin tubes channeling a milky white substance. A bulbous hump protruded from its back. A tattered shroud, draped over the hump, hid most of its body. Two massive, oversized metal hands stuck out from the openings in the shroud, and, like the legs, consisted of a chaotic jumble of different parts. The creature's folded, wrinkled neck, made of an alien rubber-like substance, seemed too long. A helmet that slightly resembled a medieval plague doctor's face mask concealed the alien's face. Three faceted high tech "eyes," pale yellow and round, pierced the helmet. The whole thing looked like someone had scooped handfuls of garbage out of some cosmic trash heap and formed a vaguely humanoid creature out of it.

A Hiru. I didn't realize any of them were left.

The thing saw us and turned, creaking. Thick lubricant squirted onto the gears, pinkish and greasy. The body clanked, ground, and moved, the metal protesting. The wind brought its noxious odor our way and I nearly gagged.

Next to me Sean had gone completely still.

"What the hell is that?"

"That's a Hiru. They are completely harmless, but most of the creatures in the galaxy find them revolting. Please try not to gag."

The Hiru slowly made its way to us and halted five feet from me.

I bowed my head and smiled. "Welcome to Gertrude Hunt."

Something screeched within the Hiru, like nails on a chalkboard.

Don't wince. Don't vomit. Don't offend the guest.

A tenor voice came forth, quiet and sad. "I have come with an offer for you."

"It will be my pleasure to hear it out. Please, follow me."

The Hiru walked into the stables, one tortured step at a time.

⚜ ⚜ ⚜

I led the Hiru into the front room. To do anything else would be an insult. Helen was still under the table. My niece had gone very quiet.

Maud met us in the doorway of the kitchen. She saw the Hiru and smiled. Not a wince, not a blink, nothing to indicate that she found anything about the guest distasteful.

"Would you like to share our meal?" I asked.

"No. I do not consume carbon-based compounds."

"Is there a particular dish that I may prepare for you?"

The Hiru shook its head. The gears screeched. "Thank you for your kindness. It is not necessary."

In my entire life I had only seen two Hirus. One stayed at my parents' inn and the other had ground and stumbled his way through the streets of Baha-char. Creatures from all over the galaxy had given it a wide berth and not just because they found it revolting. Standing next to a Hiru was as dangerous as running into an advancing enemy on the battlefield.

I concentrated and pulled part of the wall out, shaping it to fit the Hiru's body. "Please, sit down."

The Hiru bent its body the way a human would when doing a squat and carefully lowered himself onto the new seat. Helen pulled the tablecloth aside, peeked out, sneezed, and vanished back under the table.

"You said you had an offer for me?"

"Yes."

I wasn't sure if it was his translator or his true emotions, but everything he said sounded sad.

"Do you require privacy for this conversation?"

"No. This concerns the werewolf as well."

Sean, who had quietly parked himself by the wall between me and the Hiru, startled. "Why?"

"She may need help," the Hiru said.

"I'm listening," I said.

"Do you know our history? Do you know of the Draziri?"

A quick glance at Sean told me he didn't.

"A screen, please. Files on the Hiru/Draziri conflict," I told the inn.

Arland joined Maud in the doorway. They stood side by side, each at their half of the door, completely ignoring each other's presence.

A screen slid from the ceiling. On it a deep orange sun, darker than our own, burned, surrounded by twelve planets.

"The Hiru lived here, on the sixth planet." I beckoned with my fingers, and the recording zoomed in on a small planet. It looked like a ball of dark smoke, its soot-choked atmosphere glowing weakly with fluorescent green. "They were an ancient civilization, capable of interstellar travel, and they mined their system and the surrounding star systems for resources. The Draziri live here."

The image zoomed out, and a second star appeared, this one a familiar yellow color. Seven planets orbited it, the fifth one a ball of magenta, green, and blue.

"The Draziri are a relatively young civilization, a martial theocracy with a religion based on admission to afterlife following a lifetime of service and piety. They discovered interstellar travel only a century ago. The planet of the Hiru was their first stop."

The dead hunk of the Hiru's planet expanded, taking up half of the screen.

"We don't know why the Draziri declared a holy war on the Hiru. They are moderately xenophobic, as are most theocracies, but they have since interacted with the rest of the galaxy and while they keep to themselves, they haven't attempted to exterminate anyone else. We do know the Draziri invaded the Hiru star system and detonated some sort of device that caused a chain reaction in the planet's atmosphere."

"Millions died in one hour," the Hiru said.

"Directly after, the Protopriest of the Draziri proclaimed the Hiru to be an abomination. The Draziri spent the next fifty years hunting the remaining Hiru across the galaxy. It is said that a Draziri who kills a Hiru is guaranteed a place in the afterlife."

"There are only a thousand of us left," the Hiru said. "Our species will become extinct in the next twenty cycles if we do not find a way to reproduce. To mate and raise our young, certain conditions must be met. We cannot meet them while we are being hunted. We have appealed for Arbitration, but the Draziri declined."

And nothing would be done about it. I dissolved the screen back into the wall.

"Can't you appeal for refuge?" Sean asked.

"We have," the Hiru said. "The Yaok system allowed us to settle within their territory. They promised us protection. We sent the first fifty colonists, but the Draziri invaded the system and wiped us out."

"They took staggering losses," Arland said. "I remember reading about it as a child. Almost two hundred thousand Draziri troops died so they could kill fifty Hiru. Our strategy manuals use it as a cautionary tale about the costs of victories."

"We are not safe," the Hiru said.

"You are safe here," I told him.

"Yes," Sean said. "You are."

His face was dark. Auul, the planet of his parents, had been destroyed too, not by an enemy but by his own ancestors. The werewolves of Auul killed their beautiful planet rather than surrender it to their enemy.

"The Arbitrator whom we had petitioned offered a solution," the Hiru said. "We have surrendered everything we have. All the treasures we possess. We paid the price in knowledge. Everything we are and everything we were, we have given up freely."

"I don't understand," I said.

"We have hired the Archivarius," the Hiru said. "We have received word that the Archivarius has found a solution."

Oh wow.

"The Archivarius is in its parts," the Hiru said.

Sean and Arland both looked at me.

"The Archivarius is a multipart being," I explained. "A hive mind possessing an incredible wealth of information about the universe. For the knowledge to be shared, all individual members of the Archivarius must come together in a single location. They do this very rarely and they reform only for a very brief time. The Archivarius will answer questions, but it is very selective about which questions it chooses and the price is beyond what most galactic states can pay."

"The Draziri cannot know or find out," the Hiru said. "They will try to stop the Archivarius from reforming. We have no safe place. The Arbitrator suggested that you might keep us safe."

"Was he a human male? Pale yellow hair?"

"Yes." The Hiru nodded.

George. George was ruthless, cunning, and calculating, and compassionate to a fault. He couldn't stand by and let them die, so he sent them my way. It was an unspoken bargain. He helped me rescue my sister. In turn, he hoped I would rescue the Hiru. He would never ask me to do it. He would never expect that I repay the favor. He left the choice to me.

"The Archivarius and my people will make an effort to deliver the individual Archivarians, which are its parts, to your inn. But it may not always be possible. Some may need to be retrieved from other worlds. All will need to be kept safe. We wish to use your inn. We wish you to help us."

That's exactly what I thought. It broke my heart to tell him no, but I couldn't. I just couldn't.

"My deepest apologies, but the security of my inn is my priority. I am bound by the innkeeper laws. These laws dictate that I keep my guests safe first and foremost. What you are suggesting - retrieving the Archivarians - would require me to leave the inn unattended. Nor am I capable of doing the retrievals. I'm an innkeeper. I'm at my most powerful here, at the inn. This is my place."

"We have seen you rescue your sister. We have observed. We know you are capable."

George must've wanted to help them desperately. I wanted to help them.

"I can't. Doing this would make the inn a target for the Draziri and they won't abide by the treaty of Earth. The secret of the existence of other galactic life must be kept. It breaks my heart to tell you no, but I must. I'm so sorry."

"The treasures we have given were our most prized possessions," the Hiru said. "Our books. Our images. Our secrets. Everything that made us. We are dying. Our culture will be gone without us. It has value. It is rare. The Archivarius prizes rare."

I bit my lip.

"Enough for two," the Hiru said.

"Two what?" Maud asked.

"Enough for answers to two questions," the Hiru said. "The Arbitrator told us."

He raised his hand. A panel on his forearm slid aside and a translucent image formed above it, woven from the tiny yellow lights. The picture of my missing parents, the one I kept hanging on the front room wall.

"Help us," the Hiru said. "And you can ask your question."

Chapter 5

Silence claimed the room.

Maud was looking at me. It was my inn and it was up to me to respond.

"Will you give us time to discuss your proposal?"

The Hiru nodded. "My time is short, but I'll wait until the beginning of the light cycle."

We had until the next morning to decide.

"Follow me, please."

I led him through the hallway, forming a new room downstairs as we walked. So little was known about the Hiru, but the one thing my mother told me was that reproducing the Hiru's native environment was beyond the inns' capacity. Gertrude Hunt could create almost anything with my direction and the proper resources, but some things, like intense heat, for example, were off-limits. The inns could handle small controlled flames, like fireplaces and pits, but large scale blazes put them under undue stress.

According to my mother, the Hiru's environment required a very specific combination of gasses, pressure, and gravity, and we simply couldn't match it. A Hiru was never truly comfortable anywhere, but they liked water. When one stayed at my parents' inn, my mother made her a room with indigo walls and a deep pool at the end. That had to be my best bet.

The Hiru moved behind me, his gait slow, ponderous, and labored. Our galaxy loved tech in all its incarnations. A high tech assault suit or a bastard sword, it didn't matter - once it was made, someone would almost immediately try to improve on it. The Hiru were the glaring exception to this rule. There was nothing sleek or efficient about them. They were clunky and slow, as if some mad genius had tried to build a robot with things he'd found at a junkyard, but died before he could improve his design past its first, barely functional prototype. Even his translator was so ancient, it failed to associate "morning" with "beginning of the light cycle."

But there was so much sadness in his voice. The translator may have been antiquated, but the emotion was there. I had to do better than an empty blue room.

I closed my eyes for a moment and tried my best to feel the being standing next to me. If I were he, what would I need?

I would want beauty. I would want hope and tranquility, and above all, safety. But what did beauty mean to a Hiru?

"Tell me about your planet?" I asked.

"There are no words."

Of course there weren't, but this wasn't my first day in the inn. "Tell me about the sky."

The Hiru paused. "Colors," he said. "Twisting and flowing into each other. Glowing rivers of colors against the dark blue sky."

Mom was close with indigo. "Red, yellow?"

"Red, yes. Lavender. And lights." The Hiru slowly raised his massive metal hand and moved it. "Tiny sparks of lights across the sky to the horizon."

"Clouds?"

"Yes. Like a tall funnel, twisting."

We reached the door. I pushed it open with my fingertips.

The round room stretched up, rising three stories high. At the very top, a maelstrom of clouds turned ever so slowly, a 3-D projection streaming from the ceiling. An aurora borealis suffused it with light, alternating among deep purple, red, pink, turquoise, and beautiful, glowing lavender. Tiny rivers of glowing dots swirled, floating gently through the illusory clouds. The chamber's walls, deep indigo stone, offered two seats shaped to accommodate the Hiru's body protruding from the far wall. In the center of the room, right under the sky, a pool of water waited, twenty feet wide, round, and deep enough to submerge the Hiru up to the chin of his helmet.

"Enjoy your stay."

The Hiru didn't answer. He was looking at the sky. Slowly, ponderously, he moved to the pool, the openings on his metal body hissing shut. He stood on the first step of the stairs, half a foot in the water. The glow of the aurora borealis played on the metal of his suit. The Hiru took another step, moving in deeper. The water lapped at his body, he turned, and collapsed into the water, floating, his face to the sky.

I stepped out and let the door shut behind me. I grinned in victory. Nailed it.

A quiet sob filtered through the room behind me. I froze. Another, sad and tortured, the sound of a being in mourning.

All my triumph evaporated.

He was all alone in the galaxy, one of the last thousand, all that was left of his species, and now he wept in my inn.

I tiptoed away, back to the front room. Maud had landed on the couch. Arland elected to stay where he was, in the doorway. Sean hadn't moved from his spot by the wall.

"You know an Arbitrator?" Maud asked.

"As much as anyone can know George. He's a complicated guy." And he had just done me an enormous favor.

"Was he the same one I met?"

"Probably." It had to be George. Only he would look at this situation and figure out a way to help me and the Hiru at the same time.

"Are you going to take the offer?" Sean asked.

"We would be fools not to," Maud said. "We couldn't afford to ask the Archivarius a question if we worked nonstop every day for the rest of our lives."

She wasn't wrong. George had given us a once-in-a-lifetime gift, but it came with serious strings attached.

"Our brother and I searched for our parents for years," I said. "We found nothing. The Archivarius has an enormous wealth of knowledge. If anyone knows, it does."

"I sense a *but* coming," Maud said.

"We would be facing the Draziri. Sooner or later they will show up. We're putting the inn at risk of exposure and the guests at risk of injury."

Maud rubbed her face.

I thought of the Hiru in the room, weeping quietly at the memory of his planet's sky. You would have to be completely heartless to say no. If the inn had no other guests... No, not even then. It would be irresponsible. Sometimes my job required me to be heartless. I knew the correct thing to do, so why was it making me feel sick to my stomach?

"Also, we don't have the manpower," I said.

"You have me," Sean said.

"I appreciate it, but you are not part of the inn."

Sean pulled his wallet out of his pants, took out a dollar, and handed it to me.

Okay. "What am I supposed to do with this?"

"Hire me."

"I will be more than delighted to lend a hand," Arland said.

"You are a guest," Maud said.

"I'm on a sojourn," he said. "Trying to improve my physical and mental state. A little exercise is good for the body. It is my understanding that an innkeeper must meet the needs of her guests. I require a battle."

"Nobody asked me," Caldenia said, gliding into the room from the kitchen. "Because I'm apparently, what is the saying, chopped kidneys."

"Liver," I said.

"Thank you, my dear. Chopped liver. However, I would welcome some excitement as well. Life can be so dreadfully dull without a little spice, especially around the holidays."

Only Caldenia would call the threat of an interstellar invasion "a little spice."

My phone rang. I stuck the dollar into the pocket of my jeans under my robe and went to pick it up.

"Dina," Brian Rodriguez said, his voice vibrating with stress. "So glad I caught you."

"Mr. Rodriguez, what's wrong?"

Mr. Rodriguez had never asked me for anything. Please don't be the Ku, please don't be the Ku...

"Do you get the Dallas station?"

"Which one?"

"Any network."

I covered the phone with my hand. "Screen. I need the feed from WFAA8 from Dallas."

A screen slid from the wall, blinked, and flared into light. A stretch of a highway, shown from above, clearly filmed from a helicopter. A pack of police cars sped down the asphalt, lights on. In front of them a pale oval of light slid at reckless speed, zigzagging back and forth among the vehicles.

"You know what, Jim, we are some distance away," a male voice said through the mild static. "We're going to try to push in on it, but so far we have been unable to see the nature of this vehicle. We are still quite a ways away, so we'll try to get close and see if we can make out what is underneath that light. We'll have to see what happens as this vehicle keeps going down the highway here."

"We know how dangerous these high-speed pursuits are," a female newscaster said. "Whether on a freeway or on surface streets. But when you have such a bright light obscuring the vehicle, that can't possibly be safe. It is clearly blinding the officers who are pursuing this person. Can you imagine seeing that in your rearview mirror?"

Sean swore.

Oh no. Please no. I was very clear when Wing checked out of the inn before we went to get Maud. Very clear. I said to stay at Casa Feliz and behave or leave the planet.

"Well, as we can see, Jean, the police aren't really following too close behind. In fact, they are giving this driver plenty of room, trying to keep him from panicking and doing something reckless…"

"I'm so sorry to ask you for a favor," Mr. Rodriquez said. "But this is one of my guests. A Ku. His name is Wing."

Damn it!

"He checked into my inn last night, went out just before sunrise, and now we have this mess happening. I have no idea where he is going."

I knew exactly where he was going. He was heading down I45 toward me. He was coming back to Gertrude Hunt.

"Thank God someone fitted his boost bike with a daytime obfuscator," Mr. Rodriguez said.

I looked at Sean.

He raised his hands and mouthed, "It was all you had in the garage."

"I was his last stop," Mr. Rodriguez said. "He never checked out."

Wing was still a guest. If Wing was caught, Mr. Rodriquez would be hauled before the Assembly, and the Assembly wouldn't be kind.

"He's barreling down the highway toward you and he's got half of the Dallas PD behind him. He's about to clear the city limits and then the State Troopers are going to get involved. I can't get to him fast enough. We'd have to get in front of him to grab him. Any vehicle we'd have to use to get to that kind of speed would be too attention-grabbing in daylight, and the news channels are having a feeding frenzy. Is there any way you could help me?"

⚜ ⚜ ⚜

"Why in the world would you put an obfuscator on his boost bike?"

Sean and I sat in the back of the Ryder truck we had rented forty minutes ago. We'd attached a photon projector to it, drove here, and parked it on the grass well away from the road, on the side of I45. In front of us the highway rolled into the distance, completely empty.

"Because he had nothing at all, and he is a Ku." Sean rested his arms on the wheel and checked his phone.

"There were refractors in the garage. And a photon projector."

"I didn't see those, but even if I did, I wouldn't have put one on his bike."

"Why not?"

"Because he is a Ku. We used them as scouts on Nexus. He barely follows the rules as is and he drives like a maniac. If he got it through his thick skull that his boost bike was now invisible, he would zip around in daylight. We'd have a pileup on every major interstate after he was through. I put the obfuscator on there and told him it was only for emergencies and if he used it, law enforcement would come and hunt him."

Put that way, I had to agree. Wing was a menace. He wouldn't just cause accidents. He would cause many accidents. People would be hurt, possibly die.

Sean growled under his breath. "Arland is ignoring my texts."

"Have you tried sending a kissy face?"

Sean looked at me for a moment.

"Maybe he's just not that into you."

He tapped his ear piece. "They've just passed Madisonville. They threw out the spike strips, but of course he blasted right through them since he's riding two feet above the ground. He should be in range in about two minutes."

The Texas State Troopers must've reasoned that eventually the unknown vehicle would run out of gas, because all indications said they resolved to run it to ground. They also blocked the highway in both directions around Madisonville, and we had to creep past their road block. I held my breath the whole time. A photon projector could do wonders for making you near invisible, but it didn't mask sound. Every time the truck springs creaked, I'd braced myself.

We were up against eight police cars and a helicopter. They had helpfully exiled the news helicopters 'in the interests of public safety,' so at least we didn't have to worry about that.

I got my phone out and dialed Arland's phone. I'd given him one of the spares we kept for guests and showed him how to use it. He didn't seem enthusiastic.

Beep.

Beep.

Beep.

Come on, Arland.

Beep.

"This is a ridiculous communicator," Arland's voice said into the phone.

I put him on speaker.

"What is with the swiping and the pushing? Why isn't it simply voice activated?"

"The Ku will be in range in one minute and forty-five seconds," I told him.

"Understood." He hung up.

The phone might have been ridiculous, but it was safer than radio transmissions.

I dialed my sister. She picked up on the first ring.

"A minute and a half."

"Got it."

I drummed my fingers on the wooden floor of the truck's back. It would work. It was a simple plan, and it relied on the thing vampires did best - hunting. Arland would apprehend the Ku, my sister would run interference against the cops, and we were the getaway drivers.

"Are you going to help the Hiru?" Sean asked.

"I want to."

"What's stopping you?"

"It would be a logistical nightmare. It would require me to be away from the inn, probably on short notice. The Draziri would invade in force, and I don't think they care about being discreet. As an innkeeper, I'm supposed to avoid situations that put the inn at risk of exposure."

"Mhm," he said. "What's the real reason?"

"Those are the real reasons."

"I saw your face," Sean said. "You almost cried when he told his story."

So much for my inscrutable innkeeper face. "Just because I sympathize, doesn't mean I can't objectively evaluate the situation."

He didn't say anything.

On my left, in the distance, a dark dot appeared in the sky, quickly growing larger. The helicopter.

"Three... two..."

"One," Sean said.

A white ball engulfed the helicopter. Maud had fired the white-out.

The ball expanded, turning gray and growing denser in mid-air. A second explosion flared, also blinding white and low on the road. The State Troopers had crossed the white-out anti-personnel mines we seeded minutes ago. The fleet of cop cars had just been blinded.

The explosion solidified, losing its brightness. The first pale ball from the white-out fell into it, pulled like iron to a magnet. The caravan of police vehicles would come to a gentle stop, with the helicopter softly landing somewhere, hopefully not on top of them. The sphere would hold them for up to six minutes, just long enough to knock out everyone within the cars, and then dissipate into empty air. The white-out tech was developed a few centuries ago by an enterprising galactic criminal cartel specializing in kidnappings. It cost an arm and a leg. I was watching two hundred thousand credits worth of ammunition in action. A good chunk of my peace summit profits. Two steps forward, one step back. But even so, I still came out ahead.

Here's hoping the mines worked as advertised. Don't get caught, Maud. Don't get caught.

I jumped out of the truck, ran along the side, climbed into the cab, and pushed the off switch on the refrigerator-sized photon projector we had strapped to the truck's cab. If someone had been watching us from the highway, they would see the Ryder truck suddenly pop into existence out of nowhere.

A lone rider shot into view on a monstrous-looking anti-gravity glider bike, pulling a net behind him. Arland, riding a cre-cycle and dragging the boost bike and the Ku behind him in a black net. He screeched to halt in front of me. "Bagged and delivered."

Wing stared at me with terrified eyes.

Behind Arland, a second cre-cycle sped toward us. Maud. My heart hammered in my chest. She was in one piece. It was okay. Everything was okay.

Sean jumped to the ground, pulled out the retractable ramp, and lowered it to the pavement. Arland drove the cre-cycle into the truck, dragging the Ku behind him. I pulled a capsule out of my pocket.

"No!" Wing cried out.

"Yes. You're in so much trouble."

I stuck the capsule under his nose and broke it open. Green gas puffed and the Ku passed out.

"Nice," Sean said. He and Arland grabbed the net containing Wing and the boost bike and heaved it into the truck.

"Sadly this doesn't work on human anatomy." Otherwise Officer Marais would've been much less of a problem.

Maud pulled up, the big white-out cannon slung over her shoulder, and drove into the Ryder truck, wedging her cre-cycle next to Arland's. I handed her two more capsules. "If Wing stirs, drug him."

She nodded.

Sean slammed the door closed. I dashed to the cabin, opened the door, climbed up, and punched in the code in the photon projector. The unit's pale blue light blinked. I jumped down and took a few steps back, careful to walk in a straight line.

The Ryder truck vanished. If you looked very closely, you could see the slight wavy disturbance, but you had to be only a few feet away.

"Are we good?" invisible Sean asked.

"We're good." I walked straight back and almost jumped when the truck popped into existence eighteen inches in front of me. I climbed into the passenger seat. Sean eased the truck out of park and we crept across the grass onto the interstate. Sean picked up speed.

"How are we doing?" Sean asked.

I checked my phone. "Two more minutes before the mine effects dissipate. Twenty-three minutes before the photon projector runs out of charge."

He stepped on it. The Ryder rocked and rolled. It was just me and him in the cabin. This whole thing wasn't just risky, it was reckless. If we were caught, there would be hell to pay.

Sean sat in his seat, focused on driving. He didn't say anything to reassure me. He just projected a quiet, competent calm. I had a feeling that if a spaceship suddenly appeared in the sky and fired at us, Sean would somehow pull a massive gun out, shoot it down, and keep going, the same calm expression on his face. If Sean wasn't here, I would've done all of it myself, but right now I was glad he was in the cab with me.

"You asked why I have to turn the Hiru down," I said.

"I did."

"Maud. And Helen. I just rescued my sister and my niece after they lived through hell. Maud deserves some peace and quiet."

"Your sister looked pretty excited when you handed her the white-out warhead."

"I know. That's what I'm afraid of. If I put the inn in harm's way, she'll be on the front line cutting off heads."

"It's her choice," Sean said.

My alarm chimed. I flicked it off. The highway patrol was about to wake up.

"I know it's her choice. My brother-in-law brought a lot of what happened to him on his own head. Melizard was responsible for their exile, and once on the planet, he lost his mind. From what Maud said, he grew desperate and wasn't thinking clearly, and eventually he betrayed the House that hired him and got himself killed. A normal human thing for Maud to do would've been to try to get off the planet or try to establish some safety net for herself and Helen. Instead, my sister declared a blood feud and pursued it for months."

"Like a proper vampire," Sean said.

"Yes. We're not in the Holy Anocracy now. We're on Earth. This is her home. It will take time for her to remember what it's like to be human. I'm not going to make her choices for her or tell her what to do. I just don't want to thrust her into another bloody fight with no breathing room between that and what she went through. I want to give her a chance to adjust to humanity." I sighed. "The Draziri are single-minded. They will go to any lengths to kill the Hiru. You went through...things. How do you deal with it?"

"I can't speak for your sister," Sean said. "Everyone deals with it in their own way. People say you need peace and quiet and while you're there, in the thick of it, when everything is death and blood, you think so, too, because you idealize that. And then you get home."

He fell silent for a moment.

"It feels fake," he continued. "I get up, I wave at neighbors, I go to the grocery store, I gas up my car. The whole time I'm pretending to be someone else and I worry I might get my lines wrong."

"Sean..." I had no idea he felt that way.

He glanced at me, his face resolute, his eyes clear. "Peace and quiet doesn't help, because what's wrong isn't out there. It's inside me. This right here is the most normal I've felt since I got home."

I reached out and took his hand. He took his gaze off the road and looked at me. His eyes caught the light, their irises golden-brown amber. "And this." He squeezed my hand. "This feels normal. This feels like coming home."

Sirens blared behind us. He was still holding my hand, his strong fingers wrapped around mine. I remembered him walking away from me into the tear between the worlds. He'd wanted to see the galaxy and he owed Wilmos a favor. He went through it and was gone, and I'd stood on the grass, hugging myself. Guests left and we stayed. That was the fact of the innkeeper's life. My parents vanished, my brother left to look for them and disappeared, Maud had gotten married...But I got Sean back. He was in the cab with me, holding my hand and not wanting to let go.

"Slow down," I said. "It's coming up."

We passed a sign for Leona.

The sirens chased us, getting louder. I glanced into the side mirror. The police cars were right behind us. Half a minute and they would ram right into the back of the Ryder.

"Make a right," I told him.

Sean let go of my hand and cut across the grass. The Ryder rocked side to side, struggling with uneven ground, and pulled onto a narrow access road. The fleet of State Troopers tore past, wailing in fury.

Sean laughed a happy wolfish laugh under his breath.

"Don't go back to Wilmos." I hadn't meant to say it. At least not like this, but I'd started it and now I had to finish it. "Stay here with me. At least for a little while."

"I'll stay," he promised.

I looked away.

He eased off the brakes.

"Keep going down this road," I told him. "It will come out at a Buc-ee's."

"I love Buc-ee's," Sean said.

Everyone loved Buc-ee's. A chain of massive gas stations that doubled as restaurants and travel centers, Buc-ee's offered everything from parfaits and fifty different types of jerky to Texas themed merchandise. They were always full of cars and travelers who enjoyed easy access to the gas pumps and clean bathrooms. All we had to do was creep past any State Troopers guarding the exit and blend into the crowd.

Finally, Mr. Rodriguez would owe me a favor instead of the other way around.

"Why do you want to help the Hiru?" I asked Sean as we pulled into the huge parking lot.

"Because someone blew up their planet and is hunting them to extinction. Somebody needs to do something about it. Also, because you'll take them up on their offer and get involved, and I don't want you to deal with all that on your own."

"What makes you so sure I'll take them up on it?"

He grinned at me, turning into the old Sean Evans. The transformation was so sudden, I blinked to make sure I didn't imagine it.

"You're a carebear."

"What?"

"You're the type to get out of a perfectly dry car in the middle of a storm in your best dress so you can scoop a wet dog off the road. You help people, Dina. That's what you do. And the Hiru need help."

"I'm sensible," I told him.

"I'll give you till tonight," he said. "You won't even last twenty-four hours. I bet my right arm on it."

⚜ ⚜ ⚜

Sean backed the truck up my driveway and paused for a moment, pondering something.

"What?"

"I'm wondering if your sister murdered Arland in the back."

"Did she?"

He tilted his head, listening. "No. I still hear both of them. Damn it. Oh well, a man can dream."

We parked the truck. I got out and opened the back. Maud hopped onto the grass, shielded from the street by the bulk of the vehicle. Her face was a cold neutral mask.

Arland heaved the Ku and the bike to the edge of the truck. I waved my hand. Long flexible shoots burst out of the ground, wrapped around Wing and the bike and dragged them under. "Take him to the stables," I murmured. "And keep him there."

Arland jumped off the truck. "I quite enjoyed that. Thank you for this pleasant diversion."

"Thank you for your assistance."

Arland smiled, displaying sharp fangs, and went inside the inn.

I closed the truck back up and waved to Sean. He drove out. He'd return the truck and drive his car back.

Beast exploded out of her doggie door and jumped into my arms. I hugged her, but she was wiggling too hard, so I set her down and she streaked away in a fit of doggie excitement, tucking her tail between her legs for extra speed.

"Where is Helen?" Maud frowned.

"In the kitchen." I pointed. A window opened in the wall. Helen was perched precariously on a stool above a large pot. Someone had trimmed one of my old aprons, the one with sunflowers, and put it on her. She was stirring the stuff in the pot with a big spoon. The inn's tendrils hovered on both sides of her, ready to catch her if she fell.

I dug my phone out of my pocket and took a picture.

"He put her to work?" Maud stared.

Orro said something in his gravelly voice.

Helen nodded and sprinkled something into the soup and squeaked, "Yes, chef!"

"Give me that phone!" My sister grabbed the phone out of my hand and started snapping pictures.

Maud couldn't feel her daughter in the kitchen. It would come back. It had to come back. She'd spent years at our parents' inn and she never had any problems connecting to it.

"So what did you and the vampire talk about in the truck?" I asked.

"Nothing."

"Was it a small talk kind of nothing or not going to tell you kind of nothing?"

"It was a keeping my mouth shut nothing. We didn't speak. I have no interest in vampires. I've had enough of them for a lifetime."

I smiled at her.

"Have you decided what to do about the Hiru?" she asked.

"Not yet."

"Dad would approve," she said. "He never could resist a down-on-your-luck story and there is no one more down than the Hiru."

"Mom wouldn't," I said.

"Mom would, too. After the first Draziri showed up on the doorstep and issued threats."

"I pity any Draziri who tried to threaten Mom." If anyone could make them rethink an invasion of Earth, it would be our mother.

Our mother and our father. This was the entire point of the inn. This was why I had come back to Earth and hung their portrait in the front room. I'd planned to grow Gertrude Hunt into the kind of inn that was flooded with visitors. Sooner or later one of them would recognize my parents and tell me what happened to them. The galaxy was huge and the chances of that happening were tiny, but it was all I had.

"What do you think I should do?"

Maud pursed her lips, pretending to be deep in thought. "I think you should do what you think is right."

"And you said *I* turned into Mom!"

Maud headed for the kitchen door. "You're not pawning the decision off on me. You're the innkeeper."

I rolled my eyes and followed her into the kitchen.

"Mommy!"

Helen leapt off the stool, dashed across the kitchen, and jumped into Maud's arms. It would've been an amazingly high jump for a human five-year-old.

"Here is my cutey!" Maud wrinkled her face.

Helen wrinkled hers, and they rubbed noses.

"I'm a soup chef," Helen announced.

"Sous," Orro growled from the pantry.

"And I have to say 'yes, chef' real loud."

They were so cute. That's not an adjective I normally would associate with my sister. How could I possibly ruin that?

But then, the ugly truth remained: the Hiru needed help and we needed to find our parents. Maud and I had so carefully talked around it, but both of us knew what was left unsaid. This was our best chance to find Mom and Dad. And if I let my sister catch one whiff of me wavering because I worried about her safety, she would skin me alive.

"When you and Klaus showed up that time to tell me the inn disappeared, I was in a different place." Maud threw Helen up and caught her. Helen squealed and laughed. "I was the wife of a Marshal's son, who was making a bid for the post of the Marshal. My world was very defined then. I knew where we were going and how we were going to get there. I had my husband and his House, all the other knights who served with him and respected him. I had friends. We were admired, me and Melizard and our beautiful baby."

"And now?"

"And now I've learned the truth. Husbands can fall out of love. Friends can betray you. But when you're stuck in a hellhole far from home, your family will move heaven and earth to get you back. We need to get them back, Dina. They would do it for us."

The inn chimed twice, fast. Well, of course.

"Who is it?" Maud asked.

"Local law enforcement." I made a beeline for the door.

"Friendly?"

"No."

"Does he know?"

"He knows. He just can't prove it."

I composed myself, swung the door open, and smiled at Officer Marais through the screen. He didn't smile back. He was generally not in a smiley mood around me. Trim, dark-haired, and in his thirties, Officer Marais peered at me through the screen door as if I were already in the back of his cruiser with handcuffs on. Beast squeezed in front of me and let out one cautious bark.

"Officer Marais. What a pleasure."

"Miss Demille."

My father always told me that all people had magic. Most never learned they did, because they never tried to do anything out of the ordinary. But in a few gifted individuals it bubbled to the surface anyway. Officer Marais was one of those bubblers. His sense of intuition was honed to supernatural sharpness. He had identified the inn as a place where odd things kept happening and mounted a full-scale surveillance of us. Which is how he ended up getting into a fight with some vampire knights. Predictably they took a blood axe to his vehicle, and Officer Marais was deposited, trussed up like a deer, in my stables, while I twisted myself into a pretzel trying to falsify the footage from his dashcam and repair the damage to his vehicle so he couldn't prove any of it happened.

I'd managed to successfully overwrite the dash cam and the vampires did repair Marais's cruiser, hiding all traces of the damage. Unfortunately, when a vampire engineer told you that the internal combustion engine you are trying to get him to fix is an abomination and repairing it violated his oath to do no harm, he meant it. During our last meeting, Officer Marais shared with me that he'd driven his vehicle back and forth to Houston for a week and he'd yet to gas it up.

I opened the screen door. "Please come in."

Officer Marais took a careful step inside, but stayed by the door. I turned to Maud and Helen, who was hiding behind her mom's legs.

"This is my sister, Maud, and my niece, Helen."

Maud smiled at him. Helen hissed and took off like a rocket into the kitchen.

"Did that child just hiss at me?" Officer Marais blinked.

"Yes," Maud said. "She's pretending to be a cat. Children do that."

"How may I help you this time?" I asked.

"There was a disturbance here three days ago. People reported loud noises and the loss of power."

"Yes, I remember. Someone was joyriding a very loud motorcycle." And I couldn't wait to give him a piece of my mind.

"Did you see the vehicle?" His face told me that he was just going through the motions.

"No."

"Are you aware that a high-speed pursuit took place today on I45?"

"Did it?"

"Were you involved in that matter?"

"No."

"Did that pursuit have anything to do with the disturbance here?"

Officer Marais was wasted on the Red Deer P.D. We barely had any crime. In a bigger city, with his intuition, he would be knocking cases out of the park faster than they could bring them to him.

Officer Marais treated me to the serious cop stare. I did my best to keep from wilting.

"Is this the part where you tell me that you intend to get to the bottom of what's going on here?"

"What is going on here?"

"We are considering granting asylum to an alien who is a victim of a religious crusade," I told him. "We have a vampire and a werewolf on our side, but we're not sure it will be enough."

He put away his notepad. "Let me know if you see or hear anything unusual, ma'am."

Wow. I got ma'amed. "I will, Officer."

He left and even though I could feel him, I pulled the curtain aside on the front window and watched him until he got into his modified cruiser and drove away.

"Conscientious cop," Maud said. "No bigger pain. I feel sorry for you."

"Oh you don't know the half of it. You want to come with me to talk to the Ku?"

"Actually, I thought I would take a bath." She smiled.

"You should."

"What are you implying? Are you saying I stink?"

"Touchy-touchy-touchy." I stuck my tongue out at her and headed out to the stables, Beast trailing me.

Wing and his bike, still netted up, lay in the wide walkway between the stalls. He watched me approach with bright round eyes. I sat on the bench and looked at him.

"I'm sorry," he said.

Sorry was a step in the right direction. "You endangered the inn. You made trouble for Mr. Rodriguez. You almost got yourself killed. What do you think those policemen would do to you if they caught you?"

He tucked his head down as much as he could, trying to look smaller.

"What was so important that you had to run out in daylight?"

He blinked his eyes. "A present."

"What present?"

He struggled in the net.

I nodded. A narrow barrel descended from the ceiling and fired a pulse of blue light at the net. It fell loose.

The Ku rolled to his feet and opened a large compartment on his boost bike. He reached in it and took out a bright red poinsettia. It was growing from a pot wrapped in gold foil.

"This is it?"

He nodded.

"Did you steal it?"

"I bought it."

"What did you pay with?"

He reached into a pocket in his harness and showed me a handful of small gold drops shaped like tears. Well, someone got lucky today.

"Why?"

He crouched on the floor above the poinsettia, his voice hushed. "It's like home."

"Do you miss home?"

He nodded.

My righteous anger evaporated. The universe was very big and the Ku was so very small. "Why did you leave?"

"Adventures," he said.

"Can you go back?"

He nodded. "When I'm a hero."

"You know, bringing the message about my sister to me was pretty heroic," I told him.

"Not enough." He raised his arms, drawing a big circle. "Big hero."

He looked at me as if waiting for me to confirm that it was a worthy goal.

"Everyone has a dream," I said. "You're brave and kind. You'll be a big hero one day."

The Ku smiled at me, showing a mouth full of scary dinosaur teeth.

"Meanwhile, you're going to stay here at the inn," I told him. "Don't try to leave. The inn won't let you. Let's go make a nice place for your flower and give it some water. Did you know they come in white, too?"

⚜ ⚜ ⚜

Creating a room for a Ku was infinitely easier than crafting the moving ceiling for the Hiru. I'd made a few before I was even an innkeeper, while still living at my parents' inn. I went with the usual theme of wooden walls, braided together from wooden strips, and three levels; the first being the main floor, the second strewn with floor pillows, and the third a loft nest with a hammock right next to the window that let him look out onto the street. I added a few ropes and a vine swing. By the time we came to the door of his room, Gertrude Hunt had pulled plants out of stasis storage, and garlands of flowering vines and a swing greeted Wing as he came inside. He clutched his poinsettia, dashed up the rope to the loft, and landed in the hammock. Testing all the ropes and the swing would occupy him for at least a couple of hours.

I had just finished settling him in when magic chimed in my head. This chime was deeper than usual. I puzzled over it for a moment and then it hit me. Mr. Rodriguez.

I glanced out of the hallway's window. A white windowless van politely waited at the end of the driveway. When I went to see Mr. Rodriguez, I did the same thing. I stepped onto his inn's grounds and waited. When nobody came to throw me out, I went in. I didn't know what the proper etiquette was, but sitting here making them wait didn't seem like the polite thing to do.

I went down the stairs, stepped outside, and waved at the van. It reversed, turned, and rolled up my driveway. Mr. Rodriguez got out. He was in his early fifties, with bronze skin and dark hair, touched with gray. A trimmed beard hugged his jaw.

"Dina."

"Mr. Rodriguez." I stepped forward and we hugged. That was probably a breach of etiquette, too, but I didn't care.

A young version of Mr. Rodriguez hopped out of the vehicle on the passenger side.

"My son, Tony," Mr. Rodriguez said.

We shook hands. Tony seemed to be about my age, with the same dark hair and dark eyes as his father.

"Please, come in." I led them to the front room. "Would you like some iced tea?"

"I wouldn't mind," Mr. Rodriguez said.

I led them through the kitchen to the patio. Tony didn't gape at Orro, but he definitely glanced in his direction.

I settled them on the back porch, went back inside to get the tea, and had to dodge as Orro nearly knocked me over with a platter. The platter contained a pitcher of iced tea, three glasses with ice and a plate filled with tiny appetizers that looked like very small, fried to a golden crispness crab cakes topped with a dollop of some white sauce and green onions.

"Thank you," I mouthed and took the platter outside.

"Such a beautiful house," Mr. Rodriguez said.

"Thanks." I sorted out the tea and sat down.

Mr. Rodriguez and Tony both took an appetizer and chewed.

I tried one. Eating Orro's food was as close as you could get to nirvana without enlightenment.

"Did everything go well?" Mr. Rodriguez asked.

"As well as it could have gone," I said and sipped my tea. How to say this without being offensive or trying to imply. "I just settled him in his room. He seems comfortable."

"Why did he take off?" Tony asked.

"He wanted a flower. It reminded him of home."

"Ah," Mr. Rodriguez said. "He's probably on a hero's journey."

"He said as much." As soon as they left, I would look this up.

"The Ku are a hunter-gatherer society," Mr. Rodriguez said to Tony.

Tony looked at me with the long-suffering patience of an adult child who knew an educational lecture was coming and there was no way to escape.

"One can distinguish himself by being a great hunter or a great artisan. Those who can do neither sometimes decide to leave on a hero's journey through the galaxy. They must perform a great deed and bring proof to their tribe. It would bring his family a lot of honor."

Tony and I politely sipped our tea.

"I don't mind taking him off your hands," I said. "He seems comfortable here and really I have so little going on, I don't mind keeping an eye on him. We only have three other guests right now, so he won't bother anyone."

"I thought as much," Mr. Rodriguez said. "I have his things in the van."

"No Oporians?" Tony asked.

The Oporians were basically a larger version of the Ku. Although they came from a different planet, they looked remarkably similar. They also thought the Ku were a tasty snack.

"No. Our permanent guest, a vampire, and a Hiru."

"A Hiru?" Mr. Rodriguez sat up straighter. "That's rare."

"Yes, it was a bit of a surprise."

"What did you do with the room, if you don't mind my asking? The common wisdom says black and windowless, but I always felt some doubt about that."

"It's a bit difficult to explain. I can show you if you would like."

I nodded at the inn. A screen descended from the wall and the image of the Hiru's room appeared in it, with the glowing clouds. The inn always recorded still images just before a guest entered the room, so I would have a record.

Mr. Rodriguez stared at it. "Do you think I could see it? In person?"

He wasn't asking to see the actual room. That would disrupt the guest's privacy. "I'll be happy to make a duplicate."

Three minutes later we stood in an exact replica of the Hiru's suite. Tony dipped his hand into the pool. Mr. Rodriguez stared at the clouds, his face lit by their glow.

"Why the sky?" he asked.

"It seemed right. The guest liked it. He loves to float and look at the sky." He'd been doing precisely that for the last few hours.

Mr. Rodriguez frowned. "I don't know if anyone told you this, but you have a gift."

Oh wow. The highest compliment one innkeeper could give to another. "Thank you."

He looked back at the sky. "Food for thought."

"Of course, with the Hiru staying here there is the threat of Draziri," I said. "What is the Assembly's stance on Draziri?"

"Are you worried there will be repercussions against you if you continue to provide sanctuary?"

"No, but the Draziri bring a higher risk of exposure. They don't care."

"That's not your concern," Mr. Rodriguez said.

"Dad," Tony said.

"Sorry, that sounded much harsher than I intended." Mr. Rodriguez looked chastised.

"There are five of us," Tony said. "He's dealing with us all day so he can't turn the Dad Mode off."

"What I meant is, what the Draziri do is on them. You, as an innkeeper, have only one primary goal - to keep your guests safe. That is the foundation of who we are. You chose to accept the Hiru as your guest. It's now your responsibility and duty to do whatever is necessary to keep him safe. Even if the Draziri choose to invade the planet because of it, their lapse in judgment isn't your problem. Your obligation is only to your guest. The Assembly knows this. The Draziri aren't the first threat we've faced and won't be the last. We do not cower."

Okay. Nice that we cleared that up.

"It's good to know that the danger exists," Mr. Rodriguez said. "I'll help you draft a message to the Assembly. It's the least I can do. If we have to contain a large-scale event, it's always best to be prepared."

"Thank you. Would you like to stay for dinner?"

"Are you kidding me?" Tony said. "Yes."

"Apparently, we would." Mr. Rodriguez grinned.

I led them from the room.

Dangerous or not, right or wrong, the Hiru was my guest. That part wasn't in doubt. I would do whatever was necessary to keep him safe.

I still had no idea if I would take his offer.

⚜ ⚜ ⚜

We decided to eat on the porch. A Texas winter had more moods than an emo teenager, and since the day turned out to be freakishly warm and beautiful, it seemed a shame to waste it.

Orro had sprinted through the kitchen for hours, slicing, and tasting, and tossing spices, and the smell coming from his stove made me drool.

Mr. Rodriguez and his son sat outside, chatting with my sister, Arland, and Caldenia. I could hear Arland's laugh from the front room. He sounded like a chuckling tiger. Helen and Beast ran around on the lawn. I'd found a spinball in the garage. The grapefruit-sized sphere zigzagged on the grass making wild turns and changing colors, and Helen and Beast were having entirely too much fun chasing it. They had invited the Ripper of Souls, but he'd declined and now watched them from the window, scandalized.

At first Wing refused to come out because facing Mr. Rodriguez was too scary, but the aroma of Orro's cooking finally reached his room, and he too scurried to the table. Mr. Rodriguez pretended not to see him.

Everyone was here except for one.

I retreated to the kitchen and dialed Sean's cell.

"Yes?"

"What are you doing for dinner?"

"This and that."

He was probably going to eat by himself in an empty kitchen. I hadn't seen him leave the subdivision that often. He probably didn't even have groceries. I pictured Sean sitting alone at his table staring at a piece of moldy cheese.

"We are having a big dinner. You're welcome to drop by."

"I might."

"I'd like that."

"Then I'll be there."

I smiled, put the phone away, went down the hallway, and knocked on the Hiru's door.

"Enter," a quiet voice said.

The door opened and I stepped inside. The Hiru stood in the pool. The water came up to his neck.

"We are having a dinner. I know you don't consume our food, but I came to invite you for company."

"It is kind of you, but my appearance makes others uncomfortable."

He knew. "They will adjust."

"I'd rather not."

"Then I won't pressure you. On Earth, we show our friendship by sharing our food. Your presence isn't a burden.

We are happy to have you with us. If you change your mind, you are welcome to join us."

"Thank you."

I felt Sean cross the boundary, went to meet him, and led him to the table. He decided on a chair across from me. Everyone took their seats, including Orro. It had taken a few meals for Caldenia and me to convince him that we preferred he joined us at meals rather than hanging back in the kitchen by himself to observe us devour the results of his culinary wizardry. He finally condescended to make a distinction between casual and formal meals.

The feast was unbelievably delicious. Loaves of freshly-baked bread fought for space with smoked chicken and brisket so tender, it fell apart under the pressure of a fork. Big bowls offered refreshing salads, the first made with cucumber, tomato, avocado, and green onions, flavored by a delicious mix of oil and vinegar, and the second with cranberries, spinach, and some sort of honey dressing that turned me into a complete glutton.

Midway through the meal, the Hiru stepped outside. He didn't sit at the table, but I pulled a massive wicker chair out of storage and he rested nearby. He said nothing. He just watched as we talked, laughed, and reached for our food. It was still better than waiting alone in a dark room.

"If I eat another bite, I'll die," Tony declared and promptly ate more brisket.

Sean, who'd been watching him like a hawk through most of the meal, finally cracked a smile.

"I'm done!" Helen announced.

"May I be excused?" Maud corrected.

"I may be excused," Helen recited.

Maud opened her mouth and changed her mind. "Yes, you may."

She grabbed the spinball from under the table and launched it onto the lawn. Beast shot out from under the table as if fired out of a small Shih Tzu cannon. The Hiru watched them dash around the lawn.

The inn chimed. Someone had crossed the boundary. Three someones, two from the east and one from the south.

I pushed with my magic. All around the lawn, the inn's roots shivered just barely below the surface, waiting.

The southern intruder meandered up my driveway, taking his time. His two friends glided silently, moving along the edge of the inn's grounds toward the lawn where Helen was playing. They were good. I should've seen them from this spot, but the property appeared completely empty. Judging by the pattern of their movement, they must've approached and then gone to ground.

Sean looked at me, his eyes dark. He either heard them or smelled them. I shook my head very slightly.

"Please excuse me."

I picked up my broom, went to the front door, and flicked my fingers. A screen slid from the wall showing a human-shaped creature walking up the driveway, dressed in a long black trench coat. It flared as he strode forward. Rows of belts secured his sleeves. His hood was up, and pale hair, almost white, spilled from it.

Interesting. I hadn't felt a guest quite like this before.

I opened the front door, leaving the screen door closed, leaned on my broom, and waited.

He didn't walk, he glided like a graceful dancer, light on his feet.

Not a good sign.

The inn chimed in my head. The screen split, showing two shadowy figures, one lying flat on the grass and the other crouching behind a tree. Each carried a weapon, which the inn's scan highlighted with white. Long barrel and curved stock. They carried needle rifles. A single shot from a needle would paralyze and sometimes kill, if the target's weight was low enough. A needle wouldn't penetrate the Hiru's metal. The rifles were for us.

The intruder reached me. The house hid him from the street. He lowered his hood. In poor light, you could mistake him for a human. A beautiful, angelic human. His skin was an even golden tone and looked soft, like velvet. His hair, pure white, without a trace of gray or blond, streamed from his head, its ends tipped with black. His eyebrows were white too, thick, feathery, the ends touched with coal black. Large eyes looked at me from under the brows, the irises turquoise and full of inner fire, like two aquamarines. Glowing silver lines marked his forehead, curving in a complex pattern, embedded in his skin. His nose with a prominent bridge lacked curves over individual nostrils. Straight and triangular, it widened at the end into a semblance of a beak. An arrogant slash of a mouth and a human-looking jaw with a contour so crisp, it could've been carved out of stone, completed his face.

If you bumped into him in a club or saw him walking after dark, badly lit by the street lamps, you'd think, "What a handsome man." But he was standing only feet away, brightly lit by the late afternoon sunshine. That perfect skin wasn't bare epithelium, but a pelt of very short and dense down. What appeared to be hair at first glance was a mass of thin, fine feathers. A Draziri. One of the higher caste, too, judging by the rank on his forehead.

"Good evening," he said, his voice cultured and clear. Unlike the Hiru, he obviously had access to expensive tech.

"Good evening."

"I desire a room."

"We don't have one available at the moment."

He blinked, his feathered eyelashes fanning his cheeks. "I was led to believe your inn has few guests and more than ample accommodations."

"If you're familiar with innkeepers, then you must know that we reserve the right to choose our guests. At this time, unfortunately, I can't provide you with a room. Perhaps at a later date."

"I must have a room," he said.

"There is a wonderful inn over in Dallas, only a few hours from here."

The Draziri stepped closer.

"I know the Hiru is here," he said, his voice quiet but charged with menace.

"You should be on your way." Take the hint.

"Let me in. It will be over quickly."

"The Hiru is beyond your reach."

"You have a beautiful inn," he said. "I can hear other guests and a child playing on the grass."

You bastard. They would shoot Helen. That was the plan. Shoot Helen and trade her or her dead body for the Hiru.

"Your situation is complicated," he said. "I have led many raids in my lifetime. They can be easy and fast or slow and messy. There are so many beings on the grass who could accidentally get in the way. And a child. Such a lovely child. It would be a shame if she got hurt."

The two others moved toward the lawn. The roots shot out, impaling both figures. There was no sound. No screams. I pulled with my magic. The roots sank into the ground, pulling the two bodies with them.

The conversation on the lawn died.

The roots surfaced behind him with a rustle.

The Draziri turned and saw two corpses suspended above the ground, each with a thick inn root piercing its mouth and exiting out of the back of the skull.

"You're right. My niece is a lovely child. It would be a shame if something happened to her."

The Draziri stared at me, unblinking. "You're arrogant. I'll have to teach you humility."

I felt Sean behind me.

"You didn't do your homework. This is my domain. Here I own the air you breathe."

"I always get what I want. One way or—"

"Out."

He flew from the driveway as if jerked back by an invisible hand, cleared the hedges, and landed on the street in a clump. A truck roared down the street, threatening to run him over. The Draziri leapt out of the way, like a length of black silk jerked out of sight, and vanished into the Avalon subdivision.

"You should've killed the scary white one," Wing said behind me.

"Better the devil I know than the one I don't."

I turned. Wing stood in the kitchen doorway. The feathers of his crest lay so flat against his head, they looked wet. He was terrified.

"Do you know of Draziri?"

The Ku nodded. "They don't kill because they are hungry. They kill because they like it."

"You'll be safe here at the inn," I told him.

"We have his face," Sean said. "We'll know his name, and then we'll figure out what makes him tick."

I dug in the pocket of my jeans, pulled out the dollar Sean had given me, and offered it to him. "You're hired."

"You drive a hard bargain," he said and took the dollar.

"I know." I put my arm around Wing. "Come on, we haven't finished dinner."

Outside everyone at the table looked at me. Helen sat on Maud's lap.

"They found me," the Hiru said quietly. An awful finality resonated in his voice. He sounded like a being who was looking certain death in the face.

They found a world of hurt, that's what they found. "Gertrude Hunt accepts your proposition. We will grant the Archivarius sanctuary."

You could hear a pin drop.

"Why?" the Hiru asked finally.

"Because nobody threatens me or my guests in my house. They don't get to intimidate me, they don't get to harm my family, and they don't get to kill my guests. They need to learn what the word *no* means, and I'm going to teach them that lesson over and over until they get it."

Nobody said anything.

Arland reached over, speared a heap of brisket with his fork, and put it on his plate. Caldenia smiled without parting her lips and sliced through her chicken with a single, precise stroke of her knife.

"We're going to have fun, my flower," Maud told Helen.

Helen bared two little fangs.

"Dessert!" Orro announced. "Roasted pears with espresso mascarpone cream."

"I'll take two," Tony said.

Chapter 6

I closed my eyes and envisioned the inn. When one entered Gertrude Hunt through the front door, they saw a perfectly ordinary front room. Directly opposite the front door, on the wall, hung the portrait of my parents. It was unavoidable. If you entered the inn, you saw the portrait. During the peace summit, I formed a hallway behind the wall, moving the portrait back slightly. If you walked to the portrait, you had the option of turning right or left. One way would take you to the stairs leading to the Holy Anocracy's wing and the other would bring you to the barracks of the Hope-Crushing Horde. Both places opened to the Grand Ballroom. According to human science, I'd bent space in ways it wasn't supposed to function, but the inn was its own microcosm, reaching through dimensional boundaries and tangling the fabric of space.

In my mind, I pushed the Grand Ballroom back. It slid deeper into the expanse of the inn, the hallways leading to it stretching to maintain the structure of entrances and exits. Ten feet, twenty, fifty… Good enough. I reached deep below me. The core of the room pulsed and I pulled it up. A deep rumble shuddered through the inn as the chamber slid into its new place directly behind my parents' portrait. I felt the cables sliver through the walls, anchoring the room's equipment. The wall under the portrait split, pulling apart as if it were liquid to form a doorway. A wooden tendril caught the portrait before it had a chance to fall and carried it into the new chamber. I followed it.

The new space was a perfect sphere, its walls a smooth beige. In a time of need, the inn would send the feed from the outer cameras to it, giving me a 360-degree view of the inn's grounds. In the center of the room, a section of the wood lay exposed, its telltale striped texture reminiscent of mahogany and bristlecone pine. A living branch of the inn, an artery to its heart. This was the war room, the heart of the inn's defenses.

I stepped onto the wood. Magic waited, expectant. I closed my eyes and let it permeate my senses. My power stretched, connecting, flowing to the furthest branches of Gertrude Hunt. If I had wings, that's what it would be like to spread them.

The bond between the inn and the innkeeper was far greater than the bond between a servant and master or pet and its owner. We existed in symbiosis. When an innkeeper died, the inn went dormant, falling into a deep sleep. With each passing year without a bond, the inn would slip further and further away, until finally it petrified and died. When I had found Gertrude Hunt, its sleep was so deep and it had gone so far, I wasn't sure I could wake it.

The bond went both ways. Few innkeepers survived the destruction of their inn. Some died. Others lost their minds. The inn would do anything for the innkeeper, and the innkeeper had to protect the inn with their life. And that's exactly what I would do.

The inn's defenses shifted, as I realigned them. The last time I'd used the war room, I had configured Gertrude Hunt to repel a small army of bounty hunters after Caldenia arrived at the inn. The bounty hunters were truly an army of one – despite their number, every one of them was in it for themselves. They didn't trust each other and hadn't been interested in coordinating their efforts. The metal inlay on the Draziri leader's forehead meant he likely led his own flock, a clan. Flocks were highly organized and disciplined. The Draziri would attack as a team. And they likely wouldn't try to snipe the Hiru the way the bounty hunters tried to snipe Caldenia. Murdering the Hiru would be a religious triumph for them. They would try to breach the inn's defenses and close in for the kill.

I tested the feeds from the cameras, turning slowly. Night had fallen, but the inn's tech needed only a hint of light to present a clear image. The view of the orchard, the lawn, the oaks, the street, Sean's Ford F-150 truck...

Sean's truck. He'd said something about getting an overnight bag and left shortly before Mr. Rodriguez and Tony had taken off.

It was a short move, since his house was just down the street, but the truck was fully loaded and covered with a tarp. The truck springs creaked as he maneuvered it up the driveway and behind the inn.

Sean got out of the truck. He wore black pants and a skintight ballistic silk shirt, dark gray and black, designed to stop both a kinetic impact from a bullet and a low-power shot from an energy weapon. This was worth a closer look.

I waved my fingers half an inch and the inn zoomed in, expanding the image to the entire wall in front of me. The ballistic silk clung to Sean like a glove, tracing the contours of his broad shoulders and powerful back. Some men had muscular backs but a wider waist so they looked almost rectangular. The difference between Sean's shoulders and his narrow waist was so pronounced, his back tapered into an almost triangular shape. His legs were long, his arms muscular. I liked the way he moved, fast, sure, but with a natural grace that very strong men sometimes had. There was something dangerous about him and his spare, economical movements. Something that said that if violence occurred, his response would be instant and lethal, and idiot that I was, I could stare at him all day…

"So what's with you and the werewolf?" My sister asked next to my ear.

I jumped.

I didn't hear her come in. I didn't feel her come in, which was so much worse.

"Nothing."

"Mhm," Maud said. "That's why you're ogling him here on a giant screen."

"I wasn't ogling." Yes, yes I was.

"You were holding your breath, Dina."

"I wasn't."

Maud studied the screen. "He is kind of hot."

"Kind of?" There was no *kind of* about it.

"There needs to be more…" Maud held her hands wide apart.

"More what?"

"Muscle. Bulk. I like them… oversized."

"He's big enough." He was over six feet tall. "And he's very strong."

"Oh I don't doubt that he's strong and really fast, too. But… bigger."

I squinted at her. "I thought you were over your vampire fixation."

"I didn't say anything about vampires. I just like larger men."

"Sure, aha."

Sean pulled back the tarp, revealing crates and weapons. He swung a long slender weapon onto his shoulder and picked up a black crate that seemed to swallow the light.

Maud squinted at the screen. "Is that a specter sniper rifle he's packing?"

"Mhm. Looks like a recent model, too."

Specter weapons used an electromagnetic field rather than a chemical reaction to launch projectiles. Jam-proof and almost completely devoid of moving and potentially malfunctioning parts, specter sniper rifles fired bullets at just below 300m/s, under the speed of sound, avoiding the sonic boom better known as the crack of a bullet. They were completely silent.

Maud was studying at wisted shape in the truck. "You don't have a HELL unit?"

"I have two and some smaller solid lasers linked by a computer into a defense net. But he doesn't know that."

"Aw," Maud said. "He brought a High Energy Liquid Laser to protect you. Twue love."

"Shut up," I told her.

"Seriously though, that's some expensive hardware."

She was right. Liquid lasers were like computers. The smaller they were, the more they cost, and the portable unit in Sean's truck was way out of my budget. My two units were each the size of a medium-range sedan, and both were at least two centuries old. Compared to Sean's sleek modern beast, they were antiques, but they packed a hell of a punch.

"Envirosuit, camo cloak, pulse sidearm...He's got enough weapons to finish a small war. How can he afford all this? Is he secretly a prince? Are you dating a galactic weapon-lord? Does he have a rich father or possibly brother?"

"No! He isn't a prince, he isn't a gun runner, and his father isn't rich, he is a lawyer, and Sean is the only child. He did some highly paid mercenary work."

"So you are dating him."

"I didn't say that." Technically going on a date once didn't strictly qualify as dating.

"Sean and Dina sitting in a tree. K-i-s-s…"

"I will so punch you."

Sean looked up. I could've sworn he heard me, except that the inn was soundproof. I concentrated and projected my voice.

"Hey."

"Hey," he said. He didn't jump, even though I just spoke to him from seemingly thin air.

"Do you need a hand with all of that equipment?"

"Oh sure, he totally needs your help with his equipment," Maud whispered.

I stomped on her foot, but she was fast, and I only got the edge of her toes. There was no way to just project my voice. I also projected the sounds around me.

"Do you have an armory?" he asked.

"Yes."

"Can I have access to it?"

"Full access," Maud whispered and batted her eyelashes.

"Yes," I told him, opening a tunnel in the ground next to him. "Enter…" if I said tunnel, Maud wouldn't be able to contain herself. "The path I just made. Underground. The inn will move the weapons there."

"I thought I'd visit Baha-char after I'm done settling all that in," he said. "I need to talk to Wilmos."

"Sure. I'll open the door for you, but could you take Orro with you? He wants some sort of weird spices and I don't want him to go by himself."

"Will do."

He grinned at me, the look on his face positively evil, and went down into the tunnel.

I watched the inn swallow the truck whole, pulling it into the garage, and turned to my sister. "I hate you."

"Did you see how he smiled?" Maud asked. "Do you think he heard me? I wasn't projecting."

"Yeah, he heard you. My neighbors across the street heard you. Don't you know how to whisper?"

"Are you blushing?" Maud asked.

"Here!" I opened a ladder to the battle attic and dropped it into the hallway. "Since you butted in, you can check the pulse cannons instead of me. Make yourself useful."

"Yes, Mother." Maud paused in the doorway and took in the war room. Her voice turned quiet and wistful. "Brings back memories."

Yes, it did. When I had called up the war room from the depths of Gertrude Hunt for the first time, I had reshaped it to mirror the war room in our parents' inn. Mother made us do countless drills in a war room just like this one.

"We'll get them back," I said.

"Yes," she said. "We will."

Maud climbed the attic ladder. I huffed and went to splash some cold water on my face. I was blushing, and my whole face felt like it was on fire.

⚜ ⚜ ⚜

Twenty minutes later I watched Sean and Orro walk through the door into the bright sunshine of Baha-char. Sean had pulled a tattered cloak over himself, hiding his face within the depths of a hood. Orro, on other hand, held his head high, but all his spikes shivered slightly, ready to be raised at a moment's notice. I seriously doubted the Draziri would jump them there, but if they did, they would regret it.

I went back to the kitchen. In Orro's absence, Arland had brought down a grey bag, which now lay beside him in a chair, and spread his armor on the dining room table. He'd turned off the lights. Only the two table lamps were on, their warm radiance soothing and buttery yellow. A kit similar to the one he'd sent to Maud rested on the table, opened, its contents backlit by a peach glow. The tiny vials of various liquids shone weakly with borrowed light. A quiet melody was playing from the kit, the sounds of silver bells and the measured chant of female voices soothing but mysterious, as if they were weaving some secret magic.

Helen sat in the corner, quietly fascinated.

"Isn't it past your bedtime?" I asked.

"No." She yawned. "I'm not sleepy."

"Let her stay," Arland said, his voice quiet. "I remember sitting just like that watching my mother. The smells and the lights, it's comforting."

I sat in the chair. It was comforting to watch in a way. There was a meditative, unhurried quality about his movements, as if he were going through a ritual he'd done hundreds of times before. The light played on his profile and the strands of long blond hair that had escaped his ponytail. He was right. Helen probably watched her father or my sister check their armor just like this.

For a while he worked quietly. Helen's head drooped. She sighed and put her head on the table onto her arms. Her eyes closed. She wasn't quite asleep yet. I could see her eyelashes trembling. A few more minutes and I would let the inn carry her to bed.

"How well do you know Sean Evans, my lady?" Arland asked quietly.

"As well as I know you." Actually, I knew Sean better. He had shared his secrets with me. Arland hadn't.

"I don't believe he is who he presents himself to be," Arland said.

"What makes you think that?"

Arland raised his hand with a small tool in it and drew an imaginary line. It started low, climbed upward, and evened out in an arc. "This is a standard planet-to-orbit shuttle trajectory."

He moved his tool low and drew a second line. This time it kept going low, accelerated, and curved sharply, shooting up. The trajectory was almost completely inverse. "This is what Sean Evans did."

"I don't follow."

"The second trajectory sharply accelerates the craft before the drastic atmospheric climb. It's less comfortable for the passengers and it's harder on the shuttle."

I could testify to it being less comfortable. At the time, it felt like a rhino sat on my chest.

"There is only one place where that trajectory is absolutely necessary. The atmospheric anomalies there make flight unpredictable and unsafe, so it is necessary to attain the proper speed and acceleration at low altitude before punching through the atmosphere as fast as possible while at the same time ascertaining that the way is clear and you're not taking the craft straight into an anomaly that suddenly formed above your shuttle."

"And where is this place?" I knew the answer.

"Nexus," Arland said.

That's what I thought.

"I don't know what he told you he did, but I asked him where he'd learned to fly."

"I was there. I remember. He said Wilmos taught him."

Arland nodded. "I did some checking through our databanks. Wilmos isn't unknown to my House. I give you my word as a knight of the Holy Anocracy that Wilmos Gerwar knows the proper trajectory for a planet-to-orbit shuttle ascent."

"You think Sean was on Nexus."

Arland nodded. "The Merchants employed many mercenaries."

"Would it be such a bad thing if he was?"

"Nexus changes people," Arland said. "I'm concerned only for your safety."

"In that case she should be concerned about you as well," Maud said from the doorway. "After all, you've done two tours, Lord Marshal."

Arland raised his head and studied her.

My sister walked in and put her armor on the table. The inn's wall opened and the repair kit Arland had given her slipped out. She caught the heavy box and placed it on the table.

"I'm a knight. I've been conditioned to handle the rigors of war from childhood."

Maud spread her armor out, her eyes half closed under her long eyelashes as she surveyed it. "You would be surprised how many knights break under the rigors of war, my lord. They break and they run, as their honor lies dying behind them."

"I do not run, my lady."

Maud arched her eyebrow. If I didn't know, I would've sworn she was a vampire. "I have run, my lord. And I would do it again, if the circumstances called for it. Honor can't keep my daughter alive, but I can."

"There is a difference between blindly fleeing for your life and a strategic retreat because the battle is lost," Arland said, spraying pearlescent solution onto his armor.

"Sometimes it is very difficult to tell the difference between the two." Maud tapped the kit. It unfurled like a flower. She selected a narrow tool with her long elegant fingers and concentrated on some imperceptible flaw on the right shoulder.

Arland's eyes narrowed. "Although if I wore your armor, I would run, my lady. Is that a manual terminal on your vambrace?"

Maud grimaced.

"Was your crest damaged?"

"It was ripped off my armor when House Ervan exiled me and my husband, my lord. You've read the file."

"You seem very sure of that, my lady."

She shot him a quick glance. "A knight conditioned to handle the rigors of war, such as yourself, would make sure he knew exactly who he allowed on board his destroyer."

Arland opened his bag, took out a black box, and set it by his armor. Square, six inches by six, the box was completely solid. No seam, no line marking the place where the lid fit. Just a solid box that seemed to absorb the light.

Maud's eyes widened. Arland went back to working on his armor. Maud did as well. Some sort of strange vampire communication was taking place here.

"To exile a child is unprecedented," Arland said.

"It is," Maud agreed, making valiant efforts to ignore the box.

"What led to that decision?"

My sister smiled. "Perhaps, one day I will tell you, Lord Marshal."

"Regardless of the reasons, you've been wronged. The child has been wronged. The Holy Anocracy doesn't have so many children that it can throw them away. Especially one as gifted as Helen."

"You're too kind."

"Perhaps you would allow me to ask for a small kindness in return," Arland said. "Allow me to correct a small part of the injustice."

He pushed the box toward her and proceeded to ignore it.

This was better than a soap opera.

Maud touched the top of the box. The lid slid apart section by section. She dipped her fingers into it and withdrew a crest. Unlike Arland's crest, which showed a stylized snarling krahr in red on black, this crest was solid black and blank. A no-House crest. I'd seen them before. Vampires who'd left their House wore them. They functioned just like the regular House crests: they controlled the armor, sent out signals that communicated with ships and defensive networks, and stored information.

Maud pondered it as if it were a diamond.

"Thank you."

Arland inclined his head and went back to his armor.

The inn's magic chimed in my head. The Draziri were on the move.

I rose. "We have visitors."

⚜ ⚜ ⚜

It started as a single ping, an intruder brushing against the boundary. It touched the boundary and burst into half-a-dozen intruders moving fast. The Draziri weren't playing. Good, because I wasn't either.

I crossed the threshold into the war room and stepped onto the wood. Wing was in his room and Helen in hers. Maud must've taken her upstairs. Perfect. A deep chime sounded through Gertrude Hunt, a clear high sound impossible to ignore. External shutters and walls clanged, locking down. My voice carried through the inn, echoing through every room.

"Gertrude Hunt is under attack. We are under lockdown until further notice. I apologize for the inconvenience."

Thin flexible shoots spiraled from the edges of the wooden limb on which I stood, forming a two-foot-tall lattice. I held out my broom. It split into a thousand glowing blue threads that streaked into my robe, adhering to my skin and to the lattice of the inn. It would make Gertrude Hunt and I faster.

The walls around me faded, presenting a 360-degree view of the inn grounds. In the distance, from the north, six orange-sized spheres floated about two feet off the ground, slowly making their way into my territory. A quick scan told me they were rigged to explode.

Magic shifted within me, announcing another intrusion. Ha! He thought I wouldn't notice. Dear Draziri Commander had a lot to learn about the capabilities of innkeepers.

Caldenia walked through the door, carrying a glass of wine. I smiled at her and let her usual chair rise from the floor. She sat and grinned back at me, flashing her inhumanly sharp teeth.

My sister and Arland reached the doorway at the same time. They would've collided, but years of politeness ingrained in Arland took over and he smoothly halted, letting Maud burst into the room. My sister carried her sword. The Marshal of House Krahr was wearing armor.

Maud looked at Caldenia. "Your Grace? Wouldn't you be more comfortable in your rooms?"

"Nonsense, my dear." Caldenia's eyes gleamed. "I love watching her work."

"He deployed scout spheres," Arland said, watching the handful of robotic scouts meander their way into my territory. "He's trying to map your range. An expensive way to do it."

"Expensive and pointless," Maud said. "They've been in range for the last six meters. She isn't just going to destroy them the moment they touch the boundary."

I concentrated on the depiction of the grounds. An area from the west side rushed at me, zooming closer and closer. The brush grew to mountain size, the individual blades of grass became a forest, and within that forest a chain of ten ants hurried toward the inn.

I'd scanned the ants when I first felt them crossing the boundary and now I tossed the results of the scan onto the screen so the others could see it. One individual ant expanded, rotating, the analysis rolling next to its image, listing the complex readouts. I was looking at a masterpiece of cyborg technology: a living insect carrying within it roughly a million nanobots. Silent, virtually undetectable by all but the most advanced scanners, the ants were meant to reach Gertrude Hunt and let loose their horde of tiny robots, capable of everything from surveillance to sabotage. The Draziri had no idea the architecture of the inn was fluid and changed at my whim. He was trying to map out Gertrude Hunt, looking for weak points.

Arland bared his teeth. "Clever bastard."

"Not as clever as he thinks," I murmured.

Magic tugged on me. I opened a second screen in the wall. The Hiru appeared on it.

"How may I be of service?" I asked.

"I realize...this time is not the best." The Hiru's voice sounded strained. "The first Archivarian has arrived on Earth."

Not good. "Where?"

The Hiru raised his right palm. A small map of Red Deer appeared, a tiny glowing dot marking one of the streets. Walmart parking lot. Well, at least the first member of the Archivarius wouldn't stand out.

"What does it look like?"

The Hiru touched his palm and a projection appeared of a man in his mid-thirties, brown-skinned, with a bald head and an intelligent face. His features were off somehow. Something about them telegraphed alien so loudly, it practically slapped your senses. It took me a moment to figure it out. His face had no pores. No wrinkles, no small imperfections, and no variations in tone troubled his skin. He looked plastic. The effect was freakish. But in darkness he would pass for a human.

"The Archivarian must be retrieved," the Hiru said. "Immediately."

No pressure. The ants were still a good two hundred yards away. The spheres drifted perilously close to the point where they would become a problem.

"The retrieval may have to wait."

The Hiru leaned forward, his voice gasping. "The Archivarian cannot maintain its form in your planetary conditions. He must be submerged in inert gas to contain himself."

Inert gas meant an argon chamber. A piece of cake, but only on the inn grounds.

"What happens when he loses his form?" I asked.

"He is a being of energy."

Not good. So not good. The release of energy could mean anything from explosion, to bright light, to complete disintegration of the local space-time continuum.

"He must be retrieved. We have risked everything." Desperation vibrated in his voice.

This information would've been excellent to have had earlier. "How long?"

"Thirty-four minutes."

Damn it. I tossed a counter on the wall, seconds ticking back from thirty-four minutes to zero.

"Very well," I said. "How will the Archivarian know my people?"

"Take this." The Hiru's left forearm slid open, revealing a small pen-like transmitter. "He will hunt your signal."

And so would the Draziri, if they ever put two and two together. Arguing about it would waste time we didn't have. After we dealt with this initial assault, the Hiru and I would have to sit down and talk.

I nodded and cut off the communication.

"I'll take care of it," Maud said.

I loved my sister so much. "Take my car. It's bulletproof. Walmart is only seven or eight minutes from here."

"My lady," Arland said, and it took me a second to register that he wasn't talking to me. "I would be honored to assist."

"I can handle it," Maud said.

"Take the vampire, my dear," Caldenia said. "You never know when you may require muscle."

Maud's eyebrows knitted together.

I pulled the feed from the Park Street. At first glance everything appeared normal. Fortunately, the inn had been recording the street for the last four hours. A comparative analysis took only a few fractions of a second and the contours of four Draziri lit up on the screen, each wrapped in a high tech camo cloak. The cloak mimicked the surroundings the same way a chameleon would, replicating the fence and the bushes with painstaking accuracy. They must've had some way to block their body heat as well, because they didn't show up on the infrared scan.

The Draziri waited in the shadows, two by Mr. Ramirez's fence and two on the other side of the Camelot road leading into Avalon subdivision. They caught a lucky break - Mr. Ramirez had left for his weekly bowling meeting and took his dog with him.

"How much cover can you give me?" Maud asked.

"I can do Mom's Take Care," I said.

"That should be good enough."

"Exit won't be a problem," Arland said. "But the return may present a slight difficulty."

Thirty minutes. We had to decide now.

Arland was right. The Draziri wouldn't expect them to leave, but they would expect the vehicle to return. My range was limited and I was bound by the innkeeper laws. I couldn't do anything too loud or too obvious. The Draziri would ambush the vehicle on its way back. One well aimed shot from any number of fun galactic weapons, and my sister, Arland, and the Archivarian would be vaporized.

A quick calculation took place behind Maud's eyes. She turned to the vampire. "Lord Arland, it is my honor to accept your generous offer."

Arland unleashed his smile. It bounced from Maud like dry peas from the wall.

My sister strained, concentrating. I felt the inn move in response. The ceiling above us parted and car keys fell into her palm.

"Told you," I said. "Like riding a bicycle. Don't forget the Hiru's gadget."

She turned and ran. Arland followed her.

The robot spheres clicked in unison, preparing to explode. I smiled and punched a hole through reality. For an instant, an orange plain flashed under a purple sky, a vista that couldn't be found anywhere on Earth. The dimensional rip bit at the spheres. The robotic mines vanished, transported in a moment to a planet thousands of light-years away. There was no return from Kolinda.

I let the ants continue.

"You're toying with him, dear," Caldenia said.

"I'm letting him think he still has an ace up his sleeve."

"I approve." She smiled, her eyes sparkling with delight.

The image of the garage appeared on my left. Maud revved the engine. Arland sat in the passenger seat, a positron cannon in his hand.

I took in magic, building it up.

"What is 'Mom's Take Care?'" Caldenia asked.

"You will see."

The magic wound around me, tight and ready. The inn creaked.

Maud gave me an okay through the windshield. I shoved with my magic. The garage door vanished. A tunnel of dirt, stone and the inn's roots whipped into existence, spinning down the driveway and turning right, down the street. Maud gunned it. My car shot through the tunnel like a cannonball and burst onto the pavement. The Draziri stared after it, too stunned to fire off a shot. I pulled the tunnel back and dissolved it. The whole thing took two seconds. From the street, the house once again appeared normal, just as it had been a few moments ago.

The counter said twenty-nine minutes. *Good luck, Maud.*

"Our mother used this to provide additional security for high-risk guests leaving the inn," I said.

"Your mother is a remarkable woman," Caldenia said. "Now what shall we do about the ants?"

"I think they are having such a nice time walking," I said. "We should let them continue."

Caldenia leaned forward and watched as I broke the laws of physics to keep the ants moving. The soil beneath them shifted subtly, a large chunk of the lawn crawling back just as they moved forward. From their monitors, the ground would appear perfectly stationary. Eventually whoever was monitoring them would figure out that they were no closer to the house than they were ten minutes ago, but it would buy me some time.

It bought me fifteen minutes. The ants finally turned, attempting to exit and I jettisoned them into Kolinda's wastes.

Thirteen minutes.

Across the road, a Draziri abandoned subtlety, hopped onto the wooden fence, and ran along it with breathtaking grace all the way to the right, out of the range of my quiet guns. Another dashed in the opposite direction. The rest followed, splitting into two groups. They were moving through the subdivision, half to the left and half to the right, not sure from which direction the vehicle would be returning.

I launched two probes. The tiny cameras streaked along the street, tracking the Draziri and the split screen showed two groups of invaders. The one on the left holed up next to Timber Trail, a quiet street that was the newest addition to the Avalon subdivision. Lined with houses, it led to an elementary school. The group on the right crouched on the fence just behind the bend of the road. One, two, three, four... Eight on each side.

He had a lot more troops than I expected.

Eight was definitely too many and from what I had seen so far, the Draziri were well-armed. I had a choice where to send Maud. She could approach the inn from the right, coming back exactly the way she came, or from the left, after she looped through some parallel streets.

Approaching from the right was the only responsible option. On the left, the houses on Timber Trail were packed like sardines on tiny lots. There was no way a fight wouldn't be noticed, and some of the energy rifles the Draziri carried would slice through stucco and drywall like knife through butter. We would have bystander casualties.

On the right, a solid stone fence separated the bulk of the subdivision from the street, providing at least some protection for the houses. But Park Street veered slightly just past the inn. No direct shot. I had some things that could shoot around corners, but they honed in on body heat and the Draziri were masking theirs.

Magic chimed. Sean and Orro.

"In here," I called.

Sean appeared on the doorstep of the war room, a small bag in his hands, and came to stand next to me.

"My sister and Arland went to get the first Archivarian," I said.

"The counter?" Sean asked.

"Deadline to the Archivarian assuming its true form."

"What form is that?"

"Energy. There are eight Draziri waiting for them on each side of the street. Both groups are too far for any of my quiet guns. I have the needler, but its darts hone in on body heat and they are not showing up on my infrared scanner. Anything else will be too loud and too obvious."

My phone rang and I took the call. My sister's voice echoed through the war room.

"We have him."

I knew she could do it.

"Do you want me to come back the same way?"

She had to come back the same way, from the right, she would drive into an ambush. Even if I threw the tunnel as far as it could go, it wouldn't be enough. The Draziri would hit the car before it ever reached the tunnel.

I'd have to use the bats from the cave on the inn's grounds as a living shield. My heart squeezed itself into a tiny ball. The bats were a part of the inn and I would sacrifice every last one to save my sister, but they wouldn't be enough. I had no way to bring her in safely.

Seven minutes. I had to answer her.

"Let me do my job," Sean said.

"There are eight of them on each side."

He looked at me, his eyes pure wolf, and I realized it didn't matter how many of them there were. He would still go out there.

"Yes," I said to Maud. "Come back the same way."

She hung up.

"Left or right?" he asked.

"Right."

"I need the specter."

"Give him everything he wants," I told Gertrude Hunt.

He dropped his bag and left the war room. I tracked him through the inn, as he stepped out of the kitchen door, a dark shape on the screen. Sean dropped his cloak and pulled out the curved knife with a green blade. His eyes shone with bright amber, reflecting the moonlight.

He raised his hand and the specter rifle fell into it. Sean sprinted across the lawn into the trees, fast and silent like a phantom, and vanished into the woods, past the range of my scanners.

I pulled the feed from my probe, expanding it so it took up most of the wall directly in front of me. The Draziri had positioned themselves on the long wooden fence, crouching like camouflaged creepy angels. They didn't have much choice. The fence ran for the next quarter of a mile up the street.

A vehicle roared down the road. I tensed.

A white truck thundered past us. Not Maud.

Three minutes.

The first Draziri on the right dropped like a stone. Sean had fired the specter rifle.

The second Draziri, directly behind the first, fell without a sound.

The remaining Draziri leapt off the fence and dashed across the street. The night lit up with orange flashes of light as they discharged their energy rifles. Sean landed in the middle of them, fast, so shockingly fast. He gutted the third Draziri with a short precise slash, reversed the blade, and sliced the fourth attacker's throat. Blood sprayed.

The surviving Draziri spun, revealing short blades of bright pale metal. They attacked, twisting and leaping as if dancing, and Sean sliced through them, cutting a path as if he knew where they would be before they decided to move there.

Two Draziri peeled from the group on the left and dashed toward the fight right through my kill zone. Oh no, you don't. The short-range pulse cannon fired once, its invisible beam slicing through the area. Two smoking corpses crumpled to the ground.

Sean's attackers were down to one, but that last Draziri moved as if he were weightless, launching into a whirlwind of slashes and cuts and dancing away from Sean before the green blade could find him.

The phone rang. Arland's voice filled the room. "Three streets out."

Eighty seconds.

On the screen a Draziri blade caught Sean's side. My heart jumped into my throat.

Sean buried his knife in the Draziri's chest, freed it with a sharp tug, and leapt into the scraggly Texas woods bordering the inn.

"Clear," I said and hurled the tunnel down the street. It caught the car. Maud drove into the garage, the car screeching to a halt. The Archivarian stumbled out. A cylindrical vat shot out of the ground, enclosing him. The top of the vat clanged closed. Argon filled the inside.

Ten seconds.

Nine.

Five.

Three.

Two...

One.

The Archivarian looked at my sister from the inside of the vat, still humanoid.

We made it.

Sean.

I ran out of the war room and through the lawn and the woods to the east.

Be okay. Please be okay.

He crossed the boundary and I saw him running toward me. We collided and I threw my arms around him. For a second he stood there, as if not sure what to do and then he hugged me to him.

"Are you okay?" I whispered.

"I am now," he said.

⚜ ⚜ ⚜

The problem with all men, and werewolves in particular, was their odd perspective. Sean viewed the gash across his ribs as a scratch. I viewed it as an open wound made by a monomolecular blade able to cut through the werewolf armor and contaminate his body with extraterrestrial microorganisms and possibly poison. We agreed to meet somewhere in the middle. He allowed me to sterilize and seal the wound, and I promised to stop threatening to restrain him.

"I'm curious," Maud said, when I was finished. "Do you always threaten people who try to help you or is he special?"

"He isn't," Arland volunteered. "She threatened to drown me in sewage once."

"The Lord Marshal deserved it." I put down the surgical tool and examined my handiwork. The wound was reduced to a hair-thin red scar. Considering how well werewolves had been bioengineered, it would likely heal fast. In a few days, you wouldn't even be able to tell that someone tried to kill him.

We were in the front room. It had enough seating for everyone and I had formed three different screens to watch the surroundings. On the front screen, the six remaining Draziri were carefully retrieving the bodies of their dead. They had given the inn a wide berth, using back streets to skirt it and stay out of the range of my guns.

They shouldn't have bothered. As an innkeeper, my job was to respond to threats, not to initiate an attack. Once the skirmish ended, they were safe. As long as they didn't try to shoot at the inn, they could parade in front of it all day long.

Sean pulled his T-shirt back on. I wouldn't have minded if he had kept it off a few minutes longer, but with my sister here, there would be hell to pay later if I looked at him too long or noticed how muscular his back was. Or noticed his abs. I had taken a close look at his stomach while working on the gash, but it wouldn't hurt to give it a second glance.

"Did you find what you were looking for at Baha-char?" I asked.

"Yes." Sean pulled a small square of a data chip from his pocket and offered it to me. I took it off his finger, called up a terminal from the wall, and deposited the chip onto it. The terminal's surface swallowed the chip. The face of the Draziri who'd come to talk to me appeared on the center screen.

I rose. "Let me get the Hiru for this."

I walked into the depths of the inn past the Hiru's quarters to a narrow chamber protected by a door. A series of recesses waited in the wall, the first filled with an argon tank. The Hiru stood by it, looking at the humanoid creature inside.

I fought a valiant battle against the smell. The human nose was supposed to stop recognizing an odor when exposed to it for several minutes, but the scent of the Hiru pretty much destroyed that rule. Only sheer willpower prevented me from gagging. The Hiru didn't notice, absorbed in watching the tank.

"What do you see?" I asked.

The awkward alien sighed, his voice sad. "The future."

We watched the first member of the Archivarius rest on the floor in a trance. I had asked if it required anything, but the Hiru told me the tank was sufficient.

"There are too many spaces," the Hiru said, pointing at the wall. "There are ten."

"How many should there be?"

"Nine."

That meant we still had to retrieve eight members of the hive. I had hoped for two or three.

"You must give us more of a warning next time," I said. "We need to know in advance where the next member will appear and when. If you don't give us enough warning, the Draziri will get them first or we may not be able to retrieve them in time."

"I will try," the Hiru promised. "My people are trying to make sure the Archivarius is safe but matters are complicated. They are in hiding."

And any appearance of the Hiru would draw the Draziri like moths to a flame.

"We are about to review the information about the Draziri who attacked us. Will you join us? Your input may prove valuable."

The Hiru didn't respond.

I waited. I had a feeling he wanted to stand right here and guard the tank.

"I will," he said finally.

I led him back to the front room and watched everyone attempt to keep their stomach contents where they belonged. He stopped in a corner, away from everyone. Orro watched from the kitchen doorway. Her Grace sat in her usual chair.

"We're ready now," I told Sean.

"His name is Kiran Mrak za Ezara za Krala-Kric," Sean said.

"That's a mouthful," Arland put in.

"The Draziri society is segregated into flocks," I said. "The flock usually consists of the leader and his family and the retainers who choose to serve them. The greater the leader, the bigger the flock. Some flocks have thousands of members, some only a dozen or so. The name translates into 'Kiran Mrak, the First Bird of the Flock Something'. I don't know that last word."

"Wraith," Sean said.

"High aspirations," Maud said.

"The name was chosen long before Kiran was born," Sean said. "He controls about three hundred families and a force of roughly two to three hundred mercenaries. He could have many more, but he's selective in his hiring. It's not a big flock, but it's a wealthy one," Sean continued. "Flock Wraith plays dirty. Kiran took it over from his father twelve years ago, and he's been busy."

"What is the nature of his business?" Arland asked.

"Arms dealing, espionage, but mostly assassinations. That last one bit him in the ass." Sean glanced at me. "Turn the page for me?"

"Next image," I said.

A new Draziri appeared on the screen, this one old, his skin sagging and wrinkled, his long feather-hair a dark crimson. A gold design was etched into his forehead, a stylized shape of a bird with four wings spread.

"An onizeri?" I murmured. "He killed a high priest?"

Sean nodded.

Wow.

"I thought their society was a theocracy," Arland said.

"It is," Sean told him. "The high priests are guarded so well, they're almost impossible to kill. When contracts on them pop up, the price is always outrageous. Usually nobody takes the bait and if someone does, they don't come back."

"So, he's a renegade," Caldenia said.

I startled. She had been so quiet, I forgot she was there.

"I didn't know Wilmos dealt in assassinations," I said.

"He doesn't," Sean said. "He deals in mercenary talent. He doesn't walk in the shadows, but he knows where to look. Kiran Mrak has made himself quite a name in certain circles."

"How much money did he make from that kill?" Maud asked.

"Enough to buy a lot of expensive toys," Sean said. "But I don't think he did it for money."

"He did it out of pride," Caldenia said.

Sean nodded. "He's the only one on record in the last two hundred years who managed to pull it off. The last assassin who succeeded before Kiran was named Rookar Mrak za Ezara za Krala-Kric."

"A relative," Caldenia said.

"Great-grandfather," Sean said.

"So it's a family tradition," Arland said. "Once every couple of generations they kill a holy man just to dissuade anyone from thinking they've wavered in their commitment to crime, murder, and blasphemy."

"Pretty much," Sean said. "Some of the families have been with the flock for generations. They're very good at what they do. What I killed out there tonight was hired muscle. There was only one member of the flock among them and he left me a reminder to take them seriously."

"In short, we've been targeted by a Draziri crime syndicate specializing in murder and willing to assassinate their own priests." This was just getting better and better.

Maud leaned back and laughed.

I looked at her.

"You don't do anything halfway," she said.

"Question." Arland raised his index finger. "Is he excommunicated?"

"Apparently, the Draziri don't excommunicate, they condemn," Sean said. "There are only two ways a Draziri can get into heaven and receive his wings in the afterlife. One requires an exemplary life and a lot of financial contributions. The second requires—"

"Death of a Hiru," the Hiru said quietly.

"Yes," Sean said. "Kiran is officially condemned to hell where, according to the Draziri holy texts, he will fall into darkness for eternity while snakes of fire rip his body to pieces, feeding on his insides. Everyone within his flock is condemned with him. All his followers, their spouses, their children, everyone is going to a bottomless hell, unless the flock kills a Hiru. If they manage to murder one, every member of the flock, even those who already died in pursuit of the Hiru, will be elevated to heaven."

"That is a twisted religion," Arland said.

When a vampire thought your religion went too far, you definitely had problems. "So, he's desperate."

Sean nodded. "Desperate, skilled, and well supplied. His people are motivated. He'll be a pain to kill."

Great.

"There is a silver lining to all of this," Maud said. "We don't have to worry about a full-scale invasion."

"Why?" I asked.

"Because Flock Wraith wants to be the one to kill the Hiru. They'll keep it quiet. Otherwise they risk losing their target to some other flock. They're doing this on their own."

Small comfort. I turned to the Hiru. "Do you have anything to add? Anything that could help us?"

"They will stop at nothing to kill me," the Hiru said. "They will run through fire. There is no obstacle you can put in their way that will deter them."

The room fell silent.

"I don't deal in fire," I said. "It's difficult to control and the inn doesn't like it. But I'm excellent at creating a void field."

Sean stared at me.

Arland coughed. "A void field requires a high efficiency nuclear reactor."

"Or an inn with a skilled innkeeper," Maud told him.

"You can do that?" Sean asked me.

"I already did it," I told him. "I put it in place as soon as you made it in."

Arland opened his mouth and closed it without saying a word.

The void field was difficult to maintain, but the area I needed to cover was relatively small and the peace summit had provided the inn with enough power to keep it up for the next few days.

"The void field will stop organic, inorganic, or energy based projectiles," I said. "It won't hurt you, but it won't let you pass through either. Please be aware that none of you can leave the inn grounds. I think we should call it a night. Sleep well. You are safe here."

Maud hugged me and went on to bed. Arland nodded to me and went to his room. The Hiru left as well.

Caldenia rose from her seat and approached Sean. "Be a dear. Get me everything you can on Kiran Mrak and his employees. And I do mean everything."

Sean nodded.

"Good night."

"Good night, Your Grace."

She went on her way. Orro had disappeared, too. It was just me and Sean now. He got up and walked toward me, stopping just a few inches away.

"You trapped me in the inn," he said.

"It's for your own safety."

"Are you worried about my safety?" There was a hint of a smile hiding in the corners of his mouth.

My heart was speeding up. Too much happened tonight. I wasn't scared - not exactly - but anxiety ate at me. I had to protect us from the Draziri, and retrieve the rest of the Archivarius, and keep all this a secret. I wanted to stop thinking about it just for a few hours.

Sean stood in front of me, so close that if I reached out, I would touch him. It would feel so good to touch him. It would feel even better to be in bed with him. He would hold me. I knew exactly how it would feel. It would feel safe, warm, and right. If he got in bed with me, I would forget all about the Draziri and the Hiru.

I met his gaze. There was a forest in his eyes, a deep, dark wood and on its edge a wolf waited, wondering if I would coax him out.

It would be so easy. One step, and I could run my hands up his chest to his shoulders. I would throw my arms around him and kiss him, and he would come with me.

Did I want Sean because I wanted *him* or did I want him because I was scared and exhausted and wanted to feel safe? I couldn't tell. I wasn't sure. I needed to be sure.

I was an innkeeper. I always had it together. Saving Maud really got to me. Now wasn't the time to come unglued. Sean deserved better. I deserved better.

"Good night, Sean."

The wolf melted back into the woods. "It might have been," Sean said.

Chapter 7

I stood in my kitchen and drank my first cup of coffee. There was nothing quite like that first cup of coffee. For some reason, it always tasted extra delicious.

Morning light streamed through the windows. No clouds dotted the clear sky. It was going to be a beautiful warm day, one of those wonderful days in Texas when nature forgot it was winter and pretended it was May instead.

I had already done my chores for the morning. I checked the perimeter. The Draziri had tried to punch a hole in my force field during the night, but got nowhere. Then I checked on Sean. He was up but still in his room and I didn't want to intrude. I was a little abrupt last night and I didn't know how to get around it, so I avoided him and instead went to spring poor Wing out of lock up.

I had unceremoniously shut him in his room last night. Being a pragmatic creature, he decided to play with his TV and watched various TV shows for half of the night. A marathon of *Indiana Jones* movies and *Cops* were apparently his favorites. I wasn't quite sure what to think about that. We'd discussed the Draziri and the force field, and then he'd gone to play in the garage. I had a feeling open warfare wasn't something Wing looked forward to. On a planet populated with massive dinosaurian creatures, the Ku were lower level predators who sought safety in packs. Their culture was rich with many legends of great warriors who single-handedly brought down larger prey, but in reality they were small and they knew it. They followed large predators, picked off injured or weak prey by running it to ground, and fought in large groups. He asked permission to go play in the garage and I left him to it.

I savored my coffee. By the island, Orro was whipping something in a bowl, holding the whisk with his claws. At the kitchen table, Caldenia sipped her first cup of tea, a content smile on her face.

Arland strode into the kitchen. He was in his "Earth mode," a loose white T-shirt and dark pants. His blond mane was pulled back from his face into a ponytail. He was carrying his blood mace.

"Lady Dina, Your Grace, Orro, good morning all," Arland said.

Caldenia inclined her head. Orro grunted something.

"Are you going somewhere, Lord Marshal?" I asked.

"I was planning on engaging in some aerobic activity. For my health. I'm on a retreat after all."

He was going to put on a big display for the Draziri, who were likely watching the back of the inn. Vampire logic at its best: if you can't directly attack, then strive to intimidate. He was perfectly safe while within the void force field.

"Would it be helpful if I provided some objects to add variety to your exercise?"

I motioned to the inn. A rack of practice weapons surfaced on the lawn, rising from the ground like a mushroom. Maces, axes, swords, and daggers of all shapes and sizes waited in the rack, each weapon made of a tough, rubber-like substance to match the weight and dimensions of the real thing. They wouldn't cut, but they still hurt. Maud had once chased me with a rubber sword like that because I'd poured Kool-Aid powder into her conditioner. Maud had always been a hair person. She'd put conditioner on and sit outside by the pool for an hour for "deep conditioning." I'd learned two important things that day: red Kool-Aid doesn't wash out of hair and rubber swords hurt.

And now Maud had cut off all her beautiful hair.

Arland grinned. "Lady Dina, you go above and beyond as always."

"My pleasure." The weapon rack was at least two hundred years old, but the vampire weapons hadn't changed a great deal, at least from what I could see.

He marched into the yard, set his mace down, grabbed a halberd from the rack, and spun it around.

I turned around and washed my coffee cup.

"He is such a polite boy," Caldenia said.

Arland was certainly polite, but once you saw him lop off a vampire's head with one blow, it put the courtesy in a whole new light. "You're up early, Your Grace."

"It's a lovely day and we're under siege. People are trying to murder us." Her eyes shone with excitement. "Isn't it marvelous?"

She would think so, wouldn't she? "They won't succeed."

"Of course not, my dear. I intend to ensure they don't. By the way, just in case one of the corpses happens to land on inn grounds, the Draziri are delicious."

"Really, Your Grace?"

"Their meat is juicy but bland," Orro said. "They taste like small fowl and easily take on the flavor profile of the sauce."

"Have you actually cooked Draziri?"

"Of course!" He drew himself to his full height. "I was a Red Cleaver chef. I have cooked a great many beings!"

Ugh. Forget I asked.

"I never understood why you find the notion of eating sentient creatures so disturbing, Dina," Caldenia said. "After all, it isn't cannibalism. There are no health risks, provided the dish is prepared properly."

I turned to the window. "Wow, look at the sunshine. Isn't that something?"

Caldenia laughed quietly.

Olasard purred by my feet, arched his back, and rubbed his head on my ankle. I crouched and petted him, scratching behind his ears. He purred louder. His bowl was still full, so it must've been actual feline affection.

Helen crept into the kitchen, quiet as a ghost, sat on the floor by my feet, and petted Olasard. He rubbed his face on her. She giggled.

"Is your mom still asleep?"

She nodded. "I'm sneaky."

"You don't say."

"And fierce." She showed me her fangs.

"Those are sharp fangs."

She nodded and bit the air.

"Scary," I told her.

"I won't bite you, Aunt Dina. You're nice."

Outside Arland swung around a massive two-handed hammer and let out a grunt. Helen abandoned me and Olasard and went to the back door.

Arland switched to a sword. He stood still, the sword held downward, then his whole body moved at once, delivering a vicious overhead blow. He cut in the opposite direction, then reversed with devastating power. His feet moved very little, bracing him against phantom counterblows and adding momentum when he wanted to sink the entire weight of his big body into the blow. His attacks came in a controlled, precise cascade.

Helen watched him like a cat watches a bird. If I didn't let her outside, she would start making bird-call noises. I opened the door. Helen scooted out and sat on the porch, mesmerized.

"That is a vampire child," Caldenia murmured.

Tell me something I don't know.

"She will adjust," Maud said behind me.

I almost jumped. I knew the location of all guests in the inn, but calling it up required a slight effort and if necessary, I could choose to stop paying attention to a particular guest. Yesterday I made the decision to stop tracking Maud. Tracking Helen was a necessity, because she was so young, but my sister was family. My parents stopped actively tracking us when we were teens, which didn't mean that Mom couldn't zero in on us with pinpoint accuracy when we were in trouble. But both Dad and she gave us our privacy, so I gave Maud her privacy and now she snuck up on me.

"How long were you standing there?"

"For a while," she said. She was sort of looking at me, which also allowed her to covertly watch Arland through the glass door. And despite all the effort she was putting into pretending not to see him, Maud was watching him.

"Let's see what you've got," Arland told Helen.

Helen stayed on the porch.

"Come on. Or are you scared?"

Helen showed him her teeth.

Arland motioned at her. My niece stayed on the porch.

The door swung open as Maud made the inn move it. She strode out onto the porch.

"Helen, kill," my sister said.

My niece grabbed a rubber dagger from the rack and moved onto the grass, foot over foot, stalking like a cat. Arland squared his shoulders. The contrast was ridiculous. She was tiny, he was huge; she had a little dagger, and he was holding a massive sword; but the two of them looked at each other with identical expressions on their faces, like two tigers meeting on the border of their territories. Waiting. Measuring the distance with their gaze. Watching for a hint of weakness.

The attack came with blinding speed. Helen dashed forward. Her dagger sliced the front of Arland's thigh and she scuttled back around him, cutting across his calves. Arland let out a dramatic roar and fell to his knees. Helen leapt up and slit his throat. It was so fast and precise, she must've done it dozens of times. I hoped in practice. It had to be in practice.

Arland collapsed on the ground, conveniently rolling onto his back. Helen put her foot on his chest, raised her dagger, and let out a vampire roar.

Should I be horrified or cuted out? I couldn't decide.

"Good job," Maud said.

Arland grabbed at Helen's ankle. She squealed and dashed to the porch.

He sat up, a big grin on his face.

"As you can see, my daughter doesn't need any instruction from you," Maud said.

"It wouldn't hurt."

No, Arland. No, no.

"Really?" Maud asked.

Arland rolled to his feet. "Your daughter is a vampire."

"Half."

He shook his head. "She has the fangs. Humans will see her as a vampire. Vampires will see her as a vampire."

The look on Maud's face turned friendly, almost warm. If I were in Arland's shoes, I'd run now.

"And there is something wrong with the way I train my child with fangs?" Maud casually stepped toward the weapon rack.

Sean entered the kitchen and stood next to me. "What did I miss?"

"My sister is about to destroy Arland."

On the lawn Arland leaned back. "For a child this young, a challenge issued is a challenge answered."

Maud pondered the weapons. "What are you implying?"

"A properly trained vampire child wouldn't have waited for permission to kill," Arland said.

He just kept digging his own grave.

Sean opened the kitchen door.

"Where are you going?" I whispered.

"I want a front row seat to this."

I chased him outside and we sat in the chairs.

"She's too controlled. You say sit, she sits. You say wait, she waits."

More words, deeper hole.

"She should be guided by instinct. She should be a *rassa* in the grass. Instead she is a *goren* on the porch."

And he just told my sister that her daughter wasn't a wolf but a trained dog.

I braced myself.

Maud drew a sword from the rack so fast, it looked like the weapon sprang into her hand on its own. She swung it. All pretense of sweetness was gone from her face.

"Perhaps you would care to give me some instruction."

"If you wish." Arland picked up a practice mace.

My sister struck. They clashed. One moment Arland was standing and the next he staggered back, shaking his head, the red imprint of the rubber sword blade on the side of his face.

Sean laughed.

Maud lunged into the opening. Arland swung his mace as if it were light as a toothpick and parried her sword, bashing her blade to the right. She drove her left fist into his throat. He spun away from her, choking, but still striking back. She ducked under his swing and rammed the blade of her sword into his armpit.

Sean and I made *ouch* noises.

Arland roared, his fangs bared.

Maud danced around him, battering his ribs. He knocked her sword blade aside with his left arm and kicked her. My sister flew, rolled in the grass, and came back up from a crouch into a blindingly fast attack.

The sword and mace drummed, clashing. Arland and Maud rampaged across the lawn, beating on each other. Sean and I watched them, wincing when one of them grunted in pain.

Helen sat by my feet, absorbed in the violence of the fight. She was so small and our world had gotten so violent all of a sudden.

"Did you know Draziri taste like chicken?" I asked.

Sean glanced at me, as if not sure if I was okay. "I had no idea."

"Orro told me," I told him. "We're besieged by murderous poultry."

Sean reached over and took my hand. I let him.

"We've got this," he said. "It will be okay."

Both my sister and Arland were glistening with sweat. The rubber weapons weren't designed to cut, but somehow they were both bleeding from a few shallow scrapes. They danced across the lawn back and forth, gaining ground then losing it.

"It won't be much longer," Sean said. "They're getting tired."

Arland blocked Maud's sword. She reversed her hold, gripping the blade, and clubbed him with the pommel. The blow landed right between his eyes. Arland went down.

"Yield!" my sister snarled.

Arland burst from the ground, sweeping her off her feet like a charging bull, and drove her into a tree. Maud's back slapped the bark, her feet four inches off the ground. He pinned her there.

If I interfered, there would be hell to pay.

"Yield, my lady." Arland bared his teeth an inch away from her neck.

She glared at him. "I don't yield."

The ground under Arland's feet opened and swallowed him up to his knees. He let go. Maud dropped down, picked up her sword, and walked away.

I sighed and let Arland up out of the hole.

Maud threw the sword into the rack and stomped onto the porch.

"You cheated," I told her.

"Yeah, yeah." She went into the house and slammed the door behind her.

I took my hand back from Sean.

Arland stretched, wincing, picked up the practice mace and walked to the porch. Red welts covered his pale skin. He looked like someone had worked him over with a sack of potatoes.

Helen stood on her toes and punched him in the stomach.

"Ow," he said.

Helen hissed, grinned, and ran inside.

The Marshal of House Krahr opened his mouth.

I braced myself.

"Your sister is magnificent," Arland said.

⚜ ⚜ ⚜

Maud the Magnificent swished water in her mouth and spat blood out into the bathroom sink. I helpfully held out a towel for her. She looked at herself in the mirror. "No."

"Suit yourself."

She turned and took the towel. "I was talking to myself."

"Oh? Was it no as in no more sparring matches or no as in Arland Krahr is vampire sex on a stick and seducing him would be a terrible idea?" I stepped back in case I had to duck.

She blotted her face with the towel. "No, as in I won't let myself be goaded again. Also, Dina, seducing? You've been hanging out with Caldenia too long."

"Helen likes him. She punched him in the stomach after you stormed off."

"Should've aimed lower."

The inn chimed, letting me know the Hiru requested my attention.

I waved my hand. A screen opened in the side of the wall. On it the Hiru leaned forward, his mechanical wheezing fast and loud.

"The second member of the Archivarius!"

"Where and when?" I asked.

"He's unable to reach Earth. He's on Baha-char awaiting retrieval."

"Where on Baha-char?" Maud asked. "It's a big place."

"Ninth Row, past the Merchants of Death. The member is arriving in an argon tank in fifteen minutes and will need to be picked up from Aka Lorvus, merchant. Your locator will pick up the signal."

"Thank you. Will you be joining us for breakfast?"

The Hiru paused. "You do not have to continue to invite me. I know my appearance brings you discomfort."

"It's an instinctual reaction and it only lasts a few moments. We're more than our instincts."

"I will consider it," he said. "But I may remain in my room."

"I understand. Will you tell me your name, at least?"

A long silence stretched.

"Sunset," the Hiru said finally. "My name is Sunset."

"It's a beautiful name."

He severed the connection.

I waved the screen closed. At least we had a longer window this time.

"Let me get the Archivarian," Maud said.

It was the most logical choice. If I left the inn, the void field would drop. The inn wouldn't be defenseless, but why tempt fate?

"You got the last one. I hate that you're doing all the work."

Maud waved the towel. "We're a team. Look, I'll go grab that blond fool and we'll be back here in no time."

"You could take Sean."

She shook her head. "No. Arland is an arrogant, aggressive, bull-headed ass..."

"Don't hold anything back."

"...but he looks damn impressive in armor and he hits like a battering ram. I've fought more in these past years than in my whole life. I've beaten vampires that were bigger, but after sparring with him, my arms felt like they were going to fall off. If I take Arland, I won't have to fight. People see that walking castle barrel toward them and get out of the way, and if someone doesn't, he'll smash them with his mace until there is nothing left except blood and mush. Dina, I haven't been to Baha-char in years, but I've been going there longer than you. Let me do this."

"Okay."

"I'll go get my armor. I want to test the crest anyway."

She took off, marching toward Arland's rooms. A moment later I heard her voice. "Lord Marshal? Would you care for an excursion?"

Yes, he would. In fact, I had a feeling he would be thrilled.

⚜ ⚜ ⚜

Ten minutes later, I watched Maud and Arland step through the doorway at the end of the hall into the bright sunshine of the galactic market place. The door sealed shut behind them. Beast whined softly by my feet.

"I know. They will be okay."

I sighed and took a mental tally of my guests. Helen was in the garage with Wing, the Hiru was in his quarters, the first member of the Archivarius was in his tank, Sean and Caldenia were on the back porch, and Orro, predictably, lingered in the kitchen. Everyone's accounted for.

What would Caldenia and Sean be talking about? I headed toward the back porch. Beast dashed ahead of me.

Sean sat at the table, an array of parts spread before him on a green tarp. No doubt the parts fit together into some sort of deadly weapon. Caldenia sipped Mello Yello in a rocking chair. Beast wagged her tail at me from her spot on a chair next to Sean.

I turned my back to the trees in case someone decided to read my lips.

"We have the second retrieval," I said. "At Baha-char. Maud and Arland left to get it."

"How much time do they have?" Sean asked.

"It's arriving already in a tank, so plenty of time."

Sean nodded and went back to tinkering.

"It's such a lovely day," Caldenia said. "You should take your niece and your adorable dog for a walk along the force field boundary."

I looked at her.

"You should also wear some equipment so we can hear any conversations you may have." Her Grace sipped her drink.

Oh. "Would Kiran Mrak want to talk?"

"He knows nothing about you. You're a mystery. Trust me, my dear. If he's any good at what he does, he'll want to talk. He won't pass up the opportunity to gather information and take your measure."

Sean reached into the bag by his feet and pulled out a small plastic box with a clear top and a layer of complex electronics embedded in the white bottom. A flesh-colored patch the size of a penny was inside. I took the box. I could've just had my voice resonate at any point from the inn, but he went through the trouble of finding a gadget for me and I would wear it. I pried the box open and swiped the patch with my finger. It immediately mimicked my skin tone, blending so completely, I couldn't find it by looking alone.

"Where should I put this?"

"By your ear works best," he said.

I touched the patch to the spot just under my right ear. It stuck. Pale green light pulsed through the box.

"Give him as little information as possible," Caldenia said. "Don't be obvious in your questions or he'll stop talking. But do push him, dear. If you feel any splashes of emotion from him, use it and test it to see if you can get a reaction."

"Come on, Beast!" I said in stereo, one sound coming from my mouth and the other from the box.

The Shih-Tzu jumped off the chair and she and I started toward the edge of the void field.

I strolled along the boundary. Beast trailed me, stopping to sniff at random clumps of grass and fascinating sticks.

I picked one up and threw it for her. She dashed after it, a black and white blur. I looked up and saw Kiran Mrak. He stood less than a foot away, wrapped in a cloak that perfectly mimicked the shrubs around him. The void field interrupted projectiles, but it permitted sound and light. I didn't hear him. If I had been off my land, he would've killed me and I would've died never knowing what happened.

He stared at me, his turquoise eyes exquisitely beautiful. I took a step. He took one with me, perfectly mirroring my movements, as if he were a magic reflection, except he moved with the kind of grace I could never accomplish. I still couldn't hear him.

We walked along the boundary of the void force field.

There was a beauty about the Draziri, an elegance and otherworldly air. When you looked at one, it was like meeting a mystic creature from some legend.

Beast brought the stick back, saw the Draziri, but she couldn't smell him and I didn't seem alarmed. I threw the stick again and she bounced off.

"Shi-Tzu-Chi," Kiran said in his low melodious voice. "Adorable and created to kill."

"Sometimes things are not as they appear."

"So I've come to realize." He drew back his hood and tossed his cloak over his shoulder. Underneath he wore a soft gray tunic, bordered with black. A sword rested on his waist. His long white hair spilled down in a perfectly straight waterfall. The lines of his caste shone with silver on his forehead.

"A small woman in an old house on a backwater planet possessing power beyond imagination. It has an almost legendary air. A holy quest from prehistory."

"Except holy quests usually have a worthy goal and a hero. You're trying to kill a being that caused you no harm."

"He's an abomination," Kiran said. "He must die."

"Explain something to me," I said. "You kill for money."

"Yes."

"You also kill for pride and for the challenge of it."

"Yes."

"But you're not a religious man. You don't kill for the sake of your church. Why the sudden interest in the Hiru?"

"You don't know me."

"A devout man wouldn't have murdered a priest."

He smiled, revealing even, sharp teeth that didn't belong in any human's mouth. "High priest."

And he called me arrogant.

We strolled some more.

"His name is Sunset," I said.

Kiran tilted his head to look at me.

"The Hiru you're trying to kill. He has a name. He has consciousness."

"You're naive to think that should make a difference to me. I've killed hundreds of beings."

"You won't kill this one."

"I will," he promised me. "You can't maintain this force field indefinitely."

True. A week or so and it would begin to strain the inn. "I can maintain it long enough. Why not go look for an easier target?"

"Because the Hiru are rare. Locating another will take time."

"You're short on time?"

"Not me."

I took a wild stab in the dark. "Someone close to you is dying. Killing the Hiru will redeem you and them."

He didn't respond.

Who would he care about enough? Sean and I had gone over the files he brought from Wilmos until we damn near memorized them. Kiran wasn't married.

"Your lover?"

A slight hint of derision touched his mouth.

"It's your mother. Mekrikzi."

Something vicious crossed his eyes. I fought an urge to step back.

"My mother is a remarkable woman," he said quietly. "She won't spend a single moment in hell and you're not fit to sully her name with your filthy mouth."

That's just great. Now I had a filthy mouth. Well, if that wasn't a splash of emotion, I didn't know what was. "I can understand now why you have no wife."

"And why is that?"

"We have a term for men like you on our planet."

"And what that would be?"

"Momma's boy."

He smiled again. There was no humor in the smile, just a vicious baring of alien teeth. "Everyone has a weakness. We all have people who are close to us. I will find yours."

"You should look for my parents," I suggested. "Tell me what you find."

The smile faltered slightly. "You have friends. Family."

"They are all in this inn. Everyone I care about is here."

"I'll sift through your life. I'll find every guest who ever stayed in your inn."

"Start with the Khanum of the Hope-Crushing Horde and her elite warriors. You should totally pay them a surprise visit and drop some vague threats while you're at it. They love that sort of thing."

He stopped. His beautiful face turned savage. "When this is over, I'll burn your house to the ground, put a slave collar around your neck, and drag you out of here. You'll suffer for years and when I've satisfied myself with every cruelty and perversion my mind can invent, I'll sell the pitiful wreck that you'll become to the highest bidder."

His cloak flared and he vanished into the brush.

I sighed. "Come on, Beast."

We finished our walk and I came back to the porch. Sean had put together a wicked-looking gun. Caldenia was on her third can of Mello Yello.

"Well, that was that." I sat down in a chair. "I've learned nothing useful, except that Freud would love to interview him and that he has apparently given some thought to torturing me."

"On the contrary, my dear." Caldenia set the can down. "We've learned a great deal."

"What do you mean?"

"You heard, but you haven't listened. You must learn to listen, Dina."

Within the depths of the inn, the door to Baha-char opened. I felt Maud and Arland and nobody else. Crap.

"What?" Sean was on his feet.

"They're back. Alone."

The door flew open in front of me and I hurried into the kitchen and then into the front room, Sean and Caldenia behind me. Maud and Arland emerged from the hallway. Mush, fruit peels, and garbage covered their armor. Some unidentifiable sticky yellow slime stained Arland's breastplate, and pieces of some broken circuitry stuck to it. White ash filled Maud's hair. Arland was shaking with rage. Maud looked ready to rip someone's head off. The reek of rotting garbage filled the room and I gagged.

"What happened?" I squeezed out. "Where is the Archivarian?"

Maud hurled her sword onto the floor and spat a single word. "Muckrats!"

⚜ ⚜ ⚜

"You let muckrats steal the Archivarian? Are you crazy?" Of all the... How could they... Argh!

"They were already there!" Maud waved her arms. "I swear!"

"Lady Maud is correct," Arland said. "When we arrived, the merchant's shop was ransacked."

"He owed money to the muckrats," Maud added. "He missed a payment so they went through his shipment and took the Archivarian."

I put my hand over my face. Of all the creatures, it had to be muckrats.

"Why would they want the Archivarian?" Sean asked, his voice calm.

"The lights," I said.

"What do you mean?" Sean asked.

"The tank is likely big, ornate, and has blinking lights on it."

"We pursued," Arland said. "And then we tried to bargain. When reason failed, we attempted to storm their compound."

"Did you happen to storm it through a garbage compactor?" Sean asked.

Arland gave him a blank look.

"It's not his fault," Maud said. "He was brave and he tried. I tried too. They dumped garbage on us and then acid." She crouched, grabbed her sword off the floor, and stood up, all in one fluid motion, and stuck her sword under my nose. The blade resembled a half-melted candle.

"Two years." Maud's voice trembled, and I couldn't tell if it was from despair or outrage. "I've had this sword for two years. It saved my life. Look at it."

"You needn't worry, my lady," Arland said quietly. "I assure you that you will have a new blade, one suited to your skill, before nightfall."

I heaved a sigh. Berating and yelling wouldn't fix anything. It would make me feel a lot better, but we didn't have time to waste.

"We came back here as soon as we could," Maud said.

"I still think that a prolonged assault may have yielded some results," Arland said.

"No, Maud is right." I pulled my robe off and grabbed the car keys from the hook by the door. "You can't fight muckrats. You can't reason with them either. You can only trade. Maud, I need you to defend the inn. The Draziri likely won't attack. It's broad daylight."

"Where are you going?" Sean asked.

"To Walmart!"

"I'm coming with you. Kiran's fixated on you. You can't count on him being rational."

I opened my mouth... It would take longer to argue and we didn't have time. For all I knew the muckrats were prying the argon tank open as we spoke. Besides, he was right. The Draziri had made it personal during our last conversation.

"Okay." I turned to Maud. "Hold the inn. Please."

"I got it," she said.

I stuck my feet into my shoes I had left by the front door and ran for the garage. Sean followed me.

I jumped into the driver's seat, he took the passenger one, and I forced myself to casually drive out of the garage and pull into the street at a reasonable speed instead of peeling out of there like a Nascar driver. Nobody assaulted us. Nobody followed.

"What are muckrats?" Sean asked.

"Magpies of the galaxy. They have a fort at Baha-char."

Ten minutes later we marched through Walmart's doors. I headed straight for the toy aisle.

"What are we looking for?" Sean asked.

"Look for the most annoying thing you can find. Anything that's loud, has flashing lights, and complicated moving parts."

I surveyed the toys. The pickings were slim. I thought there would've been more, but with the holidays approaching, the toy isle had been picked over.

Wait. I pulled a box off the shelf. Musical Fun Hammer Pounding Toy Game. A variation on Whack-A-Mole, with plastic eggs with funny faces in bright Easter colors popping up and a hammer to whack them with. Please tell me there is a demo... There it was, at the end of the aisle, where the toy was hooked up to a cord. Four buttons on the bottom. I pushed one. Horribly loud music blared from the toy. So far so good. I grabbed the green plastic hammer and pushed the demo button. The blue egg popped up. I smacked it and it lit up from the inside with a seizure-inducing strobe light and gave a police-siren wail. I whacked another egg. A primate's screech cut my eardrums. Perfect. I grabbed the box and emerged from the aisle, almost running into Sean.

I showed the box to him. "What do you have?"

He lifted a bizarre-looking contraption that resembled a cross between a hair dryer and a megaphone with an array of lights along its plastic frame.

"What the heck is that?"

"It's a fart gun."

"A what?"

Sean pressed the trigger. The lights dramatically lit up and the gun made a loud farting noise. "A fart gun. From that kid movie. You said annoying."

He pressed the trigger again. The gun farted. A woman with a child in her cart looked at us. Sean's mouth slowly stretched into a smile.

"Okay, fine." I sped toward the checkout.

A fart.

"Will you stop doing that?"

Another fart.

"Sean! What are you, five?"

He laughed under his breath.

The express checkout lane was empty. Miracle of miracles. I slid my box onto the belt. Sean followed.

The cashier, an older plump woman, smiled at us. "Aww. You're such a cute couple buying toys. Are you expecting?"

What?

"Yes, we are," Sean said and put his arm around me. I would kill him.

"No rings?" The cashier swiped the fart gun across the scanner. "Better get on that wedding fast."

Of all the... I swiped my card and punched my code into the terminal. That's why I never came to Walmart.

The card went through. Sean grabbed the two toys and we headed out.

"Good luck, you two!" the cashier called after us.

As soon as we were out the doors, I turned to Sean. "Will you take this seriously? The future of an entire species is at stake."

"Yes, we're going to save them with a fart gun."

"Don't!"

Fart.

Ugh.

Fifteen minutes later I ran into the inn. Gertrude Hunt seemed no worse for wear. Maud was in the war room. I stuck my head in. "Anything?"

"They tried to send a probe in and I nuked it," she said. "Go, Dina! Go, we're fine."

The inn dropped my Baha-char robe, dark brown with a tattered hem, by my feet. I pulled it on, took a sack out of the closet, and held it open. Sean stuffed the toys into it and I handed it back to him. If anyone could keep it from being stolen, Sean could. The door at the end of the long hallway opened, spilling the bright sunshine of Baha-char into the inn. We stepped through the door.

Heat washed over me. We stood on pale yellow tiles lining the alley. Buildings rose on both sides of us, built with sandstone and decorated with colorful tile, fifteen floors high, each a mess of balconies, terraces, and bridges. Trees, vines, and flowers thrived in planters, adding a welcome relief from the uniformity of sandstone. Banners streamed in the breeze, burgundy, turquoise, and gold. Above, in the purple sky, a gargantuan lavender planet, cracked down the middle, oversaw it all, pieces of it floating by the main mass like misshapen moons.

I hurried out of the alley, Sean next to me. We stepped into the street, and a current of beings swept us along. Creatures in every shape and size walked, crawled, hovered, stomped, and slithered between the buildings, searching the merchants' stalls and shops for that particular something that couldn't be bought anywhere else. The street breathed and spoke in a thousand voices.

We wove our way through the current and stopped before a large building, its rectangular doorway dark. Sean grimaced. It wasn't his favorite place. Damn it, I should've thought about it before bringing him with me. Nuan Cee, one of the powerful Merchants of Baha-char, was the one who'd hired Sean to become Turan Adin. Sean was probably being hit with all sorts of memories he was trying to forget.

"I'm sorry," I told him. "But we need his help."

"It never comes without a price."

"I know."

"We could just go back, get Arland, and storm the place..."

I stepped close to him and kissed him. It was meant to be a quick kiss, a brushing of my lips on his, but the moment we touched, excitement dashed through me. The memory of what it felt like to kiss Sean Evans short-circuited my brain. I threw caution to the wind and kissed him hard. My tongue licked his lips. He opened his mouth and I tasted Sean. Like drinking fire.

We broke apart. I opened my eyes and saw the deep forest in his eyes and a scarred feral wolf looking back. He was close, much closer than he'd ever come before.

Sean wrapped his arm around my waist, and pulled me close. A little thrill dashed through me. I was caught and I didn't mind. Sean studied my face, leaned, and his mouth closed on mine. He kissed me back, deep, deliberate, seducing me right there on the street. I didn't want it to stop.

Sean broke the kiss and turned his head.

A creature had emerged from the doorway. Hulking, shaggy with long black fur, with massive arms ending in clawed fingers and a monstrous face filled with fangs, it looked like nothing Earth could produce.

"The Merchant will see you," the creature boomed.

"We should go in," I whispered.

He let me go, slowly.

We followed the bodyguard into the tall foyer lined with gray tile. A waterfall splashed from the far wall, falling into a narrow basin. Here and there plants in all shades, from purple and magenta to emerald green, flourished in ornate planters. A table of volcanic glass waited in the middle of the room. I sat on a soft purple sofa by the table. Sean remained standing.

A curtain on the right opened and a fox-like creature barely three and a half feet tall, criminally fluffy, and wearing a jeweled apron, scurried out on two legs. I opened my mouth and forgot to close it. I had expected Nuan Cee. This was…

"Cookie?"

The short fox opened his arms and ran to me. I hugged him.

"What are you doing here?" Sean asked.

Cookie reached out to hug him. Sean hugged him back.

Cookie twitched his lynx ears. "Uncle is away on business. I'm in charge until he returns."

He stepped back and very formally held his paw-hands together. With his sandy fur and bright blue eyes, he was almost too cute to be taken seriously. However, he was of clan Nuan and underestimating him would prove deadly.

"So what can the great Nuan Cee do for you?" Cookie asked.

"We need your help to bargain with muckrats," I said. "They have taken an argon tank with a creature inside it as means of payment for a debt owed by a merchant. We need to retrieve the tank."

"What do you offer in return?"

"A favor," I said. I didn't have anything else.

Cookie's blue eyes narrowed. "I shall do this. In return, I will call on you in time of need."

"Deal," I said.

Cookie rubbed his paws together. "What do you have in trade to the muckrats?"

⚜ ⚜ ⚜

Fart.

Fart.

Faaaaaaart.

"Will you please stop doing that?"

Cookie giggled and waved the fart gun around.

Males and farts. Any species, any planet, didn't matter.

We walked through the shadow area of Baha-char. The streets were narrow here, the colors duller, the canopies worn. Grime had settled on the doorways. The merchants stayed in their shops with their weapons within reach. Sean scanned the street with his gaze. I felt weary. Cookie skipped without a care in the world as if he was in the middle of a sunny meadow. Possibly because the hulking monstrosity that served as his bodyguard followed us, breathing down my neck, but most likely because his apron identified him as a scion of a Merchant clan. Harming a member of the Merchants meant signing your own death sentence.

We turned the corner. Sean stopped. High stone walls rose on both sides of us, enclosing an area about the size of a football field. Directly in front of us was an enormous metal wall, hammered together from giant rectangular hard steel plates. Smaller plates interrupted it, with rust and acid trails stretching from them over the metal. The huge gate in the center at ground level was big enough for two elephants to pass together side by side.

Cookie rubbed his hands together. "Stand back please and do not say anything."

He raised the fart gun and let it rip.

A small plate slid aside about fifty feet off the ground.

Cookie took the smashing game and pounded it with the hammer. Lights and awful screeching noises broke the silence.

More plates slid open.

Cookie raised his hands and spoke in the chirping language of the muckrats. He waved his arms. He walked back and forth. He walked some more, lecturing. He lifted the fart gun and let out another blast of sound. He smacked the game with the hammer. He spoke again, then he fell silent.

A short chirping question came from the wall. "Chichi-chichi?"

Cookie launched into a second lecture. He stood on his toes, raising his arms as far as they could go and drew a big circle. He put his arms behind his back and walked around. Then he waited.

The fortress remained quiet.

"I say we storm it," Sean whispered.

"Hush."

Another chirp.

Cookie turned to me. "Can I have your shoe?"

I reached for my sneaker.

A chorus of outraged shrieks emanated from the fortress.

"The other shoe," Cookie said softly.

I took off my left sneaker. Cookie raised it like it was a treasure and deposited it by the toys.

A metal clang echoed through the fortress, followed by rapid thuds. The gates swung open and a horde of muckrats spilled out. About four feet tall, they resembled weasels who somehow walked upright and developed monkey hands. Their sleek fur ranged from rusty brown to black, and they wore little leather kilts adorned with lights. They poured out of the gates, dragging the massive argon tank. The tank was deposited on the ground. A short muckrat dumped a pile of gold coins by the tank, another added a dead scree rat the size of a small cat, and a third put some complex electronic part on it.

The leading muckrat pointed to the pile. "Chi?"

Cookie made a great show of inspecting the goods. "Chi."

The leading muckrat grabbed my sneaker and raised it up over his head.

"Chiiiiiiiiiiii!"

The muckrats erupted in screaming. The toys vanished and the horde ran back into the fort, as if sucked into it. The metal doors clanged shut.

Sean picked up a gold coin from the pile. "Are these Spanish doubloons?"

"So sorry about the shoe," Cookie said mournfully as his bodyguard hefted the argon tank onto his shoulder like it weighed nothing, "but they wouldn't budge on it."

Chapter 8

"You're not carrying me." I pulled off my right sneaker and started down the street.

"You have no idea what's on this street." Sean wrinkled his nose. "It's disgusting."

"Then I will find a shoe merchant and buy a new pair."

"You do realize that I could carry three of you and it wouldn't slow me down?"

"You do realize that you can't even handle one of me? Three of me would be entirely too much."

Sean opened his mouth.

"I'm walking," I told him. "It won't kill me to go barefoot for a couple of blocks."

Sean muttered something under his breath.

"I heard that," I told him. I didn't, but he didn't need to know that.

Walking barefoot in this part of Baha-char was a bad idea. The big square tiles that lay in the open, baked by the sun, were too hot, which forced me to hug the edges of the street by the buildings, where trash and grime had drifted, pushed to the side by wind and the never-ending current of shoppers. Staring at the ground to make sure I didn't step on anything that would slice my feet open got old very fast. But letting Sean carry me wasn't an option. I had to preserve some dignity. Besides, being carried by him would be ... nice. I had a feeling I would like it, and we weren't out of the woods yet. I didn't need to be contemplating how exactly being that close to him felt until we were back in the safety of the inn.

I looked up long enough to see where we were going. At the end of the block, a grimy storefront under a ratty green tarp had a bright neon sign that announced FOOTWEAR in seven languages. A colorful shell, resembling that of a garden snail but five feet tall and colored in hues of brilliant red, rich brown, and lemon yellow, sat in the doorway of the shop.

"Look, shoes!"

I sped up to the stall. The merchant, a Took, sensed me coming and stretched his wrinkly neck all the way out of his snail shell. Cookie rubbed his hands together.

"I just need a pair of shoes," I told him.

"Of course," the little fox answered. "As long as we get them at the right price."

The inside of the shop contained a single massive pile of shoes made from all sorts of materials for all sorts of feet. It smelled like all sorts of feet too, but I didn't care. I dug through it, trying to find something made for humans. Sean parked himself at the front of the store, watching the street. Cookie's shaggy bodyguard stopped next to him.

I rummaged through the shoes. Too big, too small, too slimy, made for someone who only tiptoed like the elephants, too sharp, too... This pair wasn't too bad. I lifted the two sandals up, little more than soles with a string of cheap beads.

"How much?"

The Took's tentacles wavered. "Two credits."

"Two credits!" Cookie staggered back and slumped over, as if punched. "It's an outrage! Are you trying to murder us?"

Crap. I forgot he was with us. I had to cut this off now, before it devolved into bargaining. "Two credits is f—"

"Financially criminal!" Cookie announced.

The Took's squid-like eyes flared, changing color from deep red to bright green. "This is genuine okarian leather!"

Cookie plucked the sandals from my fingers and waved them around. "Yes, from the genuine ass of an okarian nifrook. Have you smelled these shoes?"

"The odor adds character!"

"Character?" Cookie bared his teeth. "My friend isn't interested in character. Do you not see that she is a young attractive female of her species? If she wears these shoes, we'll have to charge you compensation for all of the potential mates this odious footwear will repulse."

The Took's eyes narrowed. "One and three-quarters credits."

"As a matter of fact, if we were to buy these shoes, the rest of your pile would smell better. You should pay us for the service of removing these so-called sandals from your shop."

"What?"

"You heard me. Now this!" Cookie raised my right sneaker in the air. "This is a shoe."

I sighed and went to stand next to Sean.

"I should've just gone barefoot. Now he'll be haggling until the cows come home out of principle."

Sean didn't answer. He was looking down the street, back the way we came. I looked into his eyes and saw Turan Adin there. The hair rose on the back of my neck.

"What is it?"

"We're being hunted."

"Is it Draziri?"

"I don't know."

When a wolf told you that he was being hunted, only a fool ignored it. I shut up. Sean's senses were a lot sharper than mine, and distracting him right now was a dumb idea. I slipped on my glove and pulled the energy whip out of the inside pocket of my robe.

The street on both sides of us lay empty. The faint breeze that usually moved the air through the canyon-like streets of Baha-char died. The air turned hot and oppressive. I shivered. It felt wrong.

"And stay out!" the Took thundered behind me.

Cookie emerged with the sandals and deposited the shoes and a credit chip into my hand. "Here are the sandals and half a credit. I have given him your right shoe in trade."

"Thank you." I slipped the sandals on my feet.

"I had to redeem myself." Cookie smiled.

"Let's go," Sean said quietly.

We hurried down the street. Cookie started out skipping, but two turns later the fun went out of him. He slunk now, fast and silent on velvet paws.

I glanced over my shoulder. The street was still empty. The darkness seemed to pool behind us. My heart rate sped up. Maybe it was my imagination, maybe not, but I wasn't willing to take chances. We were almost running now.

We took one last turn and emerged into one of the main streets. The noise of the crowd washed over me. I exhaled. We wove through traffic, with Cookie's monster bringing up the rear.

I glanced behind me again. Nothing but the crowd.

Deep breath. Deeep breath. Almost home.

Sean's face seemed to relax slightly. Good.

Two more blocks and we would turn into the alley leading to the inn's door.

Magic crept up my spine, icy and slimy. I recoiled. It was revolting, but it felt almost... familiar? How...

The crowd in front of us thinned at an alarming speed. Creatures fled, escaping into the shops and side alleys. The street emptied, leaving a lone creature standing in front of our alley.

Eight feet tall, it wore a tattered robe with the hood pulled up. It looked like a mirror of my own, except larger, with a deeper hood, and wider sleeves. It had to be a coincidence. The galaxy had a million robes. It was highly possible that two of them would be cut and sewn together in a very similar way.

I squeezed the energy whip, releasing the thin filament. It dripped to the ground, sparking off the stone.

Next to me Cookie pulled a knife out of the jeweled sheath on his apron.

Sean looked at Cookie's shaggy bodyguard. "He's in danger."

The creature bared its fangs. A massive hand landed on Cookie's shoulder. The beast yanked the small fox up, spun, and ran down the street, carrying Cookie and the tank back the way we came, each stomp of its mammoth feet like the blow of a sledgehammer. Cookie's outraged screeches faded.

Sean pulled out his green-edged knife.

The robed creature waited between us and the alley. There was no other way to the inn's door. We had to go through it.

"Dina?" Sean asked quietly. "What is it?"

"I don't know."

The creature thrust its left arm up, exposing a humanoid hand, pale and withered, with thick yellowed claws. The veins in its arm pulsed. I felt the magic gather around it, revolting and sickening. If that magic had a body, it would've been a putrid corpse. But the pattern in which it flowed, the underlying core of it... Shock gripped me.

"It's an innkeeper."

"What?"

"It's corrupted somehow. We have to kill it. It's an abomination."

A sphere of pure energy shot out from the creature's fingers, a ball of orange lightning as big as a grapefruit. Sean leapt up and forward, but it streaked past him and curved to follow me. I couldn't outrun it.

Sean pulled a gun from within his clothes and fired, running at the robed creature. The air around the hooded figure rippled. Pulse projectiles, the deadliest in the galaxy, and it was blocking them.

The ball lightning lunged at me.

Like killed like. I flicked the energy whip.

The lightning exploded.

White haze drowned me. The magic shock wave reverberated through my bones and exploded in my chest, like my heart tried to burst. I gagged and vomited onto the ground. Sean bounced from the side of a building and landed behind the creature. He lunged, too fast to see, aiming the knife into the hooded figure's ribs. Lightning bit him. Sean flew back as if punched by a massive fist.

Oh no, you don't. I gritted my teeth and staggered forward, my whip burning with energy.

A second ball of lightning dripped from the creature's claws and shot at me. I swung my whip. It connected. The lightning burst over me. Heat and pain seared my chest and stomach. My robe caught fire. I tore at it, trying to get it away from my skin.

Sean's body blurred and a massive werewolf landed on the tiles, tall, muscular, with enormous shoulders and huge hands armed with two-inch claws. The robed figure spun toward him. The werewolf bared his fangs and lunged at the corrupted innkeeper, stabbing so fast, the knife turned into a green streak. Lightning burst from the robed figure and singed his fur, but he kept stabbing in a frenzy.

I yanked the robe over my head. The skin on my chest burned as if someone had taken a cheese grater to it, but I didn't care. I sprinted to them.

The fur on Sean's arms curled. The stench of burned hair polluted the air. The robed figure spun, trying to avoid the knife. Shreds of its robe fluttered in the air - Sean had landed some cuts.

The corrupted innkeeper raked at Sean with its withered hand, its claws dripping magic. Blood gushed from the werewolf's chest.

I flicked my whip, feeling the creature's magic shift in response. The energy whip snapped, bouncing off the empty air two inches from its head. Fast. I snapped the whip again. Somehow it slid aside. That's fine. It couldn't dodge me forever.

Sean slashed at its back.

Magic exploded from within the robe. The blast wave lifted me off my feet. I flew back, swept away like a mote of dust in a tsunami, and hit a building with my back. Oh, it hurt. It hurt so much.

Sean fell through the canopy above me and crashed next to me in the middle of broken wood and torn fabric.

The creature brought its arms together. A torrent of energy shot out from between its hands, a lance aimed at us.

I scrambled to my feet and thrust myself in front of Sean. The whip wouldn't stop it. We were dead.

It was an innkeeper.

I dropped the whip and the glove, grabbed a piece of broken railing and held it in front of me, focusing on it. It wasn't a broom, it was barely a staff, but I was an innkeeper, damn it, and he would not kill Sean.

The torrent of energy punched me and broke over the staff, the orange lightning splitting and burning with deep turquoise where it touched my staff and magic. My skin went numb. Someone had sunk tiny hooks into my veins and yanked at them, trying to rip them out of my body.

It hurt.

The hooded creature arched its back. Its robe turned pure black, as if the color had been sucked out of the fabric. The tattered hem frayed, unraveling. The torrent hit me harder.

God, it hurt. It hurt, it hurt, it hurt…

My whole body shook from the strain. Pain wrapped around each vertebra in my spine and squeezed, grinding cartilage and bone to nothing. My arms tried to wrench out of my shoulder sockets.

An eerie, unearthly shriek cut at my ears. The hooded thing was screaming.

I tasted blood in my mouth.

I couldn't hold it forever. I…

A stream of bullets hammered the creature from the left, each impact a ripple in the air, stopping just short of hitting its body. The torrent of energy weakened. It was shifting magic to cover itself.

The agony was turning my brain into mush. I gritted my teeth and stepped forward, pushing the torrent back. A step. Another step.

The hooded creature took a step back.

Yes!

It took another step, bending under the strain of shielding itself from the barrage of bullets and my magic.

Sean darted from behind me, the knife in his hand.

I screamed and sank everything I had into my staff. It split the way innkeeper's brooms did. A sharp wooden blade formed on its top. I pushed it into the torrent, until the blade pointed directly at the corrupted innkeeper, slicing through the current of energy.

The robed creature's magic tore out of it in an orange half-sphere, covering it against me and the shooter. Sean loomed behind it. The knife flashed and the robed figure collapsed in a limp heap.

The pressure of the foul magic vanished.

I sank to my knees and lay on the ground. On my left a grizzled older werewolf lowered a bizarre-looking Gatling gun. Thank you, Wilmos. Cookie stopped jumping up and down next to him and ran to me.

Sean picked me up off the ground. "Are you okay?"

I nodded. I couldn't even talk.

His lips brushed mine and he squeezed me to him gently as if I were the most important thing in the world.

⚜ ⚜ ⚜

My mouth finally obeyed. "Tank?"

"At my shop," Wilmos said. He was looking at me as if it hurt him.

Sean started down the street in the direction of the inn. "No!"

"Dina, you're badly burned. You need the inn to heal you."

"Get the tank."

"Later."

"No."

"Don't argue with me." He didn't raise his voice. He didn't look any different. But his tone severed the words like a knife. It was impossible to keep arguing. I still tried. Making words took effort and endurance I didn't have.

"Failed once. I can't…walk into the inn without the tank. Guest. Trust. Please. Please, Sean. Please."

He snarled, his wolf mouth baring his teeth.

"Please."

Wilmos looked at him.

"We'll get the tank," Sean said.

"Body…"

"And the corpse," he said, fury snarling in his voice. His gaze fixed me. It was direct and cold. A wolf gaze. "Not another word until we get to the inn. Close your eyes and rest."

The last thing I saw was Cookie's bodyguard picking up the hooded body. I laid my head on Sean's shoulder and closed my eyes, drifting, neither awake nor asleep, but stuck in a painful confusing place in between. My chest burned.

Time stretched, long and viscous.

The inn's magic touched me. I felt the cooling air on my skin - we'd passed from Baha-char's heat into my home. The walls creaked and snapped in panic. Gertrude Hunt was screaming. I opened my eyes and smiled when I saw my sister's terrified face.

"I'm okay. Everything will be fine."

The inn's tendrils wrapped around me and I sank into the depths of Gertrude Hunt, where the inn's glowing heart waited for me. It opened and embraced me. I closed my eyes and finally fell asleep.

❧ ❧ ❧

"Will Aunt Dina be okay?" Helen asked.

I opened my eyes. Helen and Maud stood together in the soothing darkness. Maud wore her armor. A sword hung in the scabbard on her hip. Helen's eyes were big and round.

Around me tendrils of smooth wood intertwined into a pillar, holding me between the floor and the ceiling. The inn's lifeblood flowed through them, wrapping me in the healing warmth, and the tendrils glowed, lit from within by green. Faint blue lights floated around me, born of pure, thick magic. The air smelled so fresh here. Clean and filled with life.

I had been here twice before. The first time when I woke Gertrude Hunt from its deep sleep. I sat right here with my hands on its heart and coaxed it back to life. The second time I had used too much power outside of the inn, and when Sean brought me back, I was almost dead. The inn healed me then as it did now.

I stirred, checking the magic within the tendrils. Strong. Much stronger than it had been after I was healed the first time. I must not have expended as much magic as I thought. Or maybe I was giving Gertrude Hunt too little credit.

"Aunt Dina will be fine, my flower," Maud said. "She's resting."

"She's awake," I said.

Beast bounded out of the darkness and Helen ran toward me and hugged the wooden pillar of tendrils holding me inside.

The inn sighed around me. It was a happy, contented sigh.

"I'm sorry," I whispered. "I'll try not to do it again."

"You better not do it again," Maud growled.

The tendrils parted, letting me step on the floor. Beast licked my feet, flopped over on her back, and then dashed away, running in a circle as if her canine feelings had gotten the better of her. I crouched and hugged Helen.

"You have flowers on your chest," my niece said.

I looked down. The inn had healed my burns - they weren't deep - and the skin was smooth but faint scars remained. They didn't look like flowers. They looked like pale swirls. And they probably wouldn't go away. I was permanently scarred.

"It doesn't look that bad," Maud said.

I looked at her.

"Oh for the love of… Stop acting like your boobs burned off. You look fine. Nothing a tanning lotion won't fix."

She marched to me, hugged me, and handed me my robe.

I slipped it on.

Beast dashed by my feet. Helen squealed and chased her.

"How's everything?"

"Sunset was overjoyed to receive another Archivarius member. The inn tried to keep the corpse of whatever you brought in out, and then when I held the door open so they could carry it in, it tried to shrink away from it. We put it into a plastic container and sealed it. That's the only way Gertrude Hunt would stop freaking out. We need to analyze it, but it won't let me go near it and it locked me out of the lab where we put it. The birds tried a direct assault just after dark. I let that idiot and your werewolf have them. I think Sean might be disturbed. He cut off their heads and put them on sticks in the back yard."

I sighed. "Can you see them from the street?"

"No. Focus. I'm telling you your boyfriend beheaded your enemies and threaded their skulls on sticks, and all you care about is if your neighbors can see them."

"Is he okay?"

"Physically, yes. Mentally... Don't get me wrong, the heads are an effective tactic. But still - disturbed. If you happen to catch his eyes in the right moment, something stares back at you."

"It's a wolf," I told her.

"What?"

"It's a wolf in the dark woods."

Maud sighed. "You see the wolf. I see cities burning. There is something not quite right about him. Something unsettling. I've been through hell before. I know that look, Dina. It's not too late to change your mind."

"I like him."

Maud rolled her eyes.

"Did the Lord Marshal deliver?"

"Deliver what?" she asked.

"You know what. He promised you a sword. I think his exact words were, 'A new blade before nightfall.'"

She clamped her mouth shut and drew a blood sword from her scabbard.

"Is it a good sword?"

"It's exquisite." She sounded like she just tasted a lemon. "He had it sent down from his ship. He made a huge scene out of it. A courier in full armor with crimson banners arrived and knelt in front of me to present it."

I wished I could've seen the look on her face.

"I tried to refuse it."

Arland could be extremely persistent when it was in his best interests. "How did that go?"

"He made it clear it was a gift from his House. If I didn't take it, I would've offended the entire House Krahr. I couldn't put us in that position. I looked up your rank while you were gone. You are at two and a half stars."

"The inn was dormant for a long time."

Maud waved her hand. "What I mean is, House Krahr publicly endorsed Gertrude Hunt. It would be both dangerous and ungrateful to offend them."

She took it. Of course, she did.

"I made it clear that I will repay this gift at the first opportunity. I don't like him," Maud said. "He is stubborn, bullheaded, and insists on doing things his way."

"You do realize all of those are synonyms?"

"I don't like him, Dina. I have a responsibility to my child. I won't risk reentering a society that threw her away like trash. We're done with vampires. Come on. We have work to do."

I took a deep breath. The void field snapped into place. I held my hand out. A broom rose from the ground and I fastened my fingers around it, feeling the worn, warm wood. I was home. It was time to soothe wild wolves and examine corrupted corpses.

⚜ ⚜ ⚜

The wolf waited for me on the second-floor balcony, in the spot I had come out to meet him in the middle of the night. It seemed like so long ago, but it was only a few days. I stepped out on to the balcony, Beast weaving around my feet.

Sean leaned against the wall on the left side of the doorway. He saw me. His eyes flashed amber, catching the light. He didn't say anything. Apparently, it was up to me to start the conversation. That was only fair. My errand almost got him killed, and without him I would've died on that Baha-char street.

I heard you killed some people and put their heads on sharpened sticks. I wanted to check to see if you are feeling okay... It was probably best to start with something simple.

"Hi."

"When you are in the inn, I trust you with my life," he said. "When you are outside, you have to trust me with yours."

"I do."

"That means when I say run, you run. You don't argue. You don't cry. You do as I tell you, or we both die."

Oh. It was that type of conversation. I crossed my arms.

He faced me. "I trust you to do your job. You have to trust me to do mine."

"I trust you. I don't trust your priorities."

I wanted to reach over and pull that stone-hard expression off his face.

"My priority is making sure you survive."

"Exactly. My priority is keeping my guests safe. They're not always one and the same."

"The Hiru was safe at the inn," Sean said. "Your insistence on bringing the tank in because you wanted to impress him—"

"It wasn't about impressing anyone. It was about trust. I promised to retrieve the tank. I had to come back with it."

"— endangered you, me, Cookie, and Wilmos. Instead of concentrating on retrieving the tank from Wilmos' shop, I had to carry you."

"I'm sorry for inflicting this horrible burden on you." I regretted it the moment the words left my mouth.

"It also endangered everyone in the inn. If you had died, Maud wouldn't be able to hold off the Draziri. The Hiru would die."

"My sister would've done just fine."

Beast barked by my feet, unsure, but feeling the pressure to provide canine support. Sean ignored her.

"I have skills and abilities you don't. More, I have experience."

"So do I."

"I've watched you kill," he said. "You kill only when you have to. Of all the responses to a threat you face, killing someone is the last choice for you. For me, it's not a choice. It's instinct. I don't think about it. I see a threat and I neutralize it. Of the two of us, I'm better equipped to handle an attack outside of the inn."

"This doesn't make you sound any more trustworthy."

"It kept me alive. And, if you let me, I'll keep you alive. I'll do everything I can to make sure you survive."

"Believe it or not, I somehow managed to survive for all these years without your help."

"Either you trust me or you don't. Decide, Dina. Because if you don't, there is no point in me being here. I can't do my job if you dig your heels in when I need you to follow my lead. I'm packed. Let me know what you decide."

He jumped off the balcony.

Great.

"Idiot werewolf."

Beast whined.

"Hush," I told her and stomped back downstairs. He had a point. One of us ran the inn and the other killed hundreds of sentient beings. Of the two of us, he was a much better killer and a much better bodyguard. He'd made the call and I should've trusted it. I implied that I would follow his lead when I hired him for a dollar. Instead I did what I had to do to ensure that Sunset didn't lose confidence in my ability to deliver. Was it truly necessary or did I do it out of pride? I didn't want to think about it.

That whole conversation didn't go the way I was hoping it would have.

A delicious smell permeated the downstairs, floating on the breeze. It smelled like... chicken.

Oh no.

I marched into the kitchen.

"Orro!" My voice cut the air like a knife.

He raised his head from a pot and turned toward me.

"Are you cooking Draziri?"

The needles stood up on his back.

"Don't lie to me. I thought I made it perfectly clear. I won't tolerate any..."

Orro jerked the oven open and yanked out a large roasting pan. On it, roasted to a golden-brown perfection, sat a medium-sized bird.

"Roasted Duck," Orro said. "With buckwheat porridge and apple stuffing."

Crap.

He drew himself to his full height, somehow taking up most of the kitchen, looming like some demon hedgehog of legend.

"In all my years, since I was a lowly apprentice barely tall enough to slide a pot onto a stove, I have broken the kitchen code only once. Once I have let a dish I hadn't tasted leave my kitchen. I have never broken it before or since. The code is my life, my religion, and my conscience. Without it," he ripped the air with his claws, "I am but a lowly savage."

There was no stopping it. I brought it on myself, I had to stand there and take it.

"Rise early to be at your station early," Orro intoned. "Keep your knives sharp. Never touch other chef's knives. Keep yourself, your station, and your food clean. Never let a dish out of your kitchen without tasting it. Know your ingredients. Respect the creatures on your prep table; honor their lives. Know your diners. Cook to the tastes of those who dine, not your own. Never serve a dish that harms your diners' health or soul. Never settle for second best. Never stop learning. These are the cornerstones of everything I am. They are the firmament of my universe."

He paused over me.

I nodded.

"Am I some vagrant you found on the street cooking rats in a rusted pot?"

Oh for the love of...

"Do you honestly think I would sink so low as to harm your soul by serving you a sentient being? Do you think so little of me?"

"I apologize."

He slapped his clawed hand over his eyes in a pose that would've made any Shakespearean actor proud. "Go. Just... go."

I fled the kitchen before he decided to continue with the speech.

So far I fought with Sean and Orro. The way today was going, if I lingered long enough, I would probably mortally offend Caldenia. Clearly there was only one place where I could safely be right now. I opened the floor and took the stairs down to the lab.

The corpse of the corrupted creature lay on the lab table. When Maud said "encased in a plastic container," I took it to mean they put it in some plastic tub. They didn't. A block of clear plastic greeted me, ten feet long and four feet wide. The corpse lay inside it, like some demented version of Snow White sleeping in a glass coffin.

How... Oh. Maud must've stuffed the corpse into an anchor tube, a clear cylinder of inert PVDF plastic. I had a whole section devoted to them in storage. They came in all sizes and were usually used to quarantine odd objects, provide microhabitats for small aquatic guests, and generally contain things when low thermal conductivity and high chemical corrosion resistance were a must. PVDF didn't conduct electricity, was impervious to most acids, and resisted radiation. The argon chamber I used for the Archivarian was made of PVDF.

Maud must've found my storage set, or Gertrude Hunt had dug up a large container in response to stress. But securing the corpse in said container didn't prove to be enough. The inn had somehow managed to encase the anchor tube in plastic.

I reached out and touched it. The inn creaked in alarm. No, not plastic. Clear resin. The inn had secreted resin and sealed the anchor tube in it until eight inches of its own sap shielded it from the corpse.

I would have to drill to get a sample and Gertrude Hunt would fight me every step of the way. I could feel it.

"We have to get a sample," I said.

The walls of my little lab wavered as if invisible snakes slid just under their surface.

"We have to do it," I said.

The walls shook.

"I know you're scared. I understand. But you have to be brave." I patted the wall. "It's dangerous. We must know what it is before it hurts us or other innkeepers and other inns. I'll be with you every step. I won't let it hurt you. I blocked it once when I was off the inn's grounds. I'll block it again. Together we are stronger."

The inn didn't answer. I sat quietly and gently stroked the wood. It moved under my fingers like a cat arching her back. I could have forced Gertrude Hunt to respond. The inn obeyed the innkeeper. Eventually there would come a time when I would have to impose my will on it. Every innkeeper faced that challenge sooner or later. But forcing the inn's compliance was a matter of last resort, used only to preserve life when no other way presented itself. I had witnessed my parents do it only twice, and it came at a great cost to them and to our inn.

"I know I'm asking a lot. But we must learn whatever we can so we'll be ready. If there are more of them, if they come calling, we can't be blind."

Silence.

The corpse of the monstrous creature lay waiting. Even in death there was something sinister about it, almost as if a dark shadow shrouded it, permeating the body and clothes. A ghost born of the cold emptiness between the stars. It lay still but aware. It might have been my imagination, but I felt like it was watching me.

I was inside my inn, where nothing could hurt me unless I allowed it, and still this thing gave me the creeps. I didn't want to open its transparent prison.

But if I didn't and it attacked again, the responsibility for the lives that might be lost would land on my shoulders. I was an innkeeper. I had a duty.

"We can do it. Together."

Silence.

I waited.

The lab's floor parted. A small plastic container rose from the floor.

"Thank you."

I raised my broom and channeled my magic into it. It split, the shaft fragmenting to expose the electric blue core of pure magic. I held it above the resin.

"Ready?"

A root slipped out of the ground, curving to hover above my broom. A viscous drop of resin formed on its tip, swelling to the size of a large grapefruit.

I set the broom on the hardened block of resin and pushed. The blue core sank into the sap, burning its way down. I let it work. There was no hurry. Coils of fragrant smoke curled from the drill site.

Quarter of the way in.

Half.

Three-quarters.

We only needed a trace of its body, just enough to run the basic analysis and scans.

Almost there.

The broom sank through the resin and met the hard resistance of the plastic. I pushed gently.

The plastic shell melted.

The black shadow I'd sensed surged up, toward the broom, covering the few inches of space between the body and the upper wall of the plastic in a blink. Foul magic clamped my broom and spiraled up. Fetid, cold, and terrifying power streamed through the broom, trying to get out.

I grasped my broom with both hands and fought back, sending my magic through it.

The shadow curved, winding around the glowing tip of the broom. It had no face, it had no substance, but there it was, right there, fighting me. It wanted out. I felt its furious hunger. It wanted to devour me and Gertrude Hunt and everything within.

I poured my power into the broom. No. Not happening.

The shadow held on for a torturous moment...and broke. I stabbed the broom into the body. A mental shriek cut across my mind like metal screeching against metal. I pierced the shadow again. It screeched and wailed, lashing in my mind.

Not in my inn. Not while I'm watching.

I stabbed and stabbed, until finally it sank deep into the body and hid there.

I dimmed the broom and slid it into the body, sliced off a small sample of the flesh, and pulled it free, depositing the sample into the plastic container and snapping the lid shut. The moment the broom came free, the inn dripped resin into the opening, sealing the shadow inside. Green and red lights flashed as the inn scanned the sample.

I waited, watching the corpse, waiting for any sign of the shadow returning.

A chime announced the DNA scan completing. Too fast. Sequencing an alien creature should've taken much longer. I turned to the screen to see the results.

Ice shot through me, from the top of my head all the way to my toes.

"We're going to need another anchor tube."

Ten minutes later Maud walked into the lab. "Here you are."

She dropped into the chair, crossing her long legs. "Helen said she heard a weird scream, so I searched the grounds, and found nothing."

"What did it sound like?"

"She said it sounded like a night shrieker. It's an ugly bird. Well, more reptile than bird really. Sounds like nails on a chalkboard."

Or metal on metal.

She nodded toward the corpse encased in plastic, sealed in resin, then encased in a larger plastic tube and sealed again. The inn was still pouring sap on it.

"Don't you think you're going overboard?"

I punctured the lid of the sample container and poured viscous purple liquid into it.

"Is that carnyte?"

"Yes."

I waved my hand. The wall in front of me flowed open, revealing a desolate landscape. I tossed the sample jar into it. The inn's wall reformed, turning transparent. The jar fell and burst into smokeless crimson fire. Carnyte was one of the worst things ever invented in the galaxy. It burned through just about everything, ripping molecules apart.

"Okay," Maud said, stretching the word out. "Mind sharing?"

The crimson fire was still burning.

"I sequenced the DNA."

"That was fast."

"There was a match in the database."

Maud stared at me. "Are you telling me that thing is...was human?"

I pointed to the corpse. "It's Michael."

She frowned. "Michael...?"

"Michael Braswell."

She drew in a sharp breath.

I waved at the screen. A picture of an innkeeper filled it, a man in his thirties, honest face, light brown hair, blue eyes.

We turned to look at the crimson fire at the same time. It was easier to watch it burn than to face that I had killed the abomination who used to be my brother's best friend.

Chapter 9

"How is this possible?" Maud paced by the body.

"I don't know."

It was too disturbing. I didn't want to think about it. I would have to, but I didn't want to. When I was twelve years old, I decided to attend middle school. I lasted one week. I desperately wanted to be accepted, but instead of making friends, I ended up being the odd kid. Middle school fights were vicious. Everyone there was a ball of insecurity and hormones, which I realized much later, and they were ready to pounce on any target that stood out from the pack. My family loved me so much. I was a sheltered kid. I couldn't even imagine that anyone could be so mean.

When I called to the house on the last Friday of my glorious middle school experience, crying and picking mashed potatoes out of my hair, my parents were out. Klaus was minding the inn and couldn't leave. It was Michael who came to pick me up in his massive pickup truck. He'd been planning to visit Klaus for the weekend, but instead he drove with me three hours to his parents' inn where I got to take a shower, have dinner with his family, and pretend that the Friday never happened, because I couldn't face my family yet. It was Michael who brought me back home the next morning and told me it would be okay.

Now he was dead and his body was a host for something too terrible to describe.

"Did he say anything? Did he recognize you?" Maud asked.

"If he did, he sure had a funny way of showing it."

"Is it related to the Archivarius? Is it the Draziri?"

"I don't know."

Maud stopped and stared at me. "What's next?"

"Next we report this to the Assembly." That part was easy.

Maud resumed her pacing. "And they come and get it? Please tell me they come and get it."

"They will eventually."

My sister paused again. "How long is eventually?"

"I don't know. I can't contact the Assembly until tonight." The rules for emergency contact weren't just strict; they were draconian. A stray transmission could give away the existence of the inns, so the session had to be no more than thirty seconds and transmission had to be sent according to the time chart provided to every inn in the beginning of the year. I had checked it before, when thinking of accepting the Hiru's bargain. My emergency session time was at 11:07 pm Central time.

"It's still alive," I said.

"What?"

"We have to store it and there is something... corrupt that's still alive inside the body. Something that wants out."

"How? Is it a creature? A parasite?"

"I don't know. It attacked me when I got the sample. I had to stab it several times to get it to retreat. That's the screech Helen heard."

Maud swore. She and I looked at the resin coffin.

"What would it be afraid of?" she asked.

I rubbed my face. "There is no way to tell unless we analyze it and Gertrude Hunt won't let me do that. Forcing the inn to take further samples is out of the question. We're not set up to do this sort of analysis safely, and I won't let this corruption infect us."

"Fire?" Maud mused.

"Too difficult. It would have to be very hot and sustainable over time, and the inn doesn't like open flames. It can deal with a small fire or even a bonfire outside, but flames of that intensity inside are a bad idea. No, we need something strong but viable long-term."

We looked at the tube again.

"Acid," we said at the same time.

It took me twenty minutes to build the chamber out of stone and fill our largest anchor tube with hydrochloric acid. We sealed the resin coffin inside another smaller tube, and suspended it in the acid. It wasn't perfect. I would've preferred dumping it on some unknown planet, but one was responsible for what one set loose, and I didn't want to shoulder the burden of unleashing this horror on anyone.

Once the tube was suspended, I set the alarms. If the plastic moved a fraction of an inch, the inn would scream in my head. We retreated to the lab, where I made the inn show me the chamber on the big screen. I sat and watched it. If it tried to break out after we left, I wanted to see it. Maud sat next to me.

Neither of us said anything.

"The Assembly will notify the family," I said.

Thinking about looking at Mrs. Braswell as I struggled to explain what her son had turned into made me nauseous.

"They should," Maud said.

We looked at the tank some more. Nothing moved. The Assembly had a lot of resources at its disposal. Some innkeepers specialized in research, and their inns had state of the art labs. And of course, there were ad-hal. When innkeeper children grew up, they had three paths open to them. A lot of us left the planet and became Travelers, bumming around the great beyond. Of those who stayed, some gave up on the innkeeper life altogether and rejoined human society, leading normal lives. But if you wanted to remain in our world, you could become an innkeeper by inheriting the inn from your parents or, very rarely, being transferred to a new inn. Or you became an ad-hal. An ancient word for secret, the ad-hal served as the Assembly's, and by extension, the Galactic Senate's, enforcers on Earth. My power was tied to the inn. The power of an ad-hal came from within them. When things went bad, terribly, catastrophically bad, an ad-hal would come and deal with it. The ad-hal knew no mercy. They would assess the situation and deliver the punishment. Seeing one was never a good sign.

Maybe the Assembly would send an ad-hal to retrieve Michael's body.

"I will stand vigil for his soul tonight," Maud said.

"I killed him."

"No, you freed him. You need your strength," she said. "He deserves a vigil."

"Okay."

Minutes crept past.

Maud finally spoke. "How are things between you and Sean?"

"Fine."

"Aha. Do you want to talk about it?"

"No."

"Because I'm right here."

"Maud..." I started, but caught myself.

"That's my name. Don't be afraid, you won't wear it out."

"You have just been through...a lot of things. You buried your husband. I don't want to dump my romantic problems on you."

"I never thought you would find someone who was in," Maud said.

"In?"

"In our world. In our little innkeeper circle. I always thought that you would go off and have a normal life with someone, I don't know, someone named Phil."

"Phil?" I blinked.

"Yes. He would be an accountant or a lawyer. You would have a perfectly normal marriage and perfectly normal children. Your biggest worry would be making sure the other PTA moms didn't outshine you at faculty appreciation day."

I blinked. "First, how do you even know about faculty appreciation day? You attended school for what, a year in high school?"

She sighed. "Would you believe me if I told you that vampires have them?"

"What do you bring to a vampire faculty appreciation day?"

"Weapons," Maud said. "Usually small knives. Ornate and pricey."

"You're pulling my leg."

"No. There is a lot of etiquette involved in deciding the exact value of a knife to bring...Okay, yes, I'm pulling your leg. Snacks. You bring snacks to a vampire faculty appreciation day. And extra school supplies are very much appreciated. I don't care how advanced your civilization is, children still want to draw on the rocks with colored chalk."

"Why did you think I would go off and marry someone normal?"

"Because you were so whiny before I left."

I stared at her.

"You were," Maud said. "It was all *me, me, me. Oh I am so put upon that I have to live in this magic house and nobody understands.* You didn't want anything to do with the inn. Making you do chores was like pulling teeth. All you wanted to do was leave the inn and hang out with your high school friends."

"I was barely eighteen. And they weren't friends; they were frenemies."

Maud grinned. "I always thought I would end up being an innkeeper."

"I always thought you'd be an ad-hal." I smiled, but I wasn't joking. She would've made an excellent ad-hal.

"You think I'm ruthless enough."

"Mhm. You have ruthlessness to spare."

She sighed. "Instead, I'm the widow of a dishonored knight, while you have an inn and are trying to date a complicated homicidal werewolf."

"You could get your own inn." It wouldn't be easy, but Maud never quit because things were a challenge.

She shook her head. "No, I don't think that's in the cards, Dina. I'm proud of you and of everything you did to get this far, but it's not for me. I was Melizard's wife for six years. I'm good at fighting. I've learned to be good at political maneuvering. If you give me a battlefield or a ballroom filled with people who want to slit my throat, I know what to do. But sitting in the inn, trying to juggle the needs of a dozen guests, with all of them wanting something at once, while keeping the whole thing a secret from the outside world isn't in me. It's going into a fight with your arms tied."

My heart sank. "Does this mean you won't stay with me here, at Gertrude Hunt?"

"It means I don't want my own inn. I'll stay with you, Dina. As long as you will have me here."

"Good. Because otherwise I'd have to kick your ass."

"I'm so sorry," she said. "Mom and Dad disappeared, and you came to me, and I was too wrapped up in my own problems. I'm sorry I wasn't there." Emotion trembled in her voice.

"You were married and just had a baby."

"It's not an excuse. You're my little sister. You needed me and I wasn't there. That's not what big sisters do."

"I wasn't by myself. I had Klaus."

She swiped moisture from her eyes. "Where is he now?"

"Who knows." I sighed.

"Do you think he's in trouble?"

"Klaus? Our Klaus? No. But before he left, he promised me he would come back when he found out something about Mom and Dad. You know how he is."

"He won't come back unless he has something." Maud looked resigned. "Men."

"Yes."

"Well, I'm here now. Tell me about your werewolf."

She didn't say it, but I heard it in her voice. Maud hated to be treated as a victim. She didn't want any allowances to be made for her. She wanted to be the big sister again. I would meet her halfway.

"I'm… conflicted. And we had a fight."

"What was the fight about?"

"I expended too much magic shielding myself and him from that thing." I nodded at the screen. "Afterward Sean wanted to take me straight to the inn and I made him go and get the tank with the Archivarian in it."

"Define 'made him.'"

"I cried and asked him to get it."

"You cried? You?"

"I think I did. I also might have implied that I wouldn't open the door to the inn without it. At least I intended to imply that. It's a bit fuzzy. So we went and got the Archivarian from Wilmos' shop. Now he is upset. He gave me an ultimatum: either I let him do his job or he will take his ball and go. He says he's a trained killer and I'm not."

"He has a point. Do you know how he got his training?"

"Yes."

"Are you going to tell me?"

"No. It's not my place to tell."

She sighed. "Fair enough. I can tell you what I saw tonight. I've spent the last few years among professional soldiers, who go to the battlefield because it's their job. When they kill, they do it efficiently and quickly. When they gather enough training and experience, they do it instinctually, like breathing. They see things in black and white, because shades of gray would kill them, and eventually they no longer agonize over it. They start out from different backgrounds, they have different personalities, they may be human, or vampire, or Otrokar, but sooner or later they all end up in a place where detachment rules. It's a way for them to survive, because we're not meant to slaughter other beings week after week."

She paused.

"Okay," I said, to say something.

"Your wolf isn't like these soldiers. He kills, because a part of him needs it. He's a predator, Dina."

"You make him sound like a maniac. He doesn't revel in it."

"I didn't say he did. He isn't cruel. But when he comes to the battlefield, he doesn't see the enemy. He sees prey. He isn't detached. He's all in. Tonight, he punished. He broke their bones, he made them scream, and then he cut off their heads and put them on a pike."

"He's been through a lot."

Maud nodded. "I know. I'm trying to explain something that I feel, and it's difficult. Despite the way the movies and books make it seem, when you're out there and someone is trying to kill you, you don't think. You just act. You kill the enemy as quickly as you can, because that's your only option. He's... Not like that. He's active. He doesn't surrender to that fight or flight response. I watched him mow through the Draziri. He looked at them for half a second, formulated a plan, and followed it. All of him is fully engaged, even the part that most people shut off."

"What are you trying to say?"

Maud sighed. "When you came to find me, you picked up Helen. Why?"

"It seemed like a natural thing to do. I could run faster carrying her than she could run alone. I could shield her."

"The moment you picked her up, neither you nor she could effectively respond to threats. You added fifty pounds to your load. You also robbed her of the only advantage she had: mobility. Helen is fast and good at dodging. She couldn't dodge while you were carrying her."

"Well..."

"Yeah."

She had a point. I didn't like it, but she was right.

"You made it to the door because, when Sean saw you scooping her up, he started cutting a way for you to get there. He didn't say anything. He just compensated. Your instincts aren't always right in a fight, Dina. But his are. Put him into any army, and in a few weeks he'll be leading it, because professional soldiers would see him fight and know that he would survive. It's something you feel. It's a lizard brain thing. If I had a strategy planned and it was the best plan in the world, and he told me to change it, I would, because he has something I don't. So when you're in danger and he tells you to follow his lead, you should."

"I don't like ultimatums."

"Neither do I. But he had a reason to give you one. I think he loves you, Dina. He's afraid of losing you."

I stared at her.

"If you're in danger and you hobble him, both of you might die. I'm not telling you anything you don't already know. That's why you gave him that dollar. What is this fight really about?"

I closed my eyes.

She waited.

"I'm afraid he'll leave." There. It came out. "I hate this."

"Why?"

"Because I sound needy and desperate."

Maud snorted. "You're the least needy person I know."

"I want him to stay here with me and run the inn. I want to wake up every day and see him there in bed with me. And I barely know him. We had one date. Am I that lonely, Maud? Because I'm all in and I don't know if he is, and I have no right to ask for that much. You know what it means to be an innkeeper. We are bound to our inns."

"If you were just lonely, you would clutch on to anybody who came along," she said. "Would you take Arland instead of Sean?"

"No."

"See?"

"You took two years to decide you loved Melizard."

She snorted again. "And look how much good it did me. I don't regret it, because I have Helen now. But it wasn't the best move. Who cares about dates? It's when you're under pressure together, that's what counts. He risked his life for you. He was ready to fight for the Hiru, because he saw an injustice. Is he kind when it's difficult? Does he still do the right thing when everything turns to shit?"

He sold himself to the Merchants for a lifetime contract to keep me from dying. "Yes."

"Then talk to him. Tell him how you feel. Nothing kills it faster than not talking. Trust me, I know. That's how my marriage died."

Her face was flat. No emotion. No tremor in her voice. She'd loved Melizard so much, she followed him across the galaxy to an alien planet, where she molded herself into a perfect vampire knight's spouse. And it ended so badly.

I wanted to hug her, but she sat stiff, her back straight. No weakness.

A screen opened in the wall. The Hiru's odd features filled it.

"What can I do for you?" I asked.

"The third Archivarian is arriving to the inn in five minutes," the Hiru said. "Please remove the void field."

⚜ ⚜ ⚜

I reached through the inn with my senses. Sean waited by the back porch.

"Sean," I whispered. "I need your help."

I felt him move toward me.

"Oh Sean..." Maud whispered in a sing-song voice, rolling her eyes.

I squinted at her. "Do you want to call Arland or should I?"

"You do it," she said.

I reached through the inn. Arland was in the kitchen, with Helen. Probably fixing his armor again.

"Lord Marshal," I said. "Could I please see you in the war room?"

Less than a minute later Sean came striding through the door. Arland was only a few steps behind. Helen rode on his shoulder like a parrot. Maud opened her mouth and clicked it shut.

"The third Archivarian is arriving to the inn in four minutes and ten seconds," I said. "I have to drop the void field. Are you in?"

"Of course." Arland gently set Helen on the floor.

"Yes," Sean said.

So much for his ultimatums.

"For the Archivarian to get here, the other side must open a door," Maud said. "A portal. If I were the Draziri, I'd try to detonate it the moment I saw it."

"The portal will open in the back field," I said. Each inn listed the official coordinates for the designated arrivals. Ours were in the back, where the house would block the view. "We must preserve the Archivarian at all costs. We need a plan. Sean?"

A calculation took place in Sean's eyes. "The Draziri are positioned all around the inn on the wooded side. They're watching the grounds."

"You want to structure our defense around the portal?" Arland asked.

"No," Sean said. "I don't want to defend it at all."

Arland mulled it over. His blond eyebrows edged together. Maud grinned like a wolf and pulled her new blood sword out.

"If they see you, they will key in on you," Sean said to me.

"He's right," Arland confirmed. "You're a high-priority target. If they eliminate you, their chances of killing the Hiru rise substantially."

"How safe would you be out in the open?" Sean asked me.

"Perfectly safe as long as I'm on the inn's grounds." I could block any kinetic projectiles and the inn could absorb most energy bombardments with my direction. "Do you want me out there to play bait?"

"Yes," Sean said. "Does the inn have something that could bombard the land outside of the boundary?"

"Can you be more specific?"

"A weapon that won't draw attention from the street but will be dangerous enough to scatter the Draziri."

Gertrude Hunt was a lot stronger than it used to be. Still, its resources were limited.

"Does it have to be precise?"

"No," Sean said. "As long as it has an impact."

It was my turn to smile. "If you want impact, I'll give you one."

A short shadow fell on the doorway.

"Wing?" I asked.

The Ku stepped into the open. His feathered crest lay completely flat on his head. He was terrified. "I fight."

"I don't think that's a good idea."

"I fight," the Ku said. "I want to help."

He wasn't looking at me. He was looking at Sean.

"We can use you," Sean told him.

※ ※ ※

The sun was setting. Twilight descended on Texas, turning harmless trees dark and twisted. I opened the kitchen door, dropped the void field, and walked out into the backyard, Beast on my right and Wing armed with one of Sean's weapons, a short simple-looking rifle, on my left. I'd asked Sean what it was and he told me it was the space equivalent of a sawed-off shotgun.

We reached the middle of the lawn. I stopped. The soil shifted and slid under me.

For a tense moment, nothing happened. Then a volley of shots, energy and kinetic, tore through the dusk, coming at me from a ragged semicircle. *There you are.*

Roots burst from the ground, dragging a wall of dirt with it to shield me from the worst of the barrage. The broom split in my hand and I plunged it into the ground. Magic poured out of me.

The lawn belched. Three rocks the size of a washing machine burst from the ground. I heaved with my magic. The boulders rolled at the Draziri. Wing fired, his rifle spitting pale blue projectiles. They landed in the trees and the brush, expanded like water balloons, and exploded silently in bursts of bright blue light. The glow caught fleeing shapes of Draziri, scattering through the brush. The boulders chased them, spinning along the boundary.

A twisted spiral of deep purple spun into existence above the ground, directly over the entrance coordinates. Individual Draziri broke free of the trees, trying to avoid my rocks and sprinting toward the forming vortex, light on their feet as if they could dance on air.

I pushed. The grass between the vortex and the boundary erupted and spat Arland in full battle armor. The Marshal of House Krahr roared and charged the ragged Draziri line. He tore into them like a bowling ball, mace swinging. A single hit sent a Draziri flying onto the inn grounds. The roots wound around her body and hurled her through the trees back the way she came.

Arland raged, loud and terrifying. The Draziri stabbed and cut at him and he tore through them, immune to fear and pain. The blood mace crashed down again and again, crushing skulls and breaking bones. I couldn't see it, but I knew that behind the battle, in the dark, my sister and Sean sliced through the Draziri ranks from the sides, like the two blades of scissors.

The vortex was almost complete.

A scream tore the night. Another. The Draziri dashed to and fro, panicking.

The vortex spat an Archivarius member. An argon tank rose from the lawn. The being stepped into it and the tank sank into the ground. Got him.

A second shape loomed within the vortex, a grotesque clunky shape. Another Hiru was coming through.

A large projectile shot out of the tree line. In the split second it flew over the inn's territory, my magic told me what it was. I shoved a doorway in its way, ripping through the fabric of our world. The missile tore through the hole in reality, sped over an orange ocean, and crashed into alien waters. Kolinda's ocean screamed. A mountain of water and vapor burst upward, blooming like some horrible flower.

Panic shot through me, a delayed response. Icy sweat drenched my skin. My heart hammered so hard, it felt like it might break my ribs. The muscles in my neck clenched so hard, vertigo gripped me.

I shut the door before the blast wave could reach us.

The Hiru landed on the grass. The vortex dissolved into empty air. I jerked the roots up, shielding the new guest from the Draziri and let Gertrude Hunt carry him away underground.

Maud leaped over the boundary. A moment later Arland emerged from the woods, dragging bodies with him, as Sean, shaggy with gray fur, all fangs and claws like some demonic nightmare, moved around the vampire knight, slicing at the Draziri. Arland punched an opponent with his left fist. Sean caught the falling Draziri, stabbing in a flurry. Another attacker lunged at Sean's back and Arland drove his mace into him.

Together Sean and Arland backed away from the woods toward the inn. Arland was breathing hard, his mace dripping blood. Dents and gashes marked his armor. The fur on Sean's right shoulder was wet and black in the light of the dying evening. I couldn't tell if it was his blood or someone else's.

Step.

Another step.

They made it over the boundary. I snapped the void field in place.

Blood dripped on Maud's cheek from a gash in her scalp. Dirt smeared her face. She saw me looking and grinned, her teeth stark white.

The tree line was littered with corpses. One, two, three... seven...

"I know this," Arland said quietly, almost to himself. "I fought against this..."

Sean straightened. His fur vanished, his body collapsing back into his human form. Slowly he wiped the blade of his green knife on his thigh.

Arland pivoted to him. His gaze snagged on the knife. A muscle jerked in his face.

Sean didn't say anything.

Rage shivered in the corner of Arland's mouth.

The Marshal of House Krahr bared his fangs and charged.

Sean moved out of the way, smooth and fast, as if he were a shadow rather than a physical being.

Arland swung again and missed.

"You!" Arland roared. "Fight me, *oryh*. Fight me!"

"No," Sean said and dropped his knife.

I took a step forward. Sean shook his head.

I could stop it, but if I did, it wouldn't be resolved. They had to fix it themselves.

"Fight me or die!"

"You're my friend," Sean said and raised his hands.

Arland swung his mace. Sean didn't dodge. The blow took him in the stomach. Sean flew back.

Arland charged after him, his eyes berserk and hot with unstoppable fury.

Maud lunged into his path and threw her arms around him. "Stop!"

He plowed on, carrying her as if she weighed nothing.

"Stop, Marshal!" Maud's voice rang. "He's unarmed. He's your friend. There's no honor in this kill."

Arland slowed.

"Honor," Maud repeated, her hands around his face, looking straight into his eyes. "*He who sheds his blood to defend my back in battle is my brother. I shall watch over him as he watches over me.*"

Reason crept into Arland's blue eyes. He pulled away from her, raised his head to the night sky, and roared.

"Innkeeper," a familiar voice called.

I turned. Kiran Mrak stood at the boundary. Behind him his clansmen waited, some with black feathers, some with bright blue, and vibrant red and rich cream. They stared at me with open hatred.

"I didn't give the order for the missile," he said.

"You fired a nuclear weapon," I said. "You broke the treaty. There will be repercussions. There is no turning back."

"There was a dissension in my ranks. It's something you and I have in common." Kiran Mrak raised his left hand. He was holding a severed Draziri head. "I've dealt with mine. It is your turn."

I turned my back to him. He laughed.

"I don't kill those I care about," I said over my shoulder.

"You're weak."

"You murder your own family. Loyalty is a two-way street."

He laughed again.

I kept walking.

Wing marched to me, stared at the Draziri behind me, turned and deliberately kicked dirt in their direction.

Sean rolled to his feet and picked up his knife.

Arland lifted his mace and stomped toward the house. Maud walked next to him, her arm wrapped around his.

Sean was waiting for me. I hurried over to him. "Are you hurt?"

"A cracked rib," he said. "It will heal. He held back."

It didn't look like he held back from where I was standing. "Come on. I'll help you with your rib. We need to talk."

"Yeah," he said. "We do."

When I walked into the kitchen, Caldenia smiled at me, clearly delighted. "Very good, dear. Just the right thing to say."

"I'm glad you approve, Your Grace."

"A creature like Kiran Mrak rules because he has the mandate of his people. His followers are his base. Crack the base, and he will come crashing down." Caldenia put the fingers of her hands together. "This will be delightfully entertaining."

I turned to the two Hiru. Sunset stood in front and the newcomer behind, as if Sunset was shielding the new guest. I had a feeling that if the Hiru weren't so bulky, the new arrival would be peeking out at us over his shoulder. It would have helped to know that the second Hiru was coming prior to the battle. I opened my mouth to tell them that.

The new Hiru pointed at me. "Is this her?" Its voice was soft, sad, and feminine.

"This is her," Sunset said. "This is Hope."

⚜ ⚜ ⚜

I stood in the middle of the empty room. A six-foot-wide circle of soft turquoise light marked the floor around me, identifying the boundary of the recording area. I wore my blue robe with the hood down and held my broom in my hand.

It took some time to settle the two Hiru. I wasn't sure if the Hiru had genders, but if they had been human, I would've guessed our new guest to be female. She was smaller than Sunset, her sad voice was higher pitched, and when the other Hiru spoke of her, his translation software used "she" as the identifying pronoun.

However, the galaxy was a big place. While dual sexes and sexual dimorphism occurred often enough, it was only one of the myriad of configurations for procreation and sex. The Garibu had three sexes and six genders, the Allui males were smaller and more fragile than females, and the Parakis formed a mating ball, where everyone went through a three-stage molting process, during which they changed sex twice. When one of these beings visited Earth, their translating software struggled to assign gender to make alien speech palatable to humans, often with hilarious results. So, I wasn't sure if the new Hiru was truly female, but since Sunset referred to her as she, I referred to her so as well. After I took her to see the Archivarians, she told me her name. She was called Moonlight-on-the-Water.

Moonlight loved Sunset's room. She walked over the threshold and gave a little gasp. He reached for her, and they walked toward the pool together, their metal arms touching. That's where I left them, floating in the basin and staring at the clouded ceiling.

The Hiru settled, I went to look for my sister and found her in the kitchen carefully spooning coffee she'd brewed into a mug half-filled with eggnog. She shrugged and told me Arland needed it. And then she took it up to his rooms. I thought about telling her that the last time the Marshal of House Krahr had coffee, he stripped off his clothes and ran around my orchard in broad daylight, flaunting the gifts the vampire goddess gave him until Sean finally tackled him, but she did make fun of me when I'd called for Sean, so I decided to let her discover the wonder that was drunk Arland on her own. She had measured that coffee very carefully, so maybe Arland would manage to keep his clothes on.

I checked on Helen, who'd fallen asleep in her room, with the cat curled up by her feet. I checked on Wing. The battle shook him up and he'd reenacted his heroic deeds for me just to make sure that they were truly heroic. Confirming the heroism took a little longer than expected. It was 10:40 pm now and my window for communication with the Assembly was approaching.

Tension twisted the muscles of my neck. This would be the third time in my life I addressed the Assembly. The first time, I just stood by my brother's side, as Klaus petitioned the Assembly for assistance in finding my parents. That time we heard nothing for over a month, after which the Assembly expressed its condolences and informed us that their investigation uncovered nothing. The second time I petitioned them for my own inn. The reply had come in twelve hours with the name of the inn and Gertrude Hunt's address.

I ran the message through my mind one more time. I'd rehearsed in my head six or seven times now. It was correctly worded: no names, no addresses, nothing that would lead back to me if it was somehow decrypted by a third party. I shouldn't have been this nervous, but tension had clamped me like a bear trap and refused to let go.

Sean slipped into the room, the wall behind him sealing the moment he entered. I'd invited him. He wanted to check the grounds first, which in his speak meant he wanted to scout the Draziri and see how much damage we'd managed to inflict. I asked him to find me when he was done and told the inn to show him the way. I'd hoped to talk to him before I sent the message, but it was too late now. We'd have to speak after. It was better this way anyway. I wasn't in any shape to talk until the message was out.

The scanner snapped to life, bathing me in the light and setting my blond hair aglow. I almost jumped. I'd programmed the scanner for 10:40, but it startled me all the same. I was wound up too tight.

The light focused on me.

The galaxy birthed many languages, but one of them was older than most, so old it was almost forgotten except by innkeepers and those like us. I opened my mouth and the lilting words of Old Galactic rolled off my tongue like a song that was as ancient as the stars.

"Greetings to the Assembly. I bring two matters before you. First, two of my guests are Hiru. Tonight the Draziri besieging my inn fired a nuclear missile at the inn's grounds. To save the lives of my guests, I directed it off world. I deeply regret the resulting loss of life and hope no sentient beings have been harmed as a result. I do not require assistance at this time."

There. I made a formal notification that the treaty had been breached. The ball was in their court. I'd included the coordinates of the nuclear explosion and they could view the evidence for themselves.

"Second, I was attacked by an unknown enemy at Baha-char. It was a creature of darkness and corruption. With the assistance of friends, it was defeated and brought to my inn, where the corruption attempted to leave its host and infect me and the inn itself. The corpse is contained, but I do not know how long the containment will last. Before sealing the body, I took a DNA sample, and a match was found in the database. The body belongs to an innkeeper, a friend of my family. I've enclosed the evidence for your review."

The blue light changed to deep indigo as the scanner encrypted my message, chewing up data and images I'd attached into a chaotic mess decipherable only by innkeeper decryption protocols.

A digital clock appeared on the wall. Thirty seconds to communication window. I cut it a little closer than I should have. Twenty seconds.

Ten.

The scanner light pulsed with white. The message was off.

"What now?" Sean asked.

"Now the Assembly has to decide what to do. I've done my part."

"How does that work?" he asked. "Do they poll all of the innkeepers?"

"They can if the matter concerns a change to innkeeper policy. This almost never happens. Most of the time, things like this are discussed among heads of the twenty-five oldest or strongest inns on the planet. I think Mr. Rodriguez is part of that twenty-five. When my parents..."

I'd almost said *when my parents were alive*. I pulled way back from that thought. I couldn't think like that. They were alive now. Until I saw evidence of their death, irrefutable evidence, I had to think of them as alive and I would look for them.

"When my parents' inn was active, my father and mother shared a single vote among twenty-five. My father was unique and his input was valued."

"When will you know something?" he asked.

"It's impossible to say." The wall parted in front of me, opening into a long hallway. I walked into it and Sean joined me. "They may choose to send some reply back, they might act on it without telling me, or they might ignore me."

"This doesn't seem like the most organized system," Sean said. "If you needed help and asked for it, there is no way to know if you'll get it."

"Each innkeeper is a world unto herself," I said. "It's the way it's always been. There were times in history when we spoke in one voice, like when we banned a species from Earth for gross disregard of the treaty."

The tunnel opened and we walked onto a wide covered balcony with a sunken fire pit in the center and a ring of couches around it, strewn with bright pillows. A kettle waited, hanging off a hook on a metal pole. Sean raised his eyebrows.

"The Otrokar quarters?"

I nodded. "I don't know why, but sitting by the fire makes me feel better."

The fire had already been laid out. Sean took a lighter from the side table and lit it. The hot orange flame licked the logs. The tinder in the center of the stack caught fire, cracking. The flames spread, gulping the logs. Warmth spread through the balcony.

I picked up the tea kettle dangling from the ceremonial stick and hung it on the metal rail above the fire.

Sean sat across from me on the bright pillows. "The Khanum would approve."

I nodded. That's how the Otrokars made their tea for hundreds of years.

"How are your ribs?" I asked.

"Not as bad as they could've been." Sean smiled.

"I have a medbay, you know. It's not as nice as what the Merchants had, but I'm sure you could slum it just this once..."

"I'm okay."

I sniffed. The water boiled and I took the kettle off the fire, hung it back on the hook, and tossed the leaves into it. Tea in winter was the best... Oh. The realization hit me like a train. Maybe I was off by a day or two... No. I was right. I felt like crying.

"What is it?" he asked, focused on me.

"It's Christmas."

Sean frowned.

"Tonight is Christmas. I don't have a tree. I didn't get any presents. I didn't decorate. I have nothing." I couldn't keep the despair out of my voice. "I missed Christmas."

It was the stupidest thing, but I had to strain to keep the tears back.

He moved over, sat next to me, and put his arm around me.

This wasn't how I planned this conversation to go. I planned on a formal detached discussion. Instead I leaned against him, because his eyes told me he understood.

"It's just a date on the calendar," he said, stroking my shoulder lightly with his fingers. "We can still have Christmas."

"It wouldn't be real."

He shook his head. "Helen doesn't care that it wouldn't be exactly on December 25th. Caldenia doesn't care. Orro will jump on any excuse to cook a feast. Your sister could use a Christmas. She hasn't had one for a while. We'll get a tree, we'll decorate, we'll wrap presents, and I'll kill any Draziri that tries to interfere…"

I stuck my head into his hard chest. He held me tighter.

"What's wrong with me?"

"Residual combat stress," he said. "Happens when a corrupted innkeeper almost kills you and then an idiot assassin shoots a nuke at you, all in twenty-four hours."

"When did you learn Old Galactic?"

"About three or four months into the Nexus tour. There wasn't much to do but fight and wait to fight. I went through a lot of manuals and brain imprints. It kept me from snapping. I'm a walking encyclopedia of random knowledge."

I let out a long slow breath. He rubbed my back.

"I thought you were packed."

One Fell Sweep

"Where would I go?" he asked me.

I leaned against him and we sat quietly for a while in front of the fire. There was no give in Sean. No softness in his body. It was all hard muscle and bones, wrapped in harsh predatory strength. The lean lone wolf trotted out of the dark woods to lay by the fire because I was here. He never abandoned who he was. He still had his sharp teeth and fiery eyes, not tame, but content to behave so I wouldn't chase him off. It made me want to go down to the kitchen and bring him something to eat.

I had put together a logical, convincing speech, but all of that seemed stupid now.

"The inn has to come first," I said. "The safety of the guests before the safety of the innkeeper."

He didn't say anything.

"It's a weird life. Once you bond with the inn, you can never truly leave. Even if you do, you still feel the pull of it. Some people view it as being trapped and they can't wait to get out. It can get boring when there are no guests. Then again, when there are guests, it can get so busy you barely have a chance to sleep. Sometimes guests want unreasonable things. Some of them listen to you explain the danger and then run straight into it. But that's your life. You take care of the inn. You keep them safe. They leave and you stay. Always."

He still wasn't saying anything.

I took a deep breath. "This is what I chose. Right or wrong, I'm here. This is my home."

Why was this so hard? I just had to say it. Even if he got up and walked away, at least I would know where we stood.

"If you're going to be an innkeeper with me—"

He pulled me closer. My voice caught. I swallowed and kept going. "—you would have to put the safety of the guests first. I will follow your lead in a fight. I won't argue or beg. I won't ask you to change your strategy. But this life would have to be enough, because I can't unchoose it. If that's not what you want..."

He didn't say anything. It felt like a lifetime. The air was viscous and heavy, like I was swimming through molasses.

I raised my gaze. He was looking at me, his amber eyes full of flames from the fire. "But would I get you, if I were an innkeeper?"

"Yes."

"That's all I want."

The weight dropped off me. I didn't realize I was carrying it. I kissed him. One moment I was looking at him and then my lips touched his, forging a connection between us.

The muscles of his arm tightened under my fingers. His lips closed on mine, hot and hungry. The kiss deepened, turning possessive, hot, heady like the intoxicating heat of strong wine gulped too quickly. He licked my tongue. He tasted so good. I slid my arms around him, wanting more. I didn't care if the whole galaxy burned, as long as he kept kissing me like that.

He broke the kiss. His eyes were completely wild. The wolf was staring back at me and he wanted me more than anything in his forest. It made me feel beautiful.

"Not tonight," he said. "You're not in the right place tonight."

He was right. I slid closer to him and put my head on his chest. "Okay."

A few seconds passed.

"I'm an idiot," Sean said. He sounded resigned.

"No," I told him. "You're my wolf."

He turned to me and a sharp humorous spark lit up his eyes. "Don't you know wolves are dangerous?"

"I do. You should kiss me again, Sean Evans. I really want you to."

He kissed me back and I melted into it.

Chapter 10

"Aunt Dina," a whisper floated into my ear.

My eyes snapped open. Helen was leaning over me, her hair all but glowing in the light of the early morning. I was laying on the pillows by a dead fire. The last thing I remembered was curling up next to Sean on the couch, but now I was on the floor on a blanket, with a pillow under my head, and another blanket over me. He must've moved me after I fell asleep. I glanced right. I glanced left. A second pillow lay next to me, the indentation from Sean's head still on it.

"What time is it?"

"Just after sunrise."

"Why are you here and not in your room?" Helen asked.

I opened my mouth.

Helen sniffed the air, wrinkling her nose. "And why is Lord Sean hiding on the balcony?"

Lord Sean chose that moment to walk back into view, since further hiding was clearly pointless.

Helen frowned. "Were you having private time?"

Um, ah ... eh.

"Mom says private time is very important."

"Where is your mom?"

"She's outside. She said to find you right away because 'that cop is about to go middle evil on Mrak.'"

I bolted off the floor. "Window to the front!"

A window opened in the wall. Maud stood at the edge of the inn's boundary, her back stiff, her arms crossed, looking across the street. On the other side of the road, the small rectangular metal cover guarding access to the water and sewer lay open. Kiran Mrak and three other Draziri, swaddled in hoodies and jeans, stood on the left side. On the right side, stood Officer Marais, one hand on his Taser.

I squeezed my eyes shut for a tiny moment and opened them. Officer Marais and the Draziri were still there.

"Shut off all water and sewer!" I sprinted out of the room and down the massive staircase. Sean swore and ran past me. Helen chased us, jumped onto the stair rail, and slid down, leaping to her feet at the bottom.

Why? Why in the world would Marais even be here the day after Christmas? Did he not have a family to go home to? Why couldn't I catch a break?

Sean grabbed my hand. "Dina, open the void field. I'll double behind them."

"Done."

His eyes flashed amber. "Please stay on the grounds. I want them to see you."

"Okay."

I tore through the house, pushed the door open, and marched across the lawn to where Maud stood. Beast trailed me.

"...understand perfectly well who you are," Kiran Mrak said, his voice suffused with derision. "You are what passes for local law enforcement. Undertrained, undereducated, likely coming from a background so poor that you view this job as a step up; a steady, respectable way to take care of your family."

"Treaty," I called out.

He ignored me. "If we had met at night, things may have been different. But here we are in broad daylight. Therefore, officer, it so happens that our interests align. You want to take care of your family, and so do I."

The moment I stepped foot off the inn's grounds, the Draziri would forget all about Marais and key in on me. I had promised Sean to stay in plain view inside the boundary and I would do it. But the urge to walk out there was strong.

"Where is your wolf?" Maud asked me under her breath.

"Sneaking around them from the back."

Marais wasn't saying anything. He clearly was determined to find out what was going on once and for all.

"So," Kiran Mrak said with the resignation of a man who'd done this hundreds of times, "how much will it take?"

"Sir, are you trying to bribe me?" Marais asked, his voice very calm.

"No. I'm trying to help you supplement your pay. It is clearly inadequate for a man of your intelligence."

Marais smiled. Oh crap.

"A man should be compensated in line with the amount of danger he faces in the course of his job," Mrak said. "And your job is exceedingly dangerous, especially at this moment."

"Oooh," Marais said, stretching the word. "I love danger."

"No, he doesn't," I called out. "If you touch a hair on that man's head, I will…"

"I believe in fairness, officer," Mrak said. "So do you want credit? Do you want currency? What is it that you value on this god-forsaken hellhole of a planet? Gold, right? You mammals like gold."

I would kill him. He had to die. Behind me the barrel of the small projectile cannon slid from under the inn's roof. It was basically a souped-up version of a rifle, and unlike energy weapons, it was very efficient. The inn had trouble loading and aiming it, but I had already loaded it and I would only need one shot.

Mrak raised his hands and one of the other Draziri put a small bag into it. The assassin pulled it open and extracted a gold nugget the size of a walnut. He looked at it, shook a few more onto his palm as if they were mints, and looked at Marais.

"Withdraw," I said. "Or I swear, I'll get your entire species blacklisted."

Next to me Helen hissed, baring her fangs. Both Mrak and Marais glanced at her. Helen stared at Mrak, raised her finger and drew it across her throat.

"What a charming child." Mrak turned to Marais. "Is this enough?"

"Sir, are you aware that bribing a law enforcement official is a crime?" Marais asked, his voice still mildly curious.

"Bribery is a crime and greed is a vice in your culture, officer, yet it rules your pathetic little lives, no matter how much you protest otherwise. I find these negotiations tedious. Yes or no?"

Marais opened his mouth. I knew exactly what would come out. It didn't matter anymore. My inn was exposed. Nobody knew how many people were watching all of this from their windows. This is how it ended. The only thing that mattered now was saving Officer Marais who had nothing to do with anything and was trying only to do his job.

"Gentlemen, this was fun." His voice rang. "Lie face-down on the ground with your hands behind your head."

Yep. That was exactly what I thought he would say.

"Really?" Mrak sighed.

"Lie down on the ground!" Marais barked. "Hands behind your head! Do it now!"

"Fine," Mrak snapped. "Kill him."

Magic moved. The ground to the left of us tore and Arland burst into the open. He wore the full suit of syn-armor, black and crimson. His golden mane fell on his shoulders. The blood mace in his hand whined, priming. He was coming, unstoppable like a battering ram. I caught a glance of Maud's face. My sister was smiling. She'd set this up.

Arland reached the edge of the inn's boundary. His mouth gaped open, his fangs on full display. The Marshal of House Krahr roared like a pissed off lion and charged. Maud grabbed Helen before she had a chance to follow.

The Draziri did what any normal sentient being would do when they saw an enraged vampire coming - they backed away, trying to scatter, and scattered straight into Sean. The first Draziri didn't know what happened when Sean broke his neck.

Arland's mace crushed the second Draziri. Both he and Sean went after Mrak. He slipped between them as if he were made of air. A blue blade appeared in his hand. He slashed with it, fast and precise. They danced across the street, Mrak avoiding their blows like a ghost. No shot.

The third Draziri lunged at Marais.

I glanced at Beast and pointed to the third Draziri. "Kill it!"

My dog dashed across the street, claws sliding out of her paws.

The officer snapped his Taser up. The Taser sparked. The Draziri jerked and ripped the metal prongs out of his body. Marais went for his gun.

Beast leapt into the air, her mouth gaping open, displaying four rows of razor sharp teeth and tore out the Draziri's throat. Blood spurted onto the asphalt at Marais's feet.

We were doomed. We were all doomed.

Kiran Mrak spun, avoiding Sean's knife. A gun barrel yawned at me. He'd walked them right where he could have the perfect shot at me.

"Now." I jerked a wall of dirt up in front of me.

The inn and Mrak fired at the same time.

Something burned my leg. I dropped the dirt in time to see Mrak jerk as if stung.

The Draziri twisted away from Sean and Arland's attacks, leapt straight up, shooting a dozen feet into the air, landed on the power line, ran across it as if it were solid ground, jumped onto the roof of a house, and disappeared from view.

Marais looked shocked, his face pale, his mouth open.

There was a hole in my robe. My leg was bleeding under the fabric. The bullet had punched through the dirt. I was lucky the soil barrier deflected it, because everything about Mrak said he didn't miss often.

Arland grabbed the first corpse by its legs and unceremoniously dragged it halfway across the road and threw it in my direction. The lawn gaped, swallowing it.

Sean grasped the second and third corpses by their feet and pulled them over. The lawn swallowed them too.

Sean and Arland walked onto the inn's grounds. Both bled from half a dozen shallow cuts. Arland looked like he hadn't gotten enough blood on his hands and was desperate to kill something. Sean looked like he was about to sprout fur any moment.

I reinstated the void field.

Sean stopped by me, inhaled, and his eyes went wild.

"It just grazed me," I told him.

He spun toward the street and I caught his arm.

"No. Please. I need you inside the house." Besides, both of them were bleeding more than me.

He snarled and went inside.

Marais finally regained control over his legs, because he was moving toward me and fast. I waited. He ran face-first into the barrier and bounced back.

"Miss Demille," he ground out through clenched teeth.

"No," I told him. "I have a child and guests to take care of. Those bastards unloaded something into the sewer system and I have no idea if the inn is filling up with some plague or if it's about to explode. I don't want your death on my hands. Go and sit in your cruiser. When it's safe, I'll come and get you."

I turned around and marched into the house, Helen and Beast in tow.

⚜ ⚜ ⚜

I walked into the inn, sending a probing pulse through the entire building. Nothing. Gertrude Hunt failed to find anything amiss in the pipes.

I pushed. The floor, walls and ceiling moved from me, distorted, as if the solid wood and stone became fluid and I was a stone cast into a placid pond.

Nothing. This would require a deeper probe.

The inn around me turned, like the inside of an enormous clock coming to life. I moved the two Hiru and Wing onto the lawn outside of the inn but still inside their own small rooms. Maud, Helen, Sean and Arland stood in the corner of the front room, next to Caldenia who sat in her chair by the window.

"Do not move," I said.

Orro emerged from the kitchen. "How can I be expected to cook without water..."

He saw my face and fell silent.

I concentrated. Pulse, another pulse...Whatever they put into the water or sewer, I would find it. It wouldn't hurt the inn. I stretched, reaching deep into the pipes. Where is it?

"What is she doing?" Arland asked.

"Diagnostics," my sister said.

"Why is the inn connected to the city water line?" Sean asked quietly.

"Because it would be suspicious if it didn't draw some water," Maud said. "The city provides only a small fraction of the inn's water supply but the meter has to show progress every month. The void field would've stopped anything the Draziri threw in there, but she had to drop it to save Marais."

"Mrak counted on it," Sean said. "Marais was bait."

"Yes," Arland agreed.

I couldn't find it. Mrak's smug face popped up in my memory. Oh no. No, you don't.

My broom split into a thousand glowing blue tendrils. They wrapped around my hand and plunged into the floor, forging a direct link between me and the inn. My hands reached through its roots. My eyes looked through its windows. I became Gertrude Hunt.

Sean was staring at me. I knew my eyes were turning bright turquoise, matching the glow of my broom as I sifted through every liquid-filled square inch inside the pipes. The house creaked and groaned around me. *Where is it?*

Helen made a small noise and stuck her face into Maud's clothes.

"Shhh, my flower," my sister whispered. "Don't worry. Let your aunt work."

Where is it?

The entire house twisted, trying to turn itself inside out to open to my inspection. Magic pulsed from me, again and again, rolling to the deepest reaches, to the smallest roots.

It touched something deep underneath within the water line. Something tiny. Something that soaked up my magic. I concentrated on the minuscule spark. It felt so much like the inn itself, it was moving right past all of Gertrude Hunt's defenses and it was growing, a tiny thread searching for the sun and warmth.

I sealed the section of the pipe, cutting it off at both ends with plastic. The thread slipped through it, as if the solid barrier wasn't there.

Magic.

If I used the void field to stop it, it would only delay the inevitable. Maybe I could jettison it once I found a way to contain it.

I followed it, tracing it. I could barely sense it. It blended so well into the very fabric of the inn, if I hadn't sunk everything into looking for it, I would've never known it was there.

Kitchen.

I pulled the broom back into its normal shape and moved into the kitchen doorway. Maud followed me.

A flower grew out of the kitchen sink, its purple stem supporting a giant blossom four feet across. Waves of petals, shimmering with delicate pink and gold, wrapped its core, which was only the size of a basketball. Parachute-like protrusions, like dandelion fuzz, thrust from the core, their feathery ends glowing gently with beautiful crimson. I'd never seen anything like it.

"*Londar Len Teles*," Arland whispered next to me.

My sister raised her eyebrows. "World killer?"

"Don't move," Arland warned, his voice an urgent whisper. "If you move, it will launch spores, sting you, and grow from your bodies."

I held perfectly still.

"Hold still, flower," Maud said without turning her head. "If you move, we all die."

"Don't raise your voice," Arland said, his lips barely moving. "It reacts to any sign of life, movement, sound, heat, change in air composition. It's a hunter. Are there any more?"

"No. This is the only one."

The soft feathers of the parachutes trembled slightly, turning toward us.

"Can you contain it?" Maud asked.

"It passed through solid plastic," I whispered.

"You can't stop it," Arland whispered. "It's impervious to fire, acid, energy weapons, and a vacuum. It will pass through whatever barrier you can summon, because it becomes flesh only when it meets its prey. If you send it to another world, you'll doom that world to extinction. It will kill and grow and kill again, until it's the only thing alive on that planet."

I couldn't be responsible for the death of an entire planet. And I couldn't contain it, burn it, or drown it.

"How do we kill it?" I asked.

"You can't," Arland said. "But I can."

"How?" Sean asked behind him.

"My blood is toxic to it," Arland said. "I'll explain if I live. The seeds should fail to implant."

"Should?" Maud whispered.

"Don't move and don't scream," Arland said. "I have to be the only target. If it keys in on anyone else, the seed will bloom inside your bodies, and the contamination will spread. I might survive one plant. I won't survive two."

"What about the void field?" I asked.

"No," Arland said. "I need to pull it out. If the void field works and you sever the stem, the flower will just grow again, in a new direction."

"This is daft," Maud said, her voice strained. "There has to be another way."

Arland's voice was eerily calm, his gaze fixed on the flower. "Lady Maud, should I die, say the Liturgy of the Fallen for me."

Maud opened her mouth. Her face turned into a bloodless mask, her eyes turned hard, and without moving a muscle, she transformed from my sister into a vampire. Her voice came out calm and even. Vampire words rolled off her tongue. *"Go with the Goddess, my Lord. You won't be forgotten."*

Arland charged into the kitchen.

The flower exploded. Every parachute sprung into the air, the bright pink seeds at the end glowing, and clamped onto the vampire. Arland snarled like a wounded animal. The parachutes engulfed him, wrapping around him like a strait jacket, the seeds pulsing with red, sinking through his armor, then falling off, black and lifeless. They battered his face, drawing blood. He gritted his teeth and locked his hands on the core of the flower. The petals flared bright red. Arland howled, his voice pure pain, and pulled the flower to him. The petals turned black. His whole body shook. The immovable mountain that was Arland barely stayed upright. The stem of the flower wrapped around his arm like a constrictor trying to choke its victim. Arland gripped it and pulled, hand over hand, his teeth bared, his eyes bulging out. The vine spilled out, coiling around him.

It whipped him, penetrating the armor like it wasn't even there. Blood drenched his face, slipping out of the dozens of tiny wounds. Arland went down to his knees, still screaming, raw and desperate, tears streaming from his eyes. I wanted to clamp my hands over my ears and curl into a ball so I wouldn't have to hear or see him. Maud stood rigid beside me, her hands locked into fists, breath hissing through her clenched teeth.

The last few feet of the stem spilled out of the drain, carrying a glowing blue bulb the size of a walnut at the end of it.

The Marshal of House Krahr gripped it. It pulsed with blinding light. He dug his fangs into it, ripping a hole in the bulb, bit his hand, and spat his own blood into its center.

The bulb turned black.

The plant convulsed, squeezing him in a last attempt to strangle its victim, turned black, and became still.

Arland raised his hand and growled a single word. "Clear."

Maud sprinted to him.

"Well," Caldenia said. "Nobody can say that this siege is boring."

⚜ ⚜ ⚜

Arland couldn't get off the floor. Welts formed on his face, swelling into blood-filled blisters in seconds. He was breathing like he'd run a sprint.

"You need to take off the armor," Maud told him. "You're bleeding under it."

"What I need...is a...moment...to catch my breath."

"Arland," I said. "You need to get out of the armor."

He didn't answer. Prying him out of the armor would be next to impossible without his cooperation. For the knights of the Holy Anocracy, armor was everything. They spent more of their lives in it than out of it, and, in times of life-threatening injuries, the urge to keep it on often overwhelmed them.

Sean stepped in front of Arland, grabbed his arm, and hauled the Marshal to his feet.

"You stay in the armor, you die," he said.

"Don't die!" Helen yelled from the front room.

Maud slapped her hand over her face. "You can move, darling."

Helen dashed into the room and hugged Arland's leg. "Don't die."

A tremor gripped Arland's body. He bit the air, as if trying to kill the pain.

Maud stepped close to him, their faces only inches apart. "I know," she said, her voice strained. "I *know*. I've been there. The last thing you want is to be without armor now. You don't want to be vulnerable. But you will die, my lord. I don't want that to happen. Helen doesn't want that to happen."

Arland looked at Helen. She clung to his armored leg, her terrified eyes opened wide. "Don't die."

Arland swallowed and hit the crest on his chest. The armor fell off him.

"Medbay!" I ordered.

A tendril sprouted from the floor, wrapped around Arland and pulled him deeper into the inn. I followed. Helen took off after me, but Maud caught her.

"No."

"But why?"

"Because he's very proud. Stay here, Helen."

I stepped into the medbay. Maud was only a step behind me. I sealed the doors behind us. The inn deposited Arland onto the metal examination table. I took a scalpel from the drawer and sliced through the black fabric of his jumpsuit.

Bloody blisters covered his entire body. Some had broken and viscous blood, tainted by something foul, leaked onto his skin. It smelled like vinegar and rot. I touched his skin. Too cold.

"What can we do?" I asked him.

"Nothing," he said. "I live or I die."

"There has to be something I can do."

He sighed. "The last time, there was a bath. With star flower."

"Mint," Maud told me as if I didn't know.

"It helped some."

I opened a screen to the kitchen, making sure Arland was out of its view. Orro was deep-frying something on the stove.

"I need mint," I said. "All of it. Everything we have."

"We have two plants," Orro said. He'd pitched a fit over fresh herbs not long after the summit was over, and I had created a hothouse, which we were slowly stocking with herbs.

"That's not enough. Take all of the mint tea we have and brew the biggest pot of tea we can."

He nodded. I closed the screen

Maud took Arland's hand.

"No," he said. "I don't want you ... to see me like this."

"Don't be ridiculous," Maud told him. "A pack of rassa couldn't make me leave."

"My lady ... "

She put her fingers on his lips. "I'm staying."

I took the handheld showerhead from the side of the bed, adjusted the water to warm, and washed the polluted blood off him.

He didn't say a word. He just lay there. No strength to protest. No energy to be embarrassed. He lay there and held Maud's hand.

We couldn't lose Arland. We just couldn't.

"I can't feel a vigil room," Maud said. "Do you have one?"

"No."

"Then I'm going to make one. Off the kitchen." She closed her eyes, concentrating.

Vampires treasured their families. The worst fate a vampire could imagine was dying alone. They fell in battle, surrounded by other vampires, or they died at home, watched over by their relatives and loved ones. Arland wouldn't be alone. It was the least we could do.

"It needs to have a tub," I told her.

She gave me a look that told me she wasn't an idiot and closed her eyes again.

I felt the inn move as parts of it shifted in response to my sister's will. There was a sluggish quality to its compliance, almost as if Gertrude Hunt hesitated before making the adjustments.

"Do what she asks," I whispered, so quiet even I couldn't hear it. It wasn't an order or a demand. It was permission.

The inn moved faster.

Arland was still bleeding. The more I washed him off and patted his wounds dry, the more polluted blood seeped from the wounds. If I sealed the wounds, I would be trapping the rot and poison inside his body.

I looked at Maud. She took the showerhead from me and kept washing.

Arland's breath slowed. His chest barely rose.

"Don't let go," Maud told him. "Hold on to me."

He smiled at her. When Arland smiled, it was a declaration of war. It dazzled. There was vigor and power in it. There was no vigor in his smile now.

"Fight it." Maud squeezed his hand.

"Everything is slowing down." He raised his hand. It shook. Maud leaned to him. His fingertips brushed her cheek.

"No time," he said.

"Fight it." Desperation pulsated in her voice. "Live."

He was dying. Arland was dying.

I felt a presence outside the door. Caldenia.

She knocked.

What could she possibly want right now? I draped a towel over Arland's hips and opened the door. Her Grace stepped inside, carrying a small wooden box in her hands. She craned her neck and glanced at Arland. "Well. As prime a specimen as I remember from your wonderful excursion to the orchard."

"I'm not dead yet," Arland's voice trembled. He was trying to snarl, but he didn't have the strength. "You can't eat me."

Caldenia raised her eyes up for a long moment. "My dear, I'm not ruled by my stomach. Right now, I'm moved by an altruistic impulse. It will be very short-lived, so you should take advantage of it while it lasts."

She opened the box and took out a small injector with clear liquid inside it.

"What is that?" Maud asked.

"This is a vaccine synthesized from a certain bacteriophage," Caldenia said, snapping the protective tip off the injector. "The same prokaryotic virus that our dear

Marshal carries in his blood." She turned to Arland. "I'm going to inject you with it, unless you just want to die on this table for the sins of your ancestors. Or, I suppose, in your case, for their ridiculous bravery and absurd ethical obligations."

She raised the injector.

"No," Arland squeezed out.

Caldenia looked at me. "He *will* die, Dina."

Arland tried to rise. His whole body trembled from the effort. He collapsed back down.

"Do you trust her?" Maud asked.

"No," I said. "She doesn't have altruistic impulses."

"I have finally taught you something," Caldenia smiled, exposing her inhumanly sharp teeth.

"But I trust her survival instinct. Without Arland the inn is more vulnerable, and if the Draziri break in, they will slaughter everyone. Her Grace didn't travel light-years across the galaxy to be murdered by some feathered religious fanatic."

Arland lay flat, his gaze on the ceiling.

"The safety of my guests is my first priority," I told him, gently brushing his hair off his face.

"She's too polite to tell you," Caldenia said. "If I were to kill you, I would be breaking my contract with Dina. The contract stipulates that the moment I kill another guest, even if I do so in self-defense, she has the right to void our agreement. I'd lose my safe haven. It would be very inconvenient for me."

Silence stretched.

Arland looked at Maud.

"Take it," she said. "Please."

"Do it," he squeezed out, his voice weak and hoarse.

Caldenia pressed the injector against a wound on his stomach and squeezed. Arland jerked and sucked in a deep breath.

"You must restrain him now," Caldenia said. "It will sting."

Maud clamped her hands on his wrists.

Arland screamed.

I thrust my broom over him. It split apart, binding him to the table. Maud threw herself over it, wrapping herself around him as much as she could.

Foam slid from Arland's lips. He flailed under the restraints.

I squeezed my hands into fists. There was nothing I could do. Maud's face was terrible, her lips a flat, bloodless slash across her face, her eyes dull as if dusted with ash.

Another convulsion... Another...

A shallow tremor.

He inhaled and lay still.

Did he die?

"Arland?" Maud called softly. "Arland?"

His eyelashes fluttered. He opened his blue eyes, looked at her, then closed them again. His chest rose and fell in an even rhythm.

She rose. I released the broom. Maud washed the blood off of him. The water ran red, then clear. The wounds stopped bleeding. That was fast. Really fast.

I pulled a clean sheet from the drawer and covered him.

"How?" I asked.

Caldenia smiled again. "Strictly speaking, that flower isn't really a plant. It's closer to a macrobacterium in structure, very heavily modified, of course. A pathogen affecting both plants and animals. The science of it is long and complicated. Suffice it to say that about three hundred years ago a naturally occurring variant was discovered by a group of enterprising vampires. It existed in a delicate balance, kept in check by virulent bacteriophages that preyed on it as it preyed on other life. The vampires colonized the pseudo-flower's planet and promptly attempted to manipulate it into a weapon to destroy their enemies once and for all. They were quite successful. It wiped out all of the native life on that world."

"It's a thing that should never have been," Arland said quietly. "It should be unmade."

He spoke. He still sounded weak, but a shadow of the power that made Arland was there. Maud took his hand in hers and stroked his fingers.

"Oh I don't know." Her Grace waved her long, elegant fingers. "There is a savage beauty to it."

It was beautiful, deadly, and had an indiscriminate appetite. Of course she would feel kinship with it.

"What happened?"

"Contact with the colony was lost, and the Holy Anocracy bestirred itself and sent a rescue fleet," Caldenia said. "The first group to land consisted of volunteers, of which several were from House Krahr and House Ilun. There was a third House, wasn't there, dear?"

"House Morr," Arland said.

"Long story short," Caldenia said, "two dozen beings went in, five came back, and then the fleet bombarded the planet's moon with nuclear and kinetic projectiles, until it shattered, causing increased volcanic activity, tsunamis, and other catastrophic developments on the surface of the planet. Gravity tore the remnants of the moon into a ring, and the Anocracy's fleet helped the resulting asteroids fall to the planet, initiating an impact winter. Nothing survived."

"Then how did the flower get here?" I asked.

"Money." Caldenia winked at me. "Given the right equipment, it can be contained. Prior to being killed by their own creation, the weapon makers sold samples to fund their research. I bought one. And the antidote, of course. One should never unleash a weapon if one cannot survive it."

I stared at her.

"It is my understanding that the two surviving members of House Krahr were so impacted by their experience, that they insisted on vaccinating their entire clan. Unfortunately, their supply of the vaccine was limited, and the potency of their defensive measures became more and more diluted with each generation. Supposedly, our darling boy here had to go through a ritual at puberty, like most of the members of House Krahr who showed potential. The ritual involved being stung by a single seed, and I use that term loosely. It is thought that this trial by fire would raise the concentration of the bacteriophage in his blood in the event he ever encountered the flower."

"Is that public knowledge?" I asked.

"No," Maud said. "I never heard of it."

Caldenia pursed her lips. "Your sister is correct. It's a closely guarded secret."

"So either Mrak didn't know that Arland was partially immune and he hoped the flower would kill all of us or he did know and wanted to specifically take Arland out," Maud said.

"Indeed." Caldenia closed her wooden box and patted Arland's leg. "Do get better. You're much more entertaining when you roar. I leave you with this parting thought. One must wonder how House Krahr keeps coming by these seeds."

The hairs on the back of my neck stood up.

I opened the door. Caldenia strode out.

"Please tell me you don't have a hothouse full of those things somewhere."

Arland shook his head. "Some things even I have no right to know."

"The vigil room is ready," Maud said.

Chapter 11

I walked over to the edge of the property, to where Officer Marais had parked by my hedges, and waved at him. He gave my innkeeper robe a once-over and got out of the car. I dropped the void force field just long enough for him to pass and put it back up. Holding it up was getting harder and harder. Soon I'd have to drop it for a while to rest.

"I want to know what's going on," he said as we walked back to the house. "I want the whole story. All the details. Who and what and when and where. Even the parts that are too ugly and parts you don't think are important. I want you to explain the robe. And if anyone comes near me with a syringe, you *will* regret it. I'll rip this place apart brick by brick."

"Technically, board by board," I told him, opening the door in front of us. "We have siding, not brick."

"Now isn't a good time to be funny..." He stepped inside the inn and froze. The far wall of the front room had dissolved. A vast desert spread beyond, a sea of shallow sand waves littered with the massive skeletons of monsters long past. Despite the sunlight, a ghostly moon, huge and striped, took up a quarter of the pale green sky. A caravan approached, massive shaggy beasts that would dwarf Earth's elephants moving ponderously through the sand, their spiked armor gleaming in the sun. Their handlers walked by the creatures' feet, their bodies draped in a light shimmering fabric. Good timing.

Hot wind fanned our faces.

Officer Marais took a few shaky steps forward, reached through the rip in the fabric of space, picked up a handful of sand, and let the grains fall from his fingers.

I came to stand next to him and waved my hand. Two fifty-five-gallon containers filled with water surfaced from the floor. When the inn first opened this door six months ago, the caravan leader gave me a gift. I didn't know what to give them back, so I shared my water with them. Predictably, the water was precious to them. They passed my way every couple of weeks, and I made it a point to have some water on hand. It cost me very little, but it meant a great deal to them.

The caravan drew closer. I could see the caravan leader now. He had skin the color of alligator hide, a long inhuman face, and big emerald-green eyes, like two jewels in the rough.

"Don't shoot," I told Marais.

He stared at the caravan open-mouthed.

The first beast approached, the metal spikes on the armor that shielded his forehead as big as a small tree. Its tusks curved outward, each tipped with gleaming metal stained with old, dried blood. We weren't tall enough to even reach its knee. An animal smell bathed us, thick and pungent. Its handler, his light blue robe stirring from the hot wind, stopped in front of the rip and drew a circle in the air with his long elegant fingers, tipped with curved silver claws.

"*Ahiar ahiar,*" he said, his voice soft like the shifting of the sand, and bowed his head. *Peace to you and yours.*

"*Ha ahiar.*" I bowed back. *Lasting peace.* "Please accept my water."

"Thank you, innkeeper. May you live a thousand years."

The inn deposited the two containers into the sand. The handler picked them up as if they weighed nothing.

"I have a gift for you, innkeeper."

The caravan leader waved his hand. Two other beings, one in a copper-colored robe and the other in rose-gold, came forth, bringing something long and wrapped in canvas. They set it into the sand and pulled back the tarp. A stasis pod. Familiar features looked back at me. An Archivarian.

How? Never mind. One didn't look a gift Archivarian in the mouth.

"I'm in your debt." I bowed my head.

"No. We're still in yours."

They pushed the stasis pod into the inn and Gertrude Hunt swallowed it, carrying it down to install it with the rest.

The caravan went on, the colossal creatures swaying. I let the door close. Marais stared at the newly formed wall.

"They come this way every few weeks," I told him. "Water is very prized in that part of their planet. This way."

He followed me into the kitchen, looked left, and did a double take. A large room stretched off the kitchen. Vines draped its walls, so dense it was hard to see the pale stone underneath. Tree limbs broke the stone, their bark rough and dark, and stretched up along the wall, supporting metal lanterns glowing with warm yellow light. Tiny white flowers bloomed on the vines. Here and there, a large yellow blossom reminiscent of a chrysanthemum somehow shaped into a lily sent a faint honey aroma into the air. The floor was moss, stone, and tree root. Turquoise flowers, five petals each, stretched from the floor on two-feet-tall stalks the color of sage. The blue blossoms were wide open, showing off the purple center. Excellent.

In the center of the room, in the large Jacuzzi tub, sat Arland. The wounds on his face had closed. The scent of mint floated to us, mixing with the aroma of the flowers.

Maud sat on a root next to the tub, her eyes closed, her face serene, her sword on her lap. Helen stood next to her, holding a stick with bells on it.

Arland reached over and flicked a few drops of water in Maud's direction. Helen shook her stick at him, the bells tinkling.

"Lord Marshal," Maud said, her eyes still closed. "I'm trying to accelerate your healing. Do take this seriously."

Marais turned to me and noticed Sean leaning against the wall, like a dark shadow. Next to him, on a windowsill, Wing was whittling something out of a piece of wood. Marais shifted his stance. Sean's tattoos expanded, spiraling up his neck as his subcutaneous armor moved to shield him against a perceived threat.

"Hey," Marais said.

Sean nodded. Wing continued his whittling.

I pulled a chair out at the table. "Please sit down."

Marais sat. Orro appeared from the depths of the pantry and advanced on Marais. Marais put his hand on his Taser. Orro swept by the table with a dramatic flourish. A covered plate landed in front of Marais. Orro reached with his long claws, plucked the white cover off and sped away.

A single golden doughnut, flecked with chocolate flakes and translucent sparkles of sugar, sat in the middle of the plate. I had to talk to Orro about his literal interpretation of our TV programming.

Marais looked at me. "Is it po-"

"No!" Sean and I hissed at the same time.

Sean leaned over Marais and said with quiet menace, "Don't say the 'p' word. Eat the doughnut. It's the best you'll ever try."

Marais picked up the doughnut and took a speculative bite. His eyes widened. He took another bite. "So," he said, chewing. "Aliens?"

"Aliens."

"Why?"

"We're a way station on the path to somewhere else," I explained. "A safe, comfortable place to stop for the night and catch your breath, before you reach your destination."

"A galactic bed and breakfast?" Marais took another bite.

"An inn," Sean said.

"And you're..."

"An innkeeper," I told him. "I keep my guests safe and their existence secret at all costs."

"Who else knows?" he asked.

"Other innkeepers like me."

"Does the President know?"

"I have no idea," I told him honestly. "Probably not."

Marais pondered the doughnut. He was taking all of this rather calmly. But then he'd had a lot of clues along the way.

"Why?" Marais asked.

"It's a bargain we made hundreds of years ago. Have you gassed up your car yet?"

"Not yet. Waiting until it gets below a quarter of a tank."

"We made the bargain, so civilizations like his-" I pointed at Arland, whose engineer had modified the car, "-don't conquer us. They have numbers and superior technology. Without the treaty that designated Earth as safe neutral ground, we'd be purged, eaten, or enslaved. The galaxy is a big and vicious place."

"So what happens when people find out?" Marais asked. "Because they will find out."

"It's been well over a thousand years and they haven't found out yet," I said. "If we break the treaty and expose the existence of our guests or fail to prevent that exposure, the consequences will be severe."

"What will happen?" Marais asked.

"Innkeepers will either kill you or leave you in some hellhole," Sean said. "You'll never get home."

I could tell by his face that Marais didn't like it.

"It wouldn't be good for people to find out," I said. "We're a young civilization. People would panic. They would lose their faith. They would want to go to war with the universe. You have police codes, because you don't want bystanders showing up to every crime scene. You restrict public access. So do we."

Marais mulled it over. "What about the pale-haired punk? What's his deal?"

It took about ten minutes to explain the Hiru and the Draziri. I had to go into detail on innkeeper's powers and inn's grounds.

"So they are in violation of the treaty and nothing happened so far. This doesn't fill me with confidence as to the effectiveness of your internal law enforcement."

"I've reported it," I explained. "It takes time."

"Is there any way I can look at this treaty?" Marais asked.

In for a penny, in for a pound. "Yes."

I opened a screen in the wall and brought the treaty up on it. Marais took out a notepad and a pen and began taking notes. We waited. Fifteen minutes later, he stood up.

"So?" I asked. "What now?"

"Now I'll have to think about it. No more acts of violence outside of the inn," he said. "At least try to keep it to a minimum. I'll let you know what I decide. I can tell you that so far you are in the clear. I sat in the cruiser after the fight and nobody came out to check with me and no emergency calls had been made. It's the morning after a holiday. Most people slept in."

He turned to leave. Orro blocked his way and thrust a paper box into his hands. "For your captain. I hope it will lessen the screaming and keep you from giving up your badge."

Marais glanced at me.

"He's been binge-watching *Lethal Weapon* movies," I explained.

"Thank you," Marais said and walked out.

"You think he'll keep quiet?" Maud asked.

"He's had a magic space car for several weeks now and, so far, hasn't said anything," I said.

"If not, I know where he lives," Sean said.

I turned to him. "How?"

"I followed him home one night when we were hunting the dahaka."

"That's creepy."

He shrugged.

"Sean, you're not killing Officer Marais."

Sean smiled a long wolf smile, reached out, and patted my hand.

"I'll help you kill him," Arland said.

"Sean Evans!" I put my hands on my hips.

"I'm trying to meditate," Maud ground out. "Can you take your lover's spat somewhere else?"

"Relax," Sean told me. "I'm pulling your leg. Marais is a good guy. I'll see him out. I've got an errand to run anyway."

He went outside. I dropped the void field, felt him and Marais pass over the boundary, and pulled it up again.

Well, one of my guests was almost murdered and the inn was pretty much exposed. This wasn't a good day so far.

Arland's crest, which he'd put on the corner of the tub, came alive with red light. Arland reached over to check it. His eyes went wide. He swore, scrambled up, and fell all the way into the tub, splashing.

Oh no.

Arland surfaced, his long blond hair stuck to his head.

"What is it?" I asked.

"What?" Maud jumped to her feet.

"Is it war?" Helen's eyes shone, catching the light.

"It's worse." Arland groaned. "My uncle is coming. Someone get me a robe. I have to get out of this tub."

⚜ ⚜ ⚜

It was late afternoon and a delectable scent floated through the kitchen. Orro was in the throes of preparing dinner. Her Grace sat at the table, delicately sipping a Mello Yello. A large straw hat lay next to her. After Arland escaped the tub, she put on her hat and announced that she would be gardening. I kept an eye on her, and her gardening mostly consisted of snipping some small branches with garden shears and talking. I couldn't see who she was talking to, but considering our situation, she was probably having discussions with the Draziri. She didn't share anything she learned, and knowing her, asking about it would do no good.

Sean sat across from her, scrolling through a personal datapad, which I had no idea he owned. His errand took almost two hours. I knew exactly when he came back because he called to let me know he was about to enter, so I would let him in. He showed no signs of telling me what the errand was about. Wing still perched on the windowsill working on his whittling project.

On the wall, on an eight-foot-wide screen, Maud and Arland sparred in the Grand Ballroom, both in armor. Once he got out of the tub and donned a robe, Arland walked to his rooms where he collapsed on the bed and passed out. Maud checked on him to make sure he didn't fall asleep facedown and suffocate. He slept like a log for five hours, then fifteen minutes ago, he came down in full armor, his hair brushed, his jaw shaved, looking like he was about to attend a parade, and announced that in half an hour his uncle would be arriving.

Maud asked him exactly how many stimulants he pumped into himself, and he told her enough to make her lower her sword in surrender. My sister did that narrow thing with her eyes that used to make me run yelling for Mom and asked him if he was willing to test his theory. Now they were beating on each other with practice weapons.

This was extremely unwise. I told him so. I told Maud so. My sister patted my shoulder and told me that he had to observe certain proprieties when he met his uncle. Meeting him while exhausted and naked in a tub of mint tea wouldn't be appropriate and a little exercise would help the stimulants spread through his system faster.

Helen and the cat sat on the dais in the ballroom and watched the fight. The dais would be a perfect place for the Christmas tree.

"I want to celebrate Christmas," I said.

"Isn't it a little late for Christmas?" Caldenia asked.

"I know, but I still want to celebrate it. I want the tree and decorations. I want gifts and Christmas music. I don't care how many Draziri are out there. They won't take Christmas from me."

"Yes, but we don't have a suitable male," Orro said. "And only one dog."

I looked at him.

"What is this Christmas?" Wing asked.

Orro turned from the stove. "It's the rite of passage during which the young males of the human species learn to display aggression and use weapons."

Sean stopped what he was doing and looked at Orro.

"The young men go out in small packs," Orro continued. "They brave the cold and come into conflict with other packs and they have to prove their dominance through physical combat. Their fathers teach them lessons in the proper use of swear words, and the young men have to undergo tests of endurance, like holding soap in their mouths and licking cold metal objects."

Sean made a strangled noise.

"At the end of their trials, they go to see a wise elder in a red suit to prove their worth. If they are judged worthy, the family erects a ceremonial tree and presents them with gifts of weapons."

Sean was clearly struggling, because his head was shaking.

"Also," Orro added, "a sacrificial poultry is prepared and then given to the wild animals, probably to appease the nature spirits."

Sean roared with laughter.

I grinned at him.

He leaned back, shaking, laughter exploding out of him.

"Your culture is so complicated," Wing said. "On my world, we just go on a quest to kill something big."

"I suppose small Helen could substitute for a male," Orro said thoughtfully. "I'm sure we can get her a proper gun."

"We can't," Sean managed between gulps of laughter. "She'll put her eye out."

"That does seem to be a prevalent concern among parents," Orro said. "Perhaps we could employ some sort of protective eye wear."

"Orro, you and I must watch *Christmas Story* together, so I can explain that movie to you." I opened another screen. "Images, Christmas feast."

Orro stared at the wall of food filling the screen.

I crossed my arms on my chest. "Officially Christmas is a religious holiday when Christians, members of one of our most popular religions, celebrate the birth of Jesus Christ. They believe that he was the son of God who sacrificed himself to absolve them of sin. Unofficially, it's the time we get together as a family and celebrate our friends. We decorate our houses, we share a meal, we give each other gifts, and we take a break from the world. Christmas is magic. It's the time of kindness when normal people allow themselves to almost believe that miracles can happen. I want to have a Christmas, Orro. And I want you to make an incredible feast for it."

The big Quillonian bowed his head. "As you wish, innkeeper."

Wing set the object he had whittled onto the table. "Done."

He'd carved a remarkably lifelike version of Kiran Mrak. It was only a foot tall, but the face was unmistakable, and the detail in the feathers and even the folds of his tunic was exquisite.

"Wing, that is beautiful. You have talent."

The small Ku regarded the statue and held out his hand. "I'm ready."

Orro put a long metal skewer into Wing's hand. The tip of the skewer glowed bright red.

"What is that for?" I asked. Wing was the last person I would trust with a heated skewer.

Wing focused, chanted something under his breath, and stabbed the statue.

Aaaa!

"Wing!"

He stabbed it again and again in a frenzy. "This is old magic. My planet's magic. My ancestors are greater than his ancestors. They will rip him apart. You will see."

I slapped my hand over my face.

He picked up the scarred statue and smashed it against the table. He jumped on it, bounced up and down, and clawed it with his foot.

"Is it working?" he asked. "Is he dead?"

"I didn't hear a scream," Orro said.

Wing's eyes shone with determination. He reached for his tunic.

"If you're going to urinate on it, go outside!" I pointed to the door. "Outside!"

Wing took his statue and went out to the back.

A chime echoed through the inn, the alarm I had set to let me know when Lord Soren was about to drop in from orbit.

"Lord Soren is inbound," I announced.

"Then I shall change." Her Grace rose and floated off. "One must observe the proprieties."

On the screen my sister and Arland were still pummeling each other.

"Everybody is so concerned with proprieties, they might just spar themselves to death," I muttered.

Sean glanced at me. "Would you like me to slip into something more comfortable?"

I pointed my broom at him. "Don't push me, Sean Evans."

He laughed.

I stepped into the backyard and dropped the void field. Around me the Texas evening was burning down, the sky a deep purple, the trees dark. A figure appeared in the branches of the trees just past the inn's grounds, as if by magic. Most likely Kiran Mrak just took off his camouflage cloak. He was letting me see him. How nice. A little reminder for me that he was always there and always watching.

A red star appeared in the sky, streaked down, flared, and released a knight of the Holy Anocracy. I raised the void field.

Vampires tended to become wider with age. Not fatter but bulkier, more muscled, more grizzled. Lord Soren was a fine example of a middle-aged vampire. Hulking, with a mane of brown hair liberally shot through with gray and a short beard, he looked as big as a tank in his armor. I had a feeling that if he planted himself and a semi rammed him at full speed, the truck would just crumple around him. Considering his serious expression, he was in no mood for nonsense.

"Lord Soren," I said, turning my back to the woods. "I wish we were meeting under different circumstances. Please come inside."

He stomped into my kitchen and I shut the door behind us.

"I apologize for the intrusion, but I have come for my nephew."

Lord Soren had two sound settings: roar and thunder. He was trying to be polite and so he confined himself to a moderate roar.

"These little vacations and excursions when he disappears without warning are becoming legendary. People are whispering. The Marshal of House Krahr is gone again. Where is he?"

I opened my mouth to tell him.

"It's time to grow up. It's time to join the House when matters of importance and state are to be discussed, in which his opinion as Marshal is required. Is there not enough at home to occupy his mind?"

I started walking toward the ballroom. Lord Soren followed me.

"He took his destroyer to Karhari for no reason. He was attacked."

"He won," I said.

"Of course he won!" Lord Soren's eyes bulged. "He is my nephew! He took them on seven at once, and he tore through them like they were children. His recording has been shared across the Anocracy."

Oh no. Arland had gone viral.

"We've received four – four! – offers of a potential match in the last two days."

I couldn't tell if he was proud or upset or both.

"The boy has potential. He has talent. But does he apply himself? No. It is time to take a wife. It's time to produce children. He isn't going to live forever and he is far too young to retire. He can't just take off whenever he wants like some sort of cosmic vagabond without a family or duty. There are certain responsibilities. If he didn't want these responsibilities, he should've thought about it before he fought the other eligibles for the post of the Marshal. Do you know what he told his aide?"

Lord Soren stared at me for a second.

"I-"

"He said to tell me that taking this holiday would make him happy. I don't want him to be happy." Lord Soren pounded his gauntleted fist into his other palm. "I want him to be an adult! I want him to deal with his duties. I want him to get a wife and make children so our House doesn't wither. He was doing so well until he visited Earth. Really, this fascination with Earth women has to end."

The ballroom door opened in front of us and I led him into the cavernous room.

"I understand the appeal. However, no Earth woman would ever make a suitable spouse for a Marshal. For one thing, they're not familiar with any of our customs. They do not understand our society. They don't grasp the significance of family ties or our politics. They are not even equipped to defend their offspring..."

Maud chose this moment to jump up and wallop the side of Arland's head with her sword. He snarled and swung his mace. She rolled out of the way and grinned at him. "Try harder, my lord."

Helen laughed like a little bell ringing.

Lord Soren closed his jaw. "Who is that?"

I gave him a sweet smile. "It's an Earth woman."

We watched Arland and Maud dance across the ballroom, Arland delivering devastating blows and Maud dancing out of the way, agile like a cat. Finally, Arland managed to slam her into the column. My sister shook her head a couple of times and said something, I couldn't tell what, since he was still pinning her to the column. He said something back. She raised her eyebrows and tapped his bicep with her hand. He let her go.

Maud started toward us. Helen jumped off the dais and snarled at Arland. Arland raised his arms to the sides and roared dramatically. They ran toward each other. Arland picked Helen up and threw her in the air about twenty feet high. I gasped. He caught Helen. She squealed.

"Lord Soren," I said. "My sister, Maud, and her daughter, Helen. Maud, this is Lord Soren, Lord Marshal's uncle and Knight Sergeant of House Krahr."

Maud smiled and bowed her head. "I believe I've met your second cousin, my lord. Lord Cherush on Karhari."

Lord Soren finally recovered. "My lady. How is my, arhm...cousin?"

"Fair as usual. He still meets with Kaylin of House Setor every fall. They talk of raiding the Karim to the south, but never do. It's not profitable. The cost in fuel alone would be higher than whatever they would get from the tribes. Lord Kaylin's ward, Eren of House Phis, is of a marriageable age and your cousin's second son is still unmarried and has expressed his interest, so I believe it is all for the best."

Lord Soren puffed his chest. "Phis? My second nephew wants to marry into the House of those cowards?"

"Not the Southern Phis, my lord. Give the poor boy some credit. Eren is from the Northern branch. Her mother was of House Toran, daughter of their Knight Sergeant. There is good blood there, and as you know, the Torans still hold the northern port. The alliance would benefit Lord Cherush in his fur trade."

Lord Soren heaved a heavy sigh. "Does she have all of her fingers and teeth, at least?"

"She is a lovely girl. Very good with an energy rifle."

"I shall have to write to my cousin," Lord Soren said. "It's been ages, after all."

"Indeed. He mentions you fondly. If you'll excuse me, my lord, I must refresh myself. Your nephew is quite vigorous. One would think that a man who had taken the full onslaught of a World Killer would be in his bed, moaning in pain, yet here he is."

"World Killer?" Lord Soren blinked.

"He has saved us all," Maud said.

Lord Soren puffed out his chest.

"A lesser knight would've died. Truly, Lord Arland is proof that an exceptional bloodline bears an exceptional fruit."

Lord Soren puffed himself even bigger. "He is the pride of our House."

"Without a doubt." Maud bowed her head. "Good day, my lord."

"Good day, my lady."

Arland turned, holding Helen while she was pretending to slice his neck with her dagger and pretended to finally notice his uncle. "Uncle! There you are."

Lord Soren pondered the two of them for a long moment and walked toward them.

"You have no shame," I murmured to Maud.

"No," she said. "Also, as vampires go, Arland isn't altogether terrible. I simply smoothed the way. That was the least I could do. He saved my baby."

My sister walked away. Lord Soren puzzled over Helen, then turned to his nephew. "Tell me of the World Killer."

Chapter 12

I walked the length of the ballroom, making sure I knew exactly what I wanted to do with it. Helen watched me, her eyes big and round. Beast lay by her, four paws in the air. When Helen forgot to pet her furry stomach, Beast wiggled until petting resumed.

I stood in the center of the floor where a mosaic depicted a stylized version of Gertrude Hunt, raised my broom, and pulled with my power. Bright tinsel and strands of golden lights spiraled out of the floor and wrapped about the beautiful columns. Garlands of pine branches studded with gold and white glass ornaments and wrapped with sparkling ribbons traced the walls. Vines sprang from the ceiling, dripping down large delicate poinsettias, their white and red petals glittering, as if dusted with fairy powder. Wing would like that.

The floor at the far wall split and a massive Christmas tree rose, growing out of a fifteen-foot-wide drum. I sank the drum just below the floor level and let the mosaic close over it. I'd gotten this tree last year, the second Christmas in the inn. It came to me cut, and then the inn touched it with its magic, and overnight it had rooted and grew. It was twenty feet tall now, full and healthy, its green needles ready for the decorations, which appeared out of the wall in a dumpster-sized bin.

I waved my hand and the inn gently plucked a five-point star from the top of the bin and lowered it onto the tree top. It blinked and glowed with golden light.

Helen stared at it in awe. "Christmas?"

"Christmas," I told her.

The look in her eyes was everything.

"Look at this." I reached into the bin and picked out a glass orb. About the size of a large grapefruit, and ruby red, it glowed gently, as if fire was trapped within. I held it out to her.

"Breathe on it."

Helen blew a puff of breath onto the glass. A tiny lightning storm burst inside, the crimson lightning kissing the glass. She giggled.

"Where should we put it?" I offered her the sphere.

She pointed to a branch seven feet off the ground. "There."

I held out the orb. "The master decorator has spoken. If you please..."

A thin tendril slipped from the wall, picked up the orb, and neatly deposited it on the branch.

"Is there more?" Helen asked.

"There is more," I told her. "This whole box is full of treasures from all around the Ggalaxy. It's a magic box for a magical tree."

I dipped my hand into the bin and drew the next ornament out. It was a little bigger and crystal clear. Inside a tiny tree spread black crooked limbs. Triangular green leaves dotted its branches and between them clusters of light blue flowers bloomed. Everything within the globe, from the details of the roots to lichen on the trunk, was amazingly lifelike.

"Oooh. Is it real?"

"I don't know. The only way to find out is to break it. But if we broke it, that would be the end of the mystery."

She put her nose to the glass. Her eyes crossed slightly, trying to focus on the tree. She was killing me with cute.

"You can keep it," I told her. "That can be Helen's ornament."

Her face lit up. Helen stepped toward the tree, turned, catlike on her toes, and looked toward the door.

The Hiru had left their room and were coming toward us.

"Don't be afraid," I told her.

"They smell," she whispered. "And they look gross."

"I know. But they are still sentient beings. They never hurt anyone. They are gentle and the Draziri hunt them and kill them wherever they can find them."

"Why?" Helen asked.

"Nobody knows. Try talking to them. Maybe they will tell you."

"Why do you protect them, Aunt Dina?"

"There are killings that are justified. Killing someone who is trying to kill you is self-defense. Killing a being who is suffering and is beyond help is mercy. Killing someone because you don't like the way they look is murder. There is no room for murder in this inn. I won't stand for it."

The two Hiru made it through the door, Sunset in the lead, moving one step at a time, their mechanical joints grinding despite lubrication. The odor of pungent rotten fish hit us. You'd think I would get used to it by now, but no. I strained to not grimace.

The Hiru came closer. Helen looked a little blue. She was trying to hold her breath. The smell must've been hell on vampire senses. Sean never gave any indication it bothered him, but it had to be terrible for him.

Helen opened her mouth with a pop, pointed at the tree, and said, "Christmas!"

"Yes," Sunset said, his voice mournful.

Sean walked into the ballroom and moved along the wall, silently, like a shadow. He leaned against a column, watching the Hiru.

"The needled one explained it," Moonlight said. "It is a time for family."

"Do you have family?" Helen asked.

"No," Sunset said.

"Where is your father?"

"He died," Sunset said softly.

"My father died too," Helen told him. "Where is your mom?"

"She died too."

Helen bit her lip. "Do you have sisters?"

"I had two."

"Where are they?"

"They are dead."

Helen hesitated. "And brothers?"

"Also dead," Sunset told her. "We are what remains of our families, little one. We are the last. We have nothing."

Helen pondered him with that odd intensity I noticed about her before, stepped toward the Hiru, and held out the ornament to him. "Here."

"What is it?" Sunset asked.

"A gift for you." Helen stepped closer. "Take it."

He reeled. Servos whirled somewhere within the Hiru, desperately trying to deal with what he was feeling. "A gift?" the translation program choked out, turning emotion into a screech.

"Yes," Helen put the ornament into his palm. "Now you have something."

Moonlight made a choking noise.

The Hiru swayed. His legs quivered. Somehow he stayed upright. "It is very beautiful," he said, his voice suffused with emotion. "Thank you."

He turned and held it out to Moonlight. Their mechanical hands touched. They held it together for a long second and then she gently pushed it back into his palm.

"That one is yours, but there is more," Helen told him. "Come, I'll show you."

She took a running start and scrambled up the side of the bin to perch on its edge.

The Hiru followed her, holding the ornament gently in his fingers.

"He is a tari," Moonlight said quietly. "His family doctored the trees."

"What did your family do?" Any crumb of information was helpful.

"We studied the pathways between the stars." Her head swiveled toward me. "We came to tell you that you don't have to help us anymore. We put you in danger. We put everyone in danger. The next Archivarian is in a place from where it cannot be retrieved. You don't have to fight anymore."

"That isn't up to the two of you. You are my guests. I have duties and responsibilities and you can't cancel them. Where is the next Archivarian?"

"In the Sanctuary of Eno. Only a select few gain access to it. We are not welcome. You are not welcome. Those of the Sanctuary will not release the Archivarian to allow us to continue."

I looked at my Christmas decorations and sighed. The last thing I wanted to do was to leave now.

"She's right," Sean said.

Moonlight made a little hop. She mustn't have realized he was there.

"The Sanctuary is run by some sort of cult," he said. "They kill anyone who enters uninvited."

"They're not cultists," I told him. "They are prophets. They see into the future. They won't release the Archivarian, but it doesn't mean what you think it means."

"Inconceivable," Sean said. "What do you think it means?"

"It means Holy Seramina wishes to see me," I told him.

⚜ ⚜ ⚜

"You're not going alone," Sean said.

"Arland is injured. He put on a good show for his uncle, but he'll need all the help he can get."

"You're an attractive target," he said. "They take you out, they take out the inn's greatest defense. Kiran Mrak is scum but he isn't stupid. You need protection. Maud can't come with you, because she's the only other innkeeper we have. Arland is recovering. That leaves me. This is my judgment as a security operative."

I told him I would follow his lead. It was time to step up. "Okay."

He nodded.

"To get to Eno, we'll need a transgate." I rubbed my face.

"You can find one at Baha-char," Moonlight said. "It will cost you many money."

"Wilmos has one," Sean said.

"Would he let us use it?"

Sean just looked at me.

"Okay," I said. "Wilmos it is."

I pulled up a screen and thought of Maud. My sister appeared on it. She was in our kitchen. Caldenia and Lord Soren sat at the table next to her, sipping something out of steaming mugs.

"I have to go out," I told her.

"Where?"

"The Sanctuary of Eno."

Maud whistled.

"I know it's a lot to ask with Arland still recovering, but can you hold the inn for several hours?"

Lord Soren squared his massive shoulders and bared his fangs in a happy grin that would give most people a lifetime of nightmares.

"Yes," Maud said. "We'll hold it. Dina, you might want to look outside. At the driveway."

"Front window," I murmured and the screen changed into the image of the street. On it, a black and white cruiser sat parked at the mouth of the Avalon subdivision. Two figures in gray hoodies stood on the sidewalk. Officer Marais loomed over them.

Oh no.

"Enlarge."

The screen grew to take up half the wall.

"...in violation of Article 3, Subsections 1 through 3, 7, 12, and 16 of the Earth Treaty," Officer Marais said with methodical precision. "You're endangering Earth's neutral status by facilitating the discovery of outside civilizations and contributing to a breach of said Article which will result in a permanent ban of your species from this waypoint. Move along."

The two Draziri made no effort to move.

A truck drove by, followed by a Ford Explorer. Nobody paid the scene any mind. The presence of a black and white was like magic - everyone concentrated on driving under the speed limit and punctuating their stops at the stop signs.

Officer Marais sighed and pulled a metal baton out. It snapped open in his hand, individual parts moving and sliding to reveal an inner core of golden light. I almost did a double take. The two Draziri froze.

"Disperse," he ordered.

The hooded killers spun around and sped off down the sidewalk.

"Sean Evans?" I asked. "How did Officer Marais get his hands on a subatomic vaporizer?"

Sean smiled.

⚜ ⚜ ⚜

We slipped into the streets of Baha-char wrapped in two nondescript brown cloaks. The day had come to an end and a short Baha-char night was just around the corner. Lights ignited on the terraces, some golden, some white, others lavender and blue. Garlands of tiny lanterns traced the contours of the stalls and elaborate lamps marked the entrances to the shops, each lamp more odd than the last. The trading was still in full swing. Life at Baha-char never stopped.

We turned the corner and blended with the multicolored crocodile of shoppers crawling through the street.

"So. An errand, huh? You gave him a subatomic vaporizer."

"He's a cop. He enforces the law. He can't enforce it if he's hopelessly outgunned."

"You gave him a weapon that can turn any living creature into a cloud of gas. Where did you even get a subatomic vaporizer?"

"I gave it to him because he won't use it unless he absolutely has to."

Nice how he ignored the question. "What if he gets confused and accidentally vaporizes his wife? Or himself?"

"How do you know he has a wife?"

"She has a knitting blog. I follow it. Stop ducking my questions. They have two kids. What if they find the vaporizer?"

"Marais knows how to store his weapons properly. I keyed the vaporizer to his DNA and his thumb print. It's double locked. It's almost impossible to accidentally discharge it. It operates on a telepathic link via an implant, so he would have to actively imagine someone blowing up for it to discharge. If one of his cop buddies finds it, they'll think it's just a novelty nightstick. A child can pick it up and whack baseballs with it all day and there is zero chance of it discharging."

Sean put his hand on my elbow and sped up.

"Are we being followed?"

"Yes."

"Draziri?"

"Yes."

"Did you actually put an implant into Officer Marais?"

"Yes."

"Sean!"

"It's a two-millimeter organic implant. It's in his scalp."

"What if he has to undergo an MRI because he has a concussion?"

"It's organic. It won't show up. Stop being a negative Nancy."

We wove through the crowd.

"I'm not a negative Nancy."

"You're just mad because I didn't tell you about it."

"Yes. Yes, I am."

"Oh baby, I do all sorts of things I don't tell you about."

Ass. "Is that so?"

"Yep."

We were almost running now. Sean's eyes flashed amber. A dark line of tattoos crawled up his neck under the skin, shielding vital points.

"I have to maintain an air of mystery. Chicks dig a man of mystery."

"You don't say."

"You know what else chicks dig?"

"Subatomic vaporizers?"

"And werewolves. Chicks really dig werewolves."

"Poor you, having to smack all of those chicks off with a flyswatter just to walk down the street."

"You don't know the half of it." He glanced back, scanning the street. "I know it's very difficult, Dina, but try to resist me. We're being chased and all."

"Are there a lot of Draziri chasing us?"

He nodded.

"How many?"

"Too many. We need to run now."

We sprinted.

Ahead a single blue lantern illuminated the entrance to Wilmos' shop.

We burst through the door and stopped.

The shop was full of werewolves. Grizzled, dressed in leather and dark clothes, they lounged in the chairs, drinking. A table to one side held *baki,* a wargame played on a large board with armies of glittering rocks. We'd run headfirst into a mercenary convention.

Sean moved in front of me on liquid joints.

"Is that him?" someone asked.

"Yes," Wilmos said from the right, where he was leaning against the counter. "That's him."

The werewolves looked at Sean. Sean looked at the werewolves. Everyone seemed calm, like nothing important was happening.

"What do you need?" Wilmos asked.

"Transgate. I'm taking my girlfriend to the Sanctuary of Eno."

He said I was his girlfriend.

Sean's voice was measured and casual. "We need some alone time but it's almost impossible for us to get away."

"What's the galaxy coming to?" someone quipped from the back.

"Something on your tail?" Wilmos asked.

"Draziri," Sean said.

"How many?" someone else asked.

"Twenty-three," he said.

"ETA?" an older female werewolf asked.

"Forty seconds," Sean said.

A massive dark-skinned werewolf gave an exaggerated sigh. "If only we had some weapons..."

Wilmos hit a switch on the counter. The walls spun around, displaying hundreds of weapons in every shape and style imaginable. The werewolves bared their teeth.

"Well, look at that," the older female werewolf said. "So many lovely toys."

Wilmos nodded toward the back room. Sean took my hand and pulled me through the room to the back.

"Hey, alpha. Let's see it," the older werewolf called.

Sean paused to glance at her.

"They won't let you into Eno in your human skin anyway," someone else said. "Let's see it."

Sean let go of my fingers. His body tore in a split-second and a huge monstrosity spilled out, shaggy, dark, a terrifying hybrid of human and wolf that somehow looked natural and whole.

Everyone stopped. They stared at him, and I saw respect in their eyes. Respect and a shadow of something deeper, a strange kind of longing, as if they were looking for someone all their lives and suddenly found him.

The monster grabbed my hand into his clawed fingers and pulled me to the back room, where the metal arch of the transgate waited by the wall.

Chapter 13

We stood on a barren plateau of dark rock. Gray boulders jutted out here and there, shot through with blue veins. Above, a night sky spread, glowing with mother-of-pearl haze, as if someone had wrapped the upper layer of the atmosphere in a pearlescent veil. Beyond the haze, the night sky spread, the kind of sky that you would never forget, alive with the light of distant stars, where nebulae rioted and clashed.

I had been here five times. I never saw the light change. It was always like this: a diaphanous haze and the universe beyond, unreachable and cold. Too big. Too vast. If you looked at it too long, it filled you with despair.

In front of us a wall rose, hundreds of feet tall and sheer, made of the same rock as the plateau. A gate punctured it. It was wide open and from where we stood, we could see that it was a hundred feet deep. I once looked at a piece of chalk under a microscope during my brief time at college. I don't know what I had expected, but I saw globules made from circles of delicate lace, except instead of thread, the lace was crafted with calcite shells shed by millions of microorganisms. The gates looked like that. Layers and layers of elaborate pale khaki lattice in dizzying patterns, some places resembling spider web, others a beehive; yet others forming delicate mandalas. Holes punctured the gates here and there, only to reveal more patterns.

"I don't like this," werewolf Sean said.

"It's a place of serenity, but not happiness. You have to turn into the wolf form now. The prophets will let you in if you look like an animal. They view animals as part of nature."

"The gates look like jaws. With teeth."

"That's because they are. If you try to enter as you are, they will close on you midway through."

He studied me for a moment. "We can go back."

"No, we can't. The Archivarian is in there."

"Tell me about this Holy Seramina."

"I met her when Klaus and I were looking for my parents. Something about my power appeals to those of Eno. They feel a kinship with me and they let me enter. I talked to three of them, and Seramina was one of those three. She's a Kelah. Her people live in large cities they call nests. Each nest is led by the royal pair and a council of advisers. Each nest also has a holy one, a spiritual leader, to whom all look for guidance. The holy ones see into the future, but they foresee only disasters, so they can save their people from misfortune. Seramina foresaw a colossal creature that would devour the nest, but she wasn't believed. The threat was too strange. Nobody had ever encountered a creature like that. And Seramina was mating at the time, and mating interferes with the holy one's ability to see into the future. The creature arrived and devoured the nest, eating everyone within except her. She watched them all die. Now she's here, among others in the Sanctuary."

"That's a lovely story," Sean said. "We should go back."

"You can wait here, but I have to go in."

He shook his head. His body blurred and a massive wolf-like creature trotted over to me. I put my hand on his furry back - he was so large, I didn't have to bend down - and took the first step through the gate. It remained open.

We walked in silence, the wolf and I. Something watched us. I couldn't see it, but I felt the weight of its gaze. I didn't want to be here.

The gate ended. A garden spread before us, filled with wide trees, their bark black and smooth. Each tree grew apart from its fellows, its blue glowing leaves shimmering within a dense canopy. Bulbous orange fruit hung from the branches, glowing like paper lanterns. Long silky grass, a dull, gunmetal gray, filled the spaces between the trees, spreading into the distance. No birds sang. Nothing disturbed the silence except for an occasional breeze that rustled the branches. I fought an urge to hug myself. When Homer wrote about the bleak plains of Elysium where the ancient Greek heroes lived after death, he must've had this place in mind.

Sean bared his teeth.

"I know," I told him.

A swirl of tiny white lights drifted from the trees, lining up to light a path in the grass. We were being summoned. I followed it, Sean moving next to me on silent wolf paws. We walked deeper into the woods, but the trees didn't become denser. It remained the same: a tree, some fruit, and the grass, then another tree…

We came to a clearing. A stone wall blocked the way, leaning to the side slightly, its surface slicked with moss. The lights flared and vanished.

A creature stepped from the shadows behind the wall. She was eight feet tall and slender, with leathery skin the color of butter. She stood upright on two long legs. Her four arms, delicate and narrow, put you in mind of a praying mantis or a damselfly, but her eyes belonged to an owl: large disks of blood-red with round black pupils. A gossamer tunic obscured her body, made with diaphanous layers of pale glittering fabric.

"Dinaaa." Her voice lingered in the air, refusing to fade.

"Holy Seramina," I said. "You called and I came."

"You brought your wolf." Seramina said. The echoes of her voice hung above the grass.

"Yes."

"It's good," she said.

She knelt by Sean and looked into his eyes. "He doesn't like me."

"He doesn't like this place."

Seramina rose. "It is calm here. It is quiet. We have serenity. Peace. You will need peace soon, Dina."

"I ask for your wisdom," I said the ritual words. "I ask for your guidance. Oh holy one, tell me what danger lies in my future."

"You will be offered that which you cannot refuse," she whispered. "It will kill everything that is alive inside you."

Fear squirmed through me. "Is there any way to avoid it?"

"No. It will come to pass. You cannot stop it, because you cannot deny the nature of who you are." She knelt by Sean again, studying him. "When her soul dies, bring her here. She will never live again, but she can exist here, with us. She can be one of us, one of the broken. She will find peace here. That is my prophecy."

She stood up and walked away into the trees.

I turned and followed the lights out. The Archivarian sat cross-legged just inside the gates. Beyond them a portal opened. Not a gate defined by a technological arc, not a tunnel, but a ragged hole punched straight through reality. At our approach, the Archivarian rose and followed us without a word.

We walked through the tear. The universe died. There was empty blackness and then the back room of Wilmos' shop burst into existence around us. The air smelled of energy discharge and gunpowder. The sounds of many weapons firing at the same time pounded on my ears.

The wolf tore and Sean spilled out, wearing nothing except his subcutaneous armor.

He grabbed me and pulled me to him, his eyes wild. "I'm never taking you back there."

His lips closed on mine. The kiss seared me and for a moment I tasted Sean and the forest inside him.

The human Sean broke free. His body blurred. The massive lupine monster brandished a green knife and burst through the door of the back room into the gunfight.

※ ※ ※

I pressed myself behind the wall and peered out through the doorway. The front wall of Wilmos' shop was gone. A ragged gap, its edges smoking and sputtering, had torn through the storefront. The werewolves had taken cover behind the counters, firing short bursts at the street, where the Draziri, hidden behind a couple of overturned merchant stalls, returned fire.

Sean flashed through the room, a dark blur that cleared the gap and burst into the street.

Sean!

"Idiot!" the older female werewolf yelled.

The werewolves line erupted with shots, as they tried to provide cover fire.

Wilmos smiled.

Somehow Sean cleared the fifty yards separating him from the overturned stalls. He leapt over the left one. Shots rang out.

"Hold your fire," the grizzled dark-skinned werewolf barked.

Across the street someone screamed, a desperate terrified shriek, cut off in mid-note.

A clump of fighters in pale Draziri cloaks burst from between the two stalls, bouncing up and down the street like an out of control spin top.

"I hope you got a DNA sample before they cut him to pieces," a blond male werewolf said.

"Watch," Wilmos said.

The clump spun, the spaces between bodies opening for a moment, and within its depth Sean moved, lightning quick. He struck, his movements short, precise, yet fluid, cutting, stabbing, severing, fast, so fast. Each vicious swipe of his knife drew blood. He was cutting the Draziri like they were mannequins standing still. Dark stains splayed over his body, turning his fur nearly black, sliding left to shield the stomach, then up to his neck to ward off a strike. It must've been his subcutaneous armor.

"Will you look at that..." someone murmured.

The Draziri tried to cut him down, but he moved among them, slicing them out of existence and moving on before they had a chance to fall. A dancer on the edge of a blade.

There was a desperate need about the way he moved, as if he was trying to rend the fabric of reality to pieces. He loved me, I realized. He loved me so much, and the wounds of Nexus had barely scabbed over. The prophecy had pushed him over the edge. He had to vent or it would tear him apart from the inside out.

The werewolves stood up. They were watching him with those odd longing expressions on their faces. Something was taking place among them, something I didn't quite understand.

Wilmos pulled a translucent datapad off the wall. His fingers danced across it.

A loud, insistent beat tore from some hidden speakers, the melody wild and frightening. A male and female chorus joined the music, singing wordlessly, their voices blending into a single powerful howl. The hair on the back of my neck rose.

Wilmos' mercenaries bared their teeth. The dark-skinned werewolf raised his head and howled. To my left, the older female mercenary howled too. All around me eyes turned amber, gold, and green.

The terraced walls on both sides of the fight rained Draziri. The reinforcements had arrived.

The werewolves blurred, shifting into their wetwork shape, and charged. I caught a glimpse of Wilmos, his eyes on fire, his fangs bared, his face human one moment and grizzled monster the next. His wolflike pet snarled and ran into the melee next to him.

They fell onto the Draziri, while the battle hymn of a dead planet howled in triumph.

Eventually there were no Draziri left to kill. The injured survivors fled. Nobody chased them. It had felt like an eternity, but my phone told me only five minutes had passed since Sean and I entered the store again.

Sean walked over to me, hulking and soaked in blood. I put my arms around his wet furry shoulders and hugged him. He sighed quietly.

"Let's go home," I said.

"I will come too," Wilmos said.

"We'll hold the shop," the female mercenary said.

The four of us, Sean, Wilmos, the Archivarian, and I weaved through the streets of Baha-char. Nobody assaulted us. We reached the door to the inn, I opened it, and we slipped inside.

A stasis tank rose from the floor, swallowing the Archivarian and carrying him to join the rest of its parts and I stood alone in the hallway with two werewolves in wetwork shape, Wimos with a graying muzzle and Sean, a full head taller. A few months ago, I'd have been mildly alarmed. Now it was just business as usual. I sighed and snapped the void field in place. When I first started, it was like slipping on a jacket. Now it felt like a car settled on my chest. Maintaining it was draining me so much, I felt the weariness all the way in my bones.

It would end eventually and then I would rest.

I started moving. I needed to get them both into showers.

"Dina!" A screen popped open in the wall and slid, matching my pace. Maud's eyes were the size of saucers. "We have a problem."

Damn it, can I just catch a tiny break? Just one? Please for the love of all that is holy in this infinite universe. "What problem?"

"A big one," my sister hissed. "Get over here."

There were strangers in my inn. In my front room. Coming through my door.

I sped up. The werewolves followed me. We burst into the front room.

Two people stood in my front room, a man and a woman, both middle-aged. There was something vaguely familiar about their faces. My sister waited on the left with a carefully neutral expression on her face. Arland stood next to her, clearly torn between pulling his weapon out and trying to remain polite.

The man and the woman looked at me, and then at the two werewolves behind me.

The man squinted. "Wilmos?"

The woman peered at Wilmos, then her gaze slid to the left. Her voice was a whisper. "Sean?"

The hulking monster unhinged his jaws. "Mom? Dad? What are you doing here?"

Oh crap.

※ ※ ※

Sean's mother was slightly plump, short, and blond. If I bumped into her during a grocery run, I would've smiled, said excuse me, and never thought of it twice. She was looking at Wilmos now, and there was a wolf in her eyes, a frightening, mad she-wolf. When she opened her mouth, her voice froze the air in the room.

"Wilmos, how do you know our son and why does he smell like blood?"

"Uh..." Wilmos said.

Sean's father dropped his bags. He looked a lot like Sean, athletic, broad-shouldered, his brown hair cut short. His gaze pinned Wilmos like a dagger.

"Four months ago Agran called me and said that there was a war on Nexus and that you've been supplying the Merchants with a general every time one of theirs took a dive. He said that the last one they got was off the charts and rumor was that the guy was an alpha-strain werewolf. I dismissed it, because every time some phantom fighter shows up, our people take credit."

Wilmos took a careful step back.

"Did you send my son to Nexus?" Sean's father growled. Black ink crept up his neck.

Oh no. No, I didn't want to do this. This wouldn't make a good impression.

Wilmos opened his mouth.

"Corwin," Sean's mother said softly. "Sean's wearing Auroon Twelve."

"Wilmos?" Sean's father snarled.

The old werewolf sighed. "Yes."

"How dare you!" Rage shivered in Sean's mother's face. "We survived. We escaped. We built a life, so our child would never have to fight the way we did. And you, you obsessive asshole, you worm, you… you sent him to Nexus!"

Sean's father blurred. A massive dark werewolf spilled out and leapt at Wilmos. I let his feet leave the ground and then the inn snatched him out of the air in mid-leap. Strong. Really strong.

A second werewolf lunged across the floor. Sean stepped forward smoothly and caught her. She snarled.

"Mom," Sean said gently. "You're not making a good first impression."

"Sean William, let go of me this instant!"

"I can't do that."

She strained against him. The muscles on Sean's arms stood out.

"That girl over there," Sean said quietly. "That's my girl. If she's forced to bury you in the floor to hold you still, it will be awkward."

His mother bared her teeth and suddenly stopped. "Wait, what?"

"I think we should all calm down," I said. "Would anyone like some tea?"

"Yes," Arland said, finally breaking his silence. "Tea would be a very good idea."

It took about half an hour for the werewolves to shower, stop snarling, and settle in the dining room. Arland, my sister, and the rest of the guests wisely decided to give them some privacy. Apparently, Sean's parents didn't react well to Arland. Sean had told them a few things that happened when Arland and he first came to the inn, and when Maud failed to produce Sean, his father had suggested that maybe Arland should run out into the orchard to find him and have a cup of coffee first if it would help. Arland discreetly informed me that in the interests of avoiding a bloody incident, he would give them some breathing space. Even Caldenia stayed away, which was for the best, because I didn't want to explain Her Grace and her comments about the deliciousness of werewolves to Sean's parents.

I made myself scarce, too, and went to finish Christmas decorating. They had a lot to talk about, and it was better if I wasn't involved.

Seramina's prophecy sat in my brain like a cold rock. I just couldn't shake it. Was it about my parents? Was it about the inn? Was it… It didn't matter. Whatever it was, it would be coming for me soon.

An hour later I was finished with the tree and the ballroom. The inn was now a Christmas wonderland. Too bad we wouldn't get any snow. Sadly, I couldn't control the weather.

The decorating didn't make me feel any better.

My cell phone rang. I answered it.

"Dina," Mr. Rodriguez said. "Good afternoon."

"Hi. Has there been any word from the Assembly?"

"Have you heard anything?"

"No. I thought maybe you did."

"It's your inn," he said gently. "When the Assembly decides on the course of action, you will know."

My heart sank.

"How are you holding up?"

"I'm tired," I said. "I've been holding the void field and it's getting harder."

"How long?" Concern vibrated in his voice.

"Several days."

"Dina, it's meant to be a short-term solution. It's not wise to hold it for longer than forty-eight hours. You know this. You can't keep this up."

"It's fine," I told him. "I just don't sleep that well, that's all."

"Tony will drive over and stay with you."

"Mr. Rodriguez, it's okay, I really am okay. My sister is here helping me."

"It's my understanding that your sister hasn't been an active innkeeper for a very long time. Tony is strong and able. It is our duty as fellow innkeepers to help in cases like this. He will help you. Besides, your chef told my chef that you are having a Christmas feast. Tony will be overjoyed. That child loves food more than fish love water. It will be all right, Dina. It will be fine."

Fatigue crept in, sapping all my strength. I didn't have the energy to argue. "Okay. Thank you."

"You're welcome."

He hung up.

I didn't need Tony. What I needed was the end to this Draziri mess. Then I would rest and sleep. For now, I would have to settle for getting out of my own head. I went back to the war room, crawled into my chair, and opened the Draziri file.

The image of the Draziri god splayed on the large screen. A beautiful creature, with an elegant neck and a small round head, it reminded me of a swan, but instead of feathers, it had membranous wings, delicate and breathtaking. Translucent, they swirled around it like the fins of a Chinese fighting fish. Like the Draziri, it had no beak, just a small mouth. A pastel blue spread down its face, with two eyes glowing like sapphires. The color rolled down its neck, darkening gradually, turning turquoise, then deep indigo, before flaring into a shocking white and then carmine on the wings.

The Draziri had no wings. Maybe they lost them during their evolution. Maybe they never had them. But the colors on the wings of their god would put a nebula to shame. It was the same reason ancient Greeks carved the pinnacle of human perfection into marble whenever they wanted to portray a god. It was an ideal and an idea, the concept of soaring through clouds on wings the color of star fire, free of gravity. Free of the world.

I'd read that file forward and backward. There was nothing I could find that told me why the Draziri had declared their holy crusade against the Hiru. The Hiru's world had a unique signature, an exceedingly rare combination of elements in the atmosphere and soil, which ensured their survival. There was nothing quite like it, which explained why despite being an advanced race, they never spread through the galaxy. They didn't present any threat. They were homeworld-bound. So why kill them? What could they possibly have done to warrant extermination?

Perhaps, it was just the principle of the thing. The Draziri lived in a theocracy, led by a God-King. Their priesthood acted as their lawmakers. Maybe when they had ventured into space, the priests became worried that their society wouldn't survive the collision with other civilizations and they would be overthrown. On Earth, when Pope Urban II wanted to consolidate his power, he started the first Crusade. Maybe the Draziri priests decided that a holy crusade would be a great way to stay in power. They looked around, saw their closest neighbors, and said, "These beings are ugly and they smell awful. They would make a handy enemy. Let's kill them in the name of our exquisite god."

"Beautiful," Sean's mother said behind me.

"The Draziri are beautiful people. It makes sense that they would have a beautiful god." It's too bad that their religion was so ugly.

"Thank you for saving my son," she said.

"No thanks are needed. I love him." That was the first time I had said it out loud. Saying it to her was easier than saying it to Sean.

"He loves you too."

"I know."

"My name is Gabriele."

I got up. "It's nice to meet you."

She stepped forward and hugged me. I hugged her back.

"I'm sorry about restraining your husband."

"You're an innkeeper," she said. "He doesn't hold a grudge. We're both sorry. He hadn't told us. About Nexus, or Wilmos, or any of that. He usually comes home for Christmas. I called him, and he sounded so distant. I felt that I was losing my child."

"It's my fault," I told her. "Nexus and Wilmos. I took him to Baha-char. I knew the moment he walked into Wilmos' shop, I'd lose him at least for a while. The universe is so big and loud."

She shook her head. "It's not you. It's in his blood. He wanted to test himself. My son has the blood of Auul in his veins. He was always restless. Earth just wasn't enough. I used to worry that I would lose him to some dumb war thousands of miles away. I had no idea I almost lost him to Nexus. I would tear Wilmos' head off, if Sean would let me. It was the perfect trap for him. He wouldn't have broken free if it wasn't for you."

"He would have eventually."

She shook her head again.

Lord Soren walked to the doorway and cleared his throat.

"Please excuse me."

She nodded.

I got up and walked over to Lord Soren.

"May I speak with you privately?" he asked.

What now? "Of course." I led him across the hallway, built a simple room, and opened a door in the wall to it. "Please."

We walked inside and I sealed the door behind us.

"How can I help you, Lord Soren?"

"I understand that your father was considered a hero by other innkeepers."

What? "Yes."

"Why?"

"My father was a guest in one of the inns, when the innkeeper and her children were attacked. He defended her. That's very unusual for a guest."

"Did he succeed?"

"In part. He bought them enough time to get out. The children survived, but the innkeeper died of her injuries. My father became trapped within the inn until my mother freed him centuries later."

Lord Soren nodded gravely. Clearly, this was terribly important.

"Do you know of your family on your father's side?"

"No."

"What about on your mother's?"

"Some. We don't keep the same meticulous records your people do." I waved my hand. A small screen opened in the wall and the picture of my grandparents appeared. They were sitting together, my grandfather in his Navy uniform and my grandmother in a lovely blue dress. When I left for college, I'd taken a lot of photographs with me. They were all I had left now. "This is my grandfather and grandmother. He was a fireman. My grandmother was a school teacher."

Lord Soren squinted. "Is that a uniform?"

"My grandfather served in the Navy during the Vietnam war."

"Are those ribbons indicative of meritorious service?"

"Yes."

"So your family understands martial traditions."

"Of course. My grandfather served in the Navy. His father was in the Marines during World War II."

"And your ancestors are long-lived?"

This was just getting weirder and weirder. "For humans, yes."

"Any genetic abnormalities?"

"Not that I know of. Lord Soren, what is this about?"

"Due diligence." Lord Soren nodded, deadly serious.

Something brushed against the void field. I turned. "Excuse me. Window, front."

A lone slender figure stood at the end of the driveway, holding a small white flag in one hand. She was wearing a backpack backwards, so it hung on her stomach. Thick, dark red belts secured it to her, wrapping tight around her slender waist and hips. On the backpack in large letters someone had written in black marker *Feel Me*. The letters were crooked and unsure, drawn rather than written.

I lowered the void field for a moment.

Something waited for me in that backpack, something warm and alive, but fragile, something that I had to nurture and take care of. It glowed like a star and it was scared. The wave of fear rolled over me. Cold sweat broke out on my forehead. I wanted to hug it to me and keep it safe. I would do anything to keep it safe.

It couldn't possibly be... No. My pulse shot up. Blood pounded through my head. No.

The inn creaked around me, stretching, reaching for the backpack, and the entirety of Gertrude Hunt focused on it. I'd never felt it want something so badly.

I slammed the void field back in place, ran to the door, burst into the hallway, and almost collided with Maud.

My sister grabbed my shoulders. "What is it? What's happening?"

"I have to go out there!"

"Why?"

I could barely speak the words. "The Draziri have an inn seed."

Chapter 14

I walked to the end of the driveway. Maud had fought with me. She wanted to go down herself, but I won. It was my inn, after all. She was watching my every move from the inside. If anything happened to me, she would keep the guests safe.

The seed was a living thing, a little baby Gertrude Hunt just waiting to be planted. The inn seeds weren't just rare; they were almost nonexistent. Sometimes we got two in a century; sometimes only one. I was a little girl the last time an inn produced a seed. It wasn't ours, but we celebrated for three days. All the chores had been canceled. We had a big dinner and my parents were so happy. A new seed was a celebration of life. It meant a new inn to be nurtured and grown. How the hell had the Draziri even found one?

I made it to the end of the driveway. The lone Draziri eyed me. She was young, probably still a teenager, with intense blue eyes, a cream-colored face, and a long mane of pale feathery hair that darkened to deep lavender at the ends. The same design of silvery threads as the one Kiran Mrak wore decorated her forehead, which meant they were related. She seemed delicate and fragile and I had the distinct impression that if I punched her, her bones would shatter.

She opened her backpack and leaned toward me. The seed lay inside, a light brown sphere about the size of a basketball lit from within by magic, cradled in a net woven of wet greenish strands. The back of the backpack was missing and the green strands burrowed straight into the Draziri's flesh.

Bile shot into my throat. I forced it back down. The seed was caught in a Gardener's web. A parasitic organism, it bound the seed and the Draziri girl, feeding on the Draziri. Now the fear made sense. The seed should've sprouted by now. It had exhausted all the nutrients within its shell and grown too large. The web had coated the shell and kept it in place, turning the protective pericarp, the outer portion of the seed, from a shelter into a prison. Trapped and unable to grow, the sprout of the new inn was slowly dying.

If I severed the seed from the girl, the web would likely pull the shell apart. The moment the seed was free, it would root and sprout. But it couldn't sprout here. This place was already occupied by Gertrude Hunt. Its roots stretched far; its branches spread through the fabric of time and space, altering it forever, and the area of that distortion was much wider than the town of Red Deer. Two inns couldn't coexist in such proximity. They had to be hundreds of miles apart.

If I let the seed sprout here, it would die. Gertrude Hunt would feel its birth and its death, and if my inn realized its presence was responsible for the death of a sprout... It would never recover. I wasn't even sure it would survive. I wasn't sure I would survive.

How do I fix this?

A Gardener's web could be removed, given time and proper feeding. I had done it before, when I was the gardener in my parents' inn. I could do it again, given the opportunity, and the Assembly would be able to do it even faster.

I had to get the seed away from this girl and I had to do it with the Gardener's web intact.

"What do you want?" I asked.

The girl held up a small screen. Mrak's face appeared, his white hair framing it.

"Do I need to explain why you can't harm her?"

"No."

"Good. She is wearing a medical unit. If you are thinking of pulling her inside and erecting that barrier, the moment the barrier cuts off my signal, the medical unit will release a hormone which will detach the web, killing it. Have I made myself clear?"

No void field, or the seed would sprout. Got it. He understood way too much about how the inns worked. Someone was supplying him with this knowledge. None of the innkeepers on Earth would help him. It had to be someone from the outside. Perhaps the same someone who sent a corrupted innkeeper after us on Baha-char. Once I resolved this mess, I would have to bring all this before the Assembly.

"What do you want?" I repeated.

"I'd like us to talk, like civilized people. Let's have a conversation, so we can come to a reasonable compromise. Please let her inside."

It was a trap. It had to be a trap of some sort.

If I let her in, I would be leaving the inn wide open. But if I said no, and the seed sprouted, even if it was five or ten miles away, it would perish. I had to preserve the seed. It was an inn, a life.

I was at my strongest on the inn's grounds. I had to get this seed away from them. Nothing else mattered.

"Decide, innkeeper. This child is terrified. It's a heavy burden for someone so young."

She did look terrified. She was actually trembling. "Don't try anything," I said. "I'm not in the mood to be kind."

"I give you my word. I simply want to converse."

I dropped the void field and watched her step onto the inn's grounds.

The seed reached for me. It was weak and pitiful, and it needed me. My magic churned. Gertrude Hunt sensed the seed and was forging a connection. I grit my teeth. *No.*

The inn tried again.

No. I erected a barrier and poured my power into it.

If it connected to the seed and the unthinkable happened, Gertrude Hunt would perish. I had to shield it from the connection. But I couldn't shield myself. The seed was reaching out and the compulsion to comfort it was overwhelming.

The Draziri pondered me. There was no way I was letting her inside the inn itself. It would be almost impossible to keep Gertrude Hunt from bonding with the seed.

"Come with me."

I led her to the backyard and waved my hand. A patio slid across the grass, carrying with it two chairs. Her eyes widened. I sat in one chair and pointed at the other. The young Draziri sat, cradling the backpack.

We were in the middle of the yard, far enough from the house.

Gertrude Hunt leaned against my barrier. The seed stirred. Weak, hesitant tendrils of its magic slipped out, seeking the connection.

I'm here. Don't be frightened.

The seed touched my magic and calmed. Just like a baby with a lullaby.

"The Hiru are an abomination," Mrak said from the screen. "They are revolting. They are everything that is wrong with life. Life is beautiful, like this girl in front of you. Like the seed she carries. The Hiru must die."

"Do you actually believe that?"

"It is enough that my people believe it."

"You've destroyed their planet," I said. "There are only a handful of them left, those who were out in space away from their home world. They are not fighting you. They just want to live in peace."

"So does my mother," Mrak said. "She wants to die in peace, knowing that she and all of her clansmen will find paradise."

"Where did you even get it?" I asked. "The seeds are very rare."

"I have connections."

"Was the dark creature that stalked me at Baha-char also yours?"

He took a fraction of a second to answer. "Yes."

He lied. He hadn't known about it. I saw the surprise in his eyes.

"Did your connection become proactive and send it to chase me?"

"As I said, the creature was mine."

"That creature is a living darkness. It is death and corruption. Whoever made it has dark designs and they won't let you live."

"You're a remarkable creature," Mrak said. "Here I am, offering you that which you hold most dear, and you're trying to get information out of me. You would make such an interesting pet."

"In your dreams."

He leaned on his elbow. "What would you let me do to you for the sake of this seed?"

And this conversation went sideways.

"You don't have to answer. You would do anything. You would debase yourself, but you don't have to. Give me the Hiru."

"There is something wrong with you," I said.

"The time for insults has passed."

"I don't mean it as an insult. There is truly something deeply wrong with you. How is it that you never learned to be a person?"

He stared at me. "I am a person."

"You flew across countless light-years to a neutral, peaceful planet to kill two creatures that haven't harmed you in any way. For that purpose, you threw away dozens of your people, and now you sit here and make nasty comments about torturing me as if it somehow fixes everything and makes you victorious. What kind of a person does that?"

He looked taken aback.

"Staying here isn't going to bring your dead to life. Killing defenseless beings who just want to be left alone won't win you any absolution. Think about it. What kind of religion mandates that? Why would anyone want to be part of it?"

"Give me the Hiru."

"Your mother is dying and that's tragic. But all things die. If you had a choice to save a child or an elderly person, you would save the child, wouldn't you? Children are the future. They are what carries us forward as people. You're throwing away your young fighters. Look at this girl you sent in here. She's terrified. You're the head of her clan. She trusts you and obeys you. Shouldn't she get something in return?"

"She knows her duty," he said.

"Let's say you kill the Hiru. Where would that leave you? You still will have lost the future of your clan. It will be generations before Flock Wraith will recover. It's your responsibility as a leader to keep your people safe and take care of them so they can prosper."

Doubt crept into his eyes. "What's a few short years in this world compared with an eternity in paradise?"

"You don't believe that. If you believed in paradise, you wouldn't have killed an onizeri. What if there is no paradise, Kiran? What if it's a lie?"

He knew. I saw it in his face. He knew their paradise was a lie, but he had come too far. "You are a heretic," he said, his voice calm. "An unbeliever."

I lost him. For a tiny moment, I got through, but now I lost him. "So are you. Why don't you just leave? Leave and live your life the way you want to. You're free to make your own choices."

"No," he said. "Freedom is an illusion. We are bound by restraints on every turn. Family, clan, religion, morals, duties; all those are restraints. For someone on the crossroads of worlds, you're naive."

"If you can't have your freedom, then what's the point of all this?"

"Give me the Hiru. Nobody has to know. We can do this in a way that leaves you blameless. I promise their deaths will be swift and painless."

I wanted the seed. It called to me. I'd been playing for time, but I thought of nothing. No brilliant plans. No elaborate ruses. I felt so helpless.

"There is nothing to think about, innkeeper," Mrak's voice floated from the screen, soft, seductive. "The seed for two lives which are lost anyway. They have no planet. Their technology is dying. They can barely keep themselves alive. Death is a mercy. Make your decision."

"Please give him what he wants," the Draziri girl whispered. "Please."

It felt like I was being ripped in two. The seed was right there, crying, begging to be saved. I could feel the two Hiru inside the inn. They were in the war room, probably watching all of this on the big screen. They stood very close. I wondered if they were holding hands.

"Please."

I heard my own voice. "The safety of the guests is my highest priority. You will find no sacrifices here."

"It is a pity, innkeeper."

The Draziri girl cried out. Web shot out from her, clutching at me, binding me and the Draziri into one. She tore at her clothes. A bumpy metal object was attached to her chest. A door-maker, a small concentrated explosive used to breach the hulls of spaceships. A faint whine cut at my ears - the bomb was armed. Detonation was imminent. I had seconds.

There was no time to get free.

I flung open a door to the farthest connection the inn had. The orange wastes of the planet Kolinda rolled in front of me under a menacing purple sky. The door opened onto a cliff.

I lunged through the gateway, taking the Draziri girl with me, and slammed the door shut behind me. We fell off the cliff and plummeted.

This was it.

I hit the ground. The impact shook my bones. The backpack with the seed landed on top of me, the web stretching, binding it to me.

I blinked, trying to regain my vision. We'd fallen onto a narrow shelf along the cliff. The chasm yawned below us.

"Help!" The Draziri screamed.

Where was she?

The green web stretched from me over the edge of the shelf.

I crawled to the edge. She hung below me. The web binding us was so thin. Gray splotches spread through it. It was dying.

I reached for her. My fingers came a foot short. If I pulled her up, I could rip the bomb out.

"Help me!"

The web snapped. She plunged down and vanished in a fiery explosion.

Behind me the seed sprouted. I sat up. A glowing shoot with two leaves stretched from the remnants of the shell. Tears rolled down my face. It was too weak.

Its magic cried out, seeking a connection. It was scared and alone. I cradled it in my arms, bonding with it, sheltering it, reassuring it that it wasn't alone. It was an inn and I was an innkeeper.

The tiny sprout wound around me.

It found peace.

And then it died.

⚜ ⚜ ⚜

There was no light. Only darkness. Neither cold nor warm. It just was. It surrounded me and I had no will to break through it. There was no point.

"Dina!"

Sean picked me up. He kissed me. He hugged me to him, but I felt nothing. The darkness was too thick.

He was calling my name, but I had no will to respond. He looked terrified. I didn't care.

"Dina, talk to me. Please talk to me. Please."

I felt nothing.

"Say something. Anything." He squeezed me to him again. "I've got you. It's okay. I've got you."

We jumped up then, and he carried me up the cliff and through the rip in reality back into Gertrude Hunt.

The inn's magic reached for me. I watched it try. It battered against the wall around me and fell back. There was no point. My little inn had died. I held it and then it died. I felt it die and I died with it. Everything was over.

My sister cried and hugged me. My niece cried, too. Orro brought me cookies. Caldenia said something, so did Arland. None of it mattered. There was only me and darkness.

⚜ ⚜ ⚜

"Fix her!"

My sister again. Some other innkeeper. Tony. His name was Tony. He looked like he saw a walking dead. That's what I was. The walking dead. Breathing. Listening. Watching. But nothing alive remained inside.

"I can't. She bonded with the seed. She couldn't let it die alone, so she connected. Her inn is dead."

"Her inn is right here," Sean snarled.

"The inns are organisms of immense power," Tony said. "They root through different dimensions, they distort reality, and they create matter out of basic components. People forget how powerful they are, because they obey the innkeepers, but their magic is immense. An inn requires an innkeeper. It can't exist without one, so it forms a symbiotic relationship with a human and then it directs all of its magic and power into strengthening that bond. The innkeepers exist in the microcosm of the inn for years, exposed to their magic and influenced by it. They undergo a change we don't fully understand, because the inns exist on planes and levels we can't comprehend. We do know that preserving and bonding with the inn becomes the very essence of the innkeeper's being."

He paused, looking them over.

"If the inn had sprouted anywhere within a ten-mile radius of Gertrude Hunt, Gertrude Hunt's magic would smother it. This inn would've felt the death of the seed and it would likely die itself and kill all of us within. She couldn't let that happen. She took the seed out of Gertrude Hunt's area, but once she'd done that, Dina was outside of her power zone.

"At the moment of its birth, the inn has only one objective: to find an innkeeper. That little inn on the cliff was weak and fragile, because it had been trapped in its shell too long, but its power was still greater than any of us could imagine. Dina couldn't let it die. It's the same instinct that would make a human dive into ice-cold water to save a drowning baby. The inn was terrified. It sought a bond, and Dina comforted it and bonded with it, because that's who she is. She couldn't let it suffer and die alone. The bond, as short as it was, was real. When the seed died, in that moment, on that cliff, she lived through the death of her inn. Innkeepers do not usually survive this. She knew it would happen. She sacrificed herself for our sake, for Gertrude Hunt, and for that little seed."

"But she's still alive," Sean said.

"Technically, yes."

"What do we do? There has to be something that can be done?" Arland demanded.

"There is nothing that can be done," Tony said. "I'm so sorry."

Above us, far within the inn, the corruption awoke within its prison. It smashed against the inside of the plastic tube, coated it, burrowed into it, and made a tiny crack. Gertrude Hunt screamed, but nobody heard it.

⚜ ⚜ ⚜

We lay in bed. He held me. His arm was around me. I couldn't feel it.

"This is the part when you tell me, 'Sean Evans, get out of my bed. You're not invited.'"

I said nothing.

"I will stay here with you," he said. "I'm not leaving. I'm not taking you to the Sanctuary."

The darkness thickened, trying to block his voice, but I still heard him.

"I love you. I won't let anyone hurt you. I won't let anyone take you away. You're not alone. Just come back to me, love. Come home."

⚜ ⚜ ⚜

Time had no meaning in darkness. The darkness was jealous. It pushed everything else out. Joy, anger, sadness. Life.

They brought me to the heart of the inn. I lay in the soft darkness, while around me the inn wept tears glowing with magic.

Maud was crying again. "Why isn't she bonding?"

"Because her inn already died," Tony said. "Right now you are the only thing keeping Gertrude Hunt from going dormant."

"But she was only bonded to it for a minute."

"It doesn't matter. She's beyond our reach. If Gertrude Hunt can't reach her, nobody can."

"I wish she never saw that fucking seed."

"She couldn't help it. No innkeeper would be able to resist a sprouting seed. It is who we are. We tend to the inns. That she saved Gertrude Hunt is a miracle."

Maud growled like a vampire. "I hate this. Fucking Draziri. Fucking Assembly. She asked you for help and you did nothing. Nothing!"

"I'm so sorry," Tony said.

The corruption slithered out of its prison, and dripped out, one molecule at a time.

Sean picked me up off the floor and carried me away.

⚜ ⚜ ⚜

"It's a simple plan," Sean said. "Simple plans are best. Tomorrow is New Year's eve. Lots of noise, lots of fireworks. The perfect cover for us. We bring all the remaining parts of the Archivarius together at the same time. Arland and Lord Soren will get one, Tony, Wing and Wilmos will take the second, my parents volunteered to bring in the third, and I will get the fourth."

"Alone?" Arland frowned.

"I'm taking Marais with me. We bring them all here at the same time and complete the Archivarius. The Hiru are on board. They know where all of the parts of the Archivarius are now."

"The Draziri will pull out all the stops," Tony said. "We'll have a full-out assault."

The corruption slithered closer.

"Let them," my sister said. "Let them all come. I can't wait."

"It will be too much," Gabriele said.

"Yes," Corwin agreed.

"I'll talk to our people," Wilmos said.

"Will we still have Christmas?" Helen asked. She was sitting on the floor by my chair, hugging my leg.

It was suddenly quiet.

"Yes," Sean said. "We will still have Christmas. It's important to her. We will kill every Draziri, until there is nothing left but blood and bodies. And then we'll have Christmas."

The darkness around me grew a little thinner.

⚜ ⚜ ⚜

He never left me. He talked to me when I lay in bed with an IV and he lay beside me and held me. He talked to me when he carried me to the bathtub. He sat with me when the inn moved me downstairs during the day. He held me when Maud cried because it hurt her to look at me.

He told me he loved me. He joked. He read books to me. He held my hand.

The world hurt. There was no pain in the darkness. I wanted to stay wrapped in it, but he refused to let me go, always there, connecting me to the outside like a lifeline.

I was lying on the blanket under the Christmas tree. Above me the lights twinkled in the branches. So many lights. Olasard, the Ripper of Souls, lay next to me, making muffins on my blanket.

"How long will you keep this up?" Sean's father asked.

"As long as it takes," Sean said next to me.

"It's been four days. Maybe…"

Sean looked at him.

"Okay," Corwin said. "Forget I said anything."

He left. The Hiru came and Sean took me to their room to float in their pool and look at the sky I made for them.

"We are so sorry we've brought this on you," Sunset said.

"You should've given us up," Moonlight whispered.

"That's not who she is," Sean said.

"We will always remember," Sunset said. "Always. Every one of us. If we survive, our children and our children's children will always remember."

"The Archivarius arrives tomorrow. Will your people be ready?" Sean asked.

"Yes," the Hiru said at the same time.

"Are you ready to go upstairs, love?" Sean asked me.

"Does she ever answer?"

"She will answer when the time comes."

"What if she won't?" Moonlight whispered.

"She will," Sean said. "She's a fighter. I have faith in her."

He picked me up out of the water. The darkness grew a little thinner.

His hands were warm.

⚜ ⚜ ⚜

"This is getting old, my dear," Caldenia said. "You and I have an agreement. I expect you to honor it. Get up, now. You don't want to spend your life like a lump of wood. The scaled creature made a totem of you and he keeps putting different medicines on it and dancing around it. It is getting annoying. Get up, dear. We do not let our enemies win. We claw their hearts out and devour them. You have work to do."

❧ ❧ ❧

"Mango ice cream. It is the best thing I've ever made. Will you please eat, small human? Please. Please eat, small human. Please."

The mango ice cream melted on my tongue and a distant echo of its taste slipped through the darkness to me.

❧ ❧ ❧

Flowers bloomed around me. I sat submerged to my neck in the tub inside the vigil room. A chorus of four voices prayed over me, urgently, forcefully, trying to pour their vitality into their words. My sister's voice blended with Arland's and Soren's, Helen's high notes underscoring the important parts.

Magic moved among them. A trace of it slipped through to me. I curled around it. It felt so warm.

The prayer ended. Maud wiped the tears from her face.

Arland stepped close to her and put his arms around her.

"Will she ever wake up?" Helen asked.

"I don't know, my flower," Maud said.

"Do not despair," Lord Soren said. "This is her home. My grandfather had all but given up on life. He lay down to die and refused to take food. Yet when House Wrir came to break down the doors, my grandfather rose from his deathbed and led our House to victory. Lived another three years after that until his heart finally gave out. You should've seen the funeral. Now that was—"

Arland looked at him.

"Right," Lord Soren said. "The point is, the Draziri will come for the Hiru. They will bring every fighter they have left. They will attack this inn. Your sister will never let that stand."

Tony walked into the room. "We're about to head out."

"We're also on our way," Arland said.

"Good luck, everyone," Tony said.

The corruption slipped through the inn, gathering above them, inching ever closer. They didn't feel it, but I did. There was something similar about the corruption and I. We existed in a similar place, shrouded in darkness, disconnected but aware. I watched it slither its way through Gertrude Hunt. It was moving through my inn.

My inn.

Tony stepped out. The corruption halted, waiting.

Arland turned and knelt on one knee before my sister. "Wish me a happy journey, my lady."

Lord Soren turned to Helen. "Come with me, little one."

"Why?"

"They need to talk."

They walked away. My sister and Arland were alone.

"Don't do that," Maud said.

"Do what?"

"Don't kneel in front of me. My husband used to kneel before me. It didn't keep us from being exiled. It didn't keep him from throwing away everything that we built together. I hate this vampire custom. It doesn't mean anything."

"I'm not your husband. It means something to me."

"Please don't." Maud sat on the root and covered her face with her hands. All her strength disappeared. I did that, I realized. A painful twinge gripped me and faded slowly.

"I will return," Arland said. "I would be by your side if you'll have me. I would have you if you allowed it."

She dropped her hands and looked at him. "Arland, I've been married and widowed. I have a child. She isn't your child…"

"Right now she's no man's child. She should have a father, who will teach her and treasure her. I will do that for her. I love you, my lady."

"Don't tell me that."

"And I would love Helen as my own."

"Don't."

Arland rose. His face was grim. "I'm no poet. I'm a soldier. So, I'll just tell you the way it is, as clumsy as it sounds. When I first saw you, it was like being thrown from a shuttle before it touched the ground. I fell and when I landed, I felt it in every cell of my body. You disturbed me. You took away my inner peace. You left me drifting. I wanted you right there. Then, as I learned more of you, I wanted you even more. You want me too. I've seen it in your eyes. You taught me the meaning of loneliness, because when I don't see you, I feel alone. You may reject me, you may deny yourself, and if you choose to not accept me, I will abide by your decision. But know that there will never be another one like you for me and one like me for you. We both waited years so we could meet."

He left the room.

Maud looked at me. "Say something, Dina. Please say something to me."

I wanted to tell her that she was afraid of being loved, because her husband betrayed her. That she shouldn't throw away this chance at being happy. But there was too much darkness between us.

⚜ ⚜ ⚜

"I will be back," Sean whispered into my ear.

A fire built inside me. A pressure that strained at the empty darkness. It hurt. The pain suffused me. I tried to escape but there was nowhere to run.

He brushed a kiss on my lips.

The pressure broke and I screamed. *Don't go! Don't leave me! I'll be all alone.*

"I'll be back soon." He let go of me and went for the door.

He didn't hear me. How could he not have heard me?

He stepped through the door.

Wait. Don't go.

It closed behind him.

Wait.

Wait for me.

⚜ ⚜ ⚜

I sat on the porch, watching late afternoon slowly bleed into the evening. Maud had put my favorite robe on me, the blue one that our mother made. I looked like an innkeeper even if I didn't feel like one. My sister had decided I should have the front row seat, so I would "snap out of it." Beast lay on my lap. At first, when Sean had brought me in, she hid as if she didn't recognize me and it scared her. Then, little by little, Sean coaxed her into my bed on the third night. Now she sat with me, sad and occasionally trembling.

Caldenia sat in a chair on my left. My sister stood on my right, holding my broom in one hand, and her sword in the other. In front of us the backyard stretched with the clearing behind it. Helen sat by my feet, holding her knives. The Hiru waited in the kitchen, out of sight.

Sean would come back. He promised to come back.

The corruption waited above me. It had flowed through the inn, filling the spaces between the branches. Gertrude Hunt had tried to stop it, but it escaped the inn's grasp. Everyone forgot about it, but it was there, biding its time. It wanted something.

Maud, feel it. You will feel it if you just reach out.

Helen hugged herself by my feet and looked up, at the inn.

Maud!

"It's about time," Maud said.

"Are you up to this, my dear?" Caldenia inquired.

"I'll have to be. What about you? Is all that plotting and talking you've been doing ever going to pay off?"

"All in good time." Her Grace smiled, showing sharp teeth.

Maud looked at me. "Dina, please help me."

I was trying. I was honestly trying.

A rift opened in the middle of the lawn. The werewolves from Wilmos' shop walked out of it dragging a big metal box. They waved at us, planted the box on the ground, and the brown-skinned werewolf armed it through the panel on the side. The box unfolded like a flower, sending out a complex antenna-like structure made of shiny small cubes and triangles, each rotating in different directions.

"What is that?" Caldenia asked.

"That's the projectile dampener," Maud said. "It disrupts the path of kinetic projectiles and negates energy and heat weapon targeting. Very short range and outrageously expensive. We're renting it for the next two hours. It cost us an arm and a leg. If... when Dina wakes up, she'll kill me. I wiped out her budget. But if the Draziri want a piece of us, they'll have to fight for it in my sword's range."

She bared her teeth.

"Were do you want us?" the female mercenary asked.

"Here is fine."

They took up positions around the porch.

"Damn the Assembly," Maud muttered. "We could've used help."

"For all the reverence Dina shows for the ad-hal, I have yet to see a demonstration of their power," Caldenia said.

"Trust me, you don't want to witness that, Your Grace."

I struggled to rise. My sister was preparing to repel an assault on my inn and all I could do was watch and scream into the silence wrapped around me. I had to move. Even if I could just twitch a finger.

A pale light ignited in the middle of the field, elongating into a glowing filament, like the wire of a lit lightbulb. The fabric of space ripped and Sean's parents burst through the gap, two massive werewolves dripping blood, one dark, the other lighter. The darker one carried an Archivarian slung across his back.

They ran across the lawn. The rapid staccato of high tech rifles chased them. None of the projectiles landed.

Move. Stand up. Do something! I had to do something. I dug my fingers into the darkness and strained to rip it.

Sean's father shook the Archivarian off at Maud's feet. My sister focused. Gertrude Hunt responded sluggishly, swallowing the Archivarian.

The two Hiru walked out onto the porch, slow, ponderous, and stopped next to me.

"What are you doing here?" Maud said. "We agreed you would stay safe in your room."

"We're the reason for this fight," Sunset said.

"Let them see us," Moonlight said. "We are not afraid."

"We will give them a target, so the Archivarians can be retrieved," Sunset said.

Maud sighed and called out, "We're about to get rushed."

The werewolves pulled out their knives.

One moment the woods were empty. The next, Draziri leapt from the branches in unison, like a flock of predatory birds taking flight. So many... They landed and sprinted across the open ground on their elegant legs, like weightless dancers, Mrak in the lead brandishing a wicked silver blade.

I tore at the darkness. It held.

Caldenia studied her nails.

A tall Draziri, his hair the same white as Mrak's, buried his knife in Mrak's back. Mrak cried out. The other Draziri pulled the knife free and flipped it in his fingers, falling into a fighting stance. Mrak spun around. "You dare!"

"You are unfit to lead!" the other Draziri snarled. "You're weak. You failed again and again. We're bankrupt, hunted, and dying, all because of you! It's time for a new power to head this flock."

They clashed, their blades meeting together with a sharp clang. The invading Draziri broke, splitting. Two-thirds tore into each other. The rest kept running toward us.

"Divide and conquer." Caldenia smiled. "I do so love that phrase."

The werewolves rushed into the approaching Draziri.

A brilliant red light pulsed above the grass and spat Arland and Lord Soren onto the lawn, an Archivarian between them, smack in the middle of the clashing Draziri. Their armor smoked. Arland roared, baring his fangs. Helen roared back from the porch, her daggers held wide by her side.

The Draziri fell on them. The two vampires cut a path to the porch, working side by side, their movements practiced and sure. Skulls crunched, blood weapons whined, attackers screamed and died.

Blood splashed on Arland's face. He snarled as a Draziri fighter buried her blade in his armor.

Maud dropped the broom and ran across the grass, slicing through the Draziri as if they were butter. Helen dashed after her mother. Beast leapt off my lap and bounded after her.

I pounded on the darkness. *What are you doing? Use the inn!*

"Right now would be an excellent time to step in, my dear," Caldenia murmured.

I ripped at the darkness with all my will.

A female Draziri blocked Helen's path, brandishing a large knife. Beast lunged at her. Her jaws with four rows of teeth locked on the Draziri's ankle. She howled as her bones crunched. Helen jumped onto the female Draziri and slit her throat.

Someone do something, damn it!

Orro ran out of the kitchen, huge, dark, all his spikes erect, thundered over the grass, snatched Helen up by her clothes and dragged her back to the inn.

"No!" Helen kicked her feet. "No!"

He opened his mouth and roared into her face. "Stop!"

She froze, shocked. He dropped her by my feet. "Protect Dina!"

Helen snapped her teeth at him, but stayed put. Beast trotted back to her and flopped on the porch, her mouth dripping blood.

My sister finally remembered that she had powers. The second Archivarian slid into the lawn, spinning like a corkscrew. Maud fought next to Arland, cutting and slicing, her blade so fast, it looked liquid. He was grinning, his face splattered with blood.

A hole opened, and Sean walked out, dragging the third Archivarian out. Marais followed, his clothes covered in soot, his hair wet with slime, his eyes far away, lost in a thousand-yard stare.

Sean.

He came back to me. He came back! The darkness in front of me shrank, thinning. I wanted to stand up so badly, everything hurt.

Marais grabbed the Archivarian by the arm and muscled him toward the porch. Sean followed, quiet and precise, cutting down opponents before they had a chance to notice.

Magic whispered through the lawn, slipping through the emptiness around me. A circular doorway opened silently and Tony, Wing, and Wilmos walked out, bringing the last Archivarian with them. Tony wore a plain brown robe. He carried a broom in his hand.

Wilmos picked up the Archivarian and ran across the grass toward me, Wing scampering after him.

Tony stayed where he was. He looked around him, his nice face oddly serious, and pulled his hood over his head. His broom darkened to black, flowing into a staff, its tip glowing with red. His robe turned the color of blood, spreading like the mantle of some king, moving seemingly on its own, and beneath that robe and inside of his hood was darkness, cold and empty darkness, the kind that lived between the stars.

I reeled back, shocked. Of all the people, I would've never guessed Tony.

The ad-hal reached out and touched Mrak's shoulder. An unearthly voice emanated from inside his hood. It was the kind of voice that stopped your heart.

"Be still."

Mrak stopped moving. His opponent stumbled back, his face horrified.

The corruption awoke and surged forward.

Magic drowned the clearing, ancient and cold. I felt it even through the darkness. The tiny hairs on the back of my neck rose. It flowed among the Draziri and held them in place.

Behind me the corruption dripped from the ceiling to pool on the kitchen floor.

Arland spun around toward the creature that used to be Tony, focusing on the new threat.

"No!" Maud threw her weight on Arland's sword arm.

"You have been judged by the Assembly," the ad-hal said. **"You have been found guilty."**

Mrak just stood there, a lost expression on his face. Nobody moved.

The corruption spilled from the doorway, rising like a foul cloud, emanating its putrid magic. I tore at the darkness. *It's coming. Look! Look, damn you!*

Someone screamed.

The foul cloud slithered toward the ad-hal across the grass. It wasn't hiding anymore. He raised his hand. His magic rose to block it, but the corruption flowed through it and kept going. I felt him pour his power out and the corruption swallowed it and wanted more.

It would infect him. It had wanted him all along.

Sean stepped between the corruption and the ad-hal and raised his knife. His eyes were pure amber.

The corruption would kill him. I would lose him and that couldn't happen. I've lost too much already. I lost my father, my mother, and my brother. Even my sister was lost for a time. I'd lost the seed of an inn.

Nobody would take Sean from me. I loved him, he loved me, and he was mine.

No. Not today. Not ever.

Not in *my inn*.

A towering wave of rage swept through me and burst through the darkness. The wall blocking me tore apart, its shreds melting into nothing. The power of Gertrude Hunt hit me all at once, the inn suddenly triumphant, giddy that it finally felt me and we connected. The broom landed in my hand. I was on my feet, and I didn't know when I got up or how. I raised the broom and poured all the inn's power and all my magic through it.

The broom glowed with bright blue. A wall of pure magic surged up in front of the corrupt cloud, a brilliant blue barrier separating it from Sean. The cloud smashed into it and recoiled.

Sean smiled at me.

A phantom wind stirred my hair and the hem of my robe - the inn's magic surging into me. The corruption shrank, hugging the ground, but there was no place to go. This was my inn. The soil, the trees, the air, all of it was mine. I wrapped the barrier around it, locking it into a sphere of magic.

It jerked up, trying to flee, but I took it into the fist of my power and squeezed, harder and harder. I squeezed it because I loved Sean, because I loved my sister and my niece, because the Draziri made me live through the death of a tiny inn, because the Hiru had sacrificed everything, and because nobody and nothing would ever get away with threatening one of mine, guest or family, on the grounds of Gertrude Hunt.

The corruption thickened under the pressure of my power, collapsing in on itself.

It hurt, but I barely noticed. I squeezed. I wanted to feel it die.

The sphere pulsed with white, contracting.

The corruption within burst into blue flame. It howled as it burned, its shriek cutting across my ears, sharp and painful.

Nobody said a word.

It burned until it disappeared into nothing.

I looked at the Draziri. My robe turned black. My face must've been terrible, because even trapped within the ad-hal's power, they tried to shrink back. He didn't let them move.

"The inn is yours, innkeeper," the ad-hal said.

"You may begin," I told Sunset.

The Hiru walked off the porch, each step a slow torturous motion. The Draziri and werewolves moved apart, giving them a wide passage, some on their own, others pushed by the ad-hal. The Hiru's mournful voice echoed through the backyard, fading into the encroaching twilight.

"You destroyed our home. You murdered our families. You almost killed our people. You sentenced us to eternal exile, because no other planet could sustain us. Today you will learn why."

The nine tubes rose from the ground, each holding a member of the Archivarius within it. The plastic tubes sank back into the earth. The nine beings stepped toward each other, their arms raised in front of them, forming a ring. Their fingers touched and melted, blending together. Flesh flowed like water, turning into a whirlpool and uniting into a whole.

I bent physics to keep the backyard hidden from the street. The residents of the Avalon subdivision were not ready for this.

A giant knelt on one knee on the lawn. He was human in shape, but his head had no features, except for a dark slash of a mouth. Werewolf fur sheathed him, each strand long and translucent. Stars and galaxies slid over the fur and his feathered Draziri mane, as if the depth of the infinite Cosmos reflected in him. A Ku crest rose on its head. Quillonian spikes burst from his shoulders. He opened his mouth, and within the darkness, two white vampire fangs gleamed. A pair of wings opened behind him, glittering with stars. The Archivarius had mirrored us the way his body mirrored the night sky.

YOU ASKED A QUESTION, a soft voice said. I HAVE THE ANSWER.

Sunset raised his head. "The innkeeper must have her payment first."

The cosmic being turned toward me. ASK YOUR QUESTION, INNKEEPER.

I would only get one question. Where, no, what, no... "How can I find my parents?"

The Archivarius paused. Silence reigned. My heart was beating too loud. Please let them be alive.

SEBASTIEN NORTH.

Who was Sebastien North? What did that mean?

The Archivarius pivoted back to the two Hiru. It was enormous and the Hiru seemed so small next to it, two ants talking to a colossus.

Around the perimeter of the backyard, ovoid portals opened, and behind each the other Hiru stood, waiting, dozens of them. We were looking at the entire species.

"Please," Moonlight said. "Where is our new home?"

A cold rush of magic tore through me in a second. A vast portal opened behind the Archivarius, as tall as he was. Beyond the portal a beautiful landscape spread under a breathtaking sky. Glowing flowers, indigo and turquoise, bloomed in the shadow of majestic burgundy trees, their long weeping willow branches shimmering with pale green leaves. Strange blossoms grew in the meadow of silver-green grass that rolled gently to a sea, the water so transparent that every vibrant burst of color underneath was crystal clear. Long emerald-green seaweed rose among the cream-colored coral in the shallows studded with underwater plants. Bright fish darted beneath the waves, and above it all, a glorious sky reigned, awash with gentle pinks, blues, and greens.

Sunset took a step forward, walking to the portal as if he were asleep. Five feet away from it he stopped. Metal clanged. His body fell apart. Pieces of machinery tumbled down, gears fell into the grass, lubricant gushed, and a luminous creature flew up from the remnants of machinery and hovered above the grass. It took my breath away.

The Draziri screamed as their god spread the delicate veils of its wings, burning with all the colors of an aurora borealis. A tiny glowing strand stretched from its graceful neck. On it Helen's Chrismas ornament dangled.

Sunset spun once and slipped through the portal, hovering just beyond its boundary, waiting.

All around us, the Hiru stepped through the portals and entered the clearing, forming a long slow line. Moonlight, the first in line, walked up to the pile of Sunset's space suit. Her metal shell fell apart and she surged up, her wings silver, black, and white, glowing like the moonlight that inspired her name. She slipped into the portal.

They came one by one, shedding their space suits, luminescent and heartbreaking in their beauty. I realized I was crying. Somehow Sean made it next to me and he held my hand. Arland put Helen on his shoulders. She watched the

Hiru assume their true form and there were stars reflected in her eyes.

Some Draziri had collapsed. Others stared, shocked, their expressions lost. Mrak wept. Tears rolled down his cheeks.

On and on the Hiru went, until the last of them paused by the portal. He was old. Burns and scars dented his space suit. He turned to me. A once-mournful voice issued forth, tuning triumphant. "Thank you, innkeeper. We will never forget."

His space suit joined the pile on the grass and a creature the color of sun fire slipped through the portal to its new world.

"Wait..." Mrak whispered to the Hiru.

The portal collapsed.

The Archivarius rose. Its wings beat once. It flew into the night sky and vanished.

Mrak's shoulders shook. He stared at the spot where the portal had been a moment ago.

"You and I have unfinished business," the ad-hal said. A gateway opened behind him, a swirling pool of darkness.

Mrak turned, like a chastised child, and together they walked into it, the ad-hal's fingers still on Mrak's shoulder.

"Where is he taking him?" Helen asked.

"Nowhere good," Maud told her.

⚜ ⚜ ⚜

The Draziri left, shell-shocked and lost, held together by the Draziri who had attacked Mrak. He turned out to be Mrak's cousin. Before Her Grace retired to make herself presentable for dinner, she informed me that she'd had several conversations with him and in her opinion he wasn't a complete idiot. I allowed them to go. The fight was over and I had never wanted this fight to happen in the first place.

The werewolves stayed. They were tired from fighting and hungry, and they wanted to talk to Sean and his parents. They crowded into my front room, loud and growly. I glanced into the front room, hoping for a glimpse of Sean, but I could barely see him, crowded by the mercenaries. It would have to wait. That was okay. We had time now.

Orro cornered me in the kitchen. "The holiday dinner was supposed to include eleven beings. Now that number is doubled!"

Aha. "Does this mean you're unequal to the task?"

Orro puffed out, looming over me. "I am a Red Cleaver chef!"

I nodded.

"I require two hours."

He spun on his foot.

"Thank you for the ice cream," I told his back. "It was the best thing I have ever tasted."

His spikes rose, shivering, and he sped off into the kitchen.

I raided Gertrude Hunt's very old wine cellar, picked several bottles at random and let the inn take them to the Grand Ballroom. The tables I used during the peace summit were still stored underneath, and I pulled two of them out, arranged the bottles there, and asked Orro to serve some bread and cheese when he got a moment.

Once he was done, I headed to the front room. "Gertrude Hunt welcomes you to our Christmas feast. We'll serve refreshments now. Follow me, please."

The werewolves fell on the wine, bread and cheese like hungry beasts. Sean brushed by me and squeezed my hand, before they dragged him with them. Wing and Marais joined them. Wing was beside himself at being treated like a hero. Marais was slowly thawing. I'd provided him with a room and a shower to freshen up, and he looked much better now, without slime covering his hair. A couple of glasses of wine and he would be able to go home to his family. He still had that owlish, not-quite-right look in his eyes, but all in all he was handling this rather well. I'd have to thank him later when things died down.

Maud stopped next to me. "Hey."

"Hey yourself."

"I'm going to pop over to Baha-char for a few minutes," she said.

"Why?"

"To buy presents." She grinned.

"Do you have money?"

"No, but I have a ton of the Draziri weapons to trade."

Ooo. "What am I getting?"

"I'm not going to tell you and I won't let you snoop either. You were always a terrible sneak, Dina."

"That's a lie. I'm an excellent sneak."

She hugged me, hard. "I'm so glad you're okay."

"I'm getting there." I was feeling kind of wobbly, and if I stopped doing things and talking, the echo of the little inn's death tore at me, but I would survive. I had a lot going for me. I had people who loved me. I mattered to them and when I fell, they caught me and put me back on my feet.

"Are you going to leave with Arland?" I asked.

"I haven't decided."

"Do you love him?"

She sighed, her face pained. "I'm trying to figure that out. He's going to ask me to marry him tonight."

"How do you know?"

"I spied on his conversation with his uncle." Maud sighed. "I'm so stupid, Dina. I stood there like some love-stricken teenager and when he told his uncle he wanted to marry me, I felt... I felt things."

"Are you going to accept?"

"No. I barely know him. I'm a mother. It's not just my life at stake here. It's also Helen's. Besides, you would be left alone again."

"I'm not alone." I tilted my head and glanced at Sean. He must've felt me looking, because he turned and looked back at me. "I have someone, too."

"It's like that then?" Maud smiled.

"It is. If you like Arland, I'm sure he will find a way to let you figure out if you love him."

"This crest—" she touched the crest on her armor "—gives me the right to enter the territory of House Krahr as a free agent. If I turn him down and he invites me to come with him anyway, I may do that."

"You will always have a place here. And it's not like you'll be far away. Arland pops over any time he pleases. If you give Arland a chance, he will take care of you and of her. You need someone to take care of you, Maud, whether you want to admit it or not."

"I want more than that." She bit her lip.

"I know." I had no questions as to why Arland threw himself at that flower. He did it for me and Sean and all the others, but most of all he did it for Maud and Helen.

Maud stared away. I glanced in the direction of her gaze and saw Arland. He was looking back at her, and his eyes were warm and wistful. He never looked at me like that.

"It's going to be difficult," she said. "I'll be an outcast again. I bring no money, no alliances, and no benefits.

Only me and Helen. It would be Melizard all over again, with having to prove my worth. His family never did accept me. It would take a lot of work to win over another vampire House."

"You will roll over them like a bulldozer. By the end of this year, they will be eating out of your hand. Lord Soren is already making plans."

"What? How do you know?"

I thought of telling her about our conversation on the subject of family military service and genetic abnormalities and decided it would be more fun to leave it a surprise. "Just a feeling I have."

She squinted at me. "What are you not telling me?"

"You should go and try it," I told her. "Gertrude Hunt isn't going anywhere. You can always come back. Once I figure out where to start looking for Mom and Dad, I'll reach out."

Her face turned grim. "Sebastien North."

"Yes."

"Do you know who that it? What that is?"

I shook my head. "No. But I will find out."

"Maybe I'll track down Klaus," Maud said. "He should be told."

"Good luck," I told her. "I've tried. If you find him, punch him for me for disappearing."

She hugged me. "I'm off to shop."

"Go!" I told her. "Time is short. Tomorrow is Christmas Day."

She grinned and took off.

A presence entered the inn. A moment later Tony stumbled into the ballroom, his face worried. "Did I miss dinner?"

"No." I grinned at him. "An ad-hal, huh?"

He shrugged. "Sorry about that. You know how it is. We can do nothing without a directive from the Assembly. I would've come sooner if they'd let me."

"Thank you for showing up."

He sighed. "The Hiru attained space flight long before the Draziri. The best we can determine is that the Hiru, in their exploration of the galaxy, stopped on the Draziri planet. Somehow the early Draziri saw them in their natural form. Concerned that they were unduly influencing an emerging civilization, the Hiru had withdrawn from the Draziri planet. They are pacifists by nature and 99.999% of the planets in our galaxy are lethal to them. They couldn't survive without their sits, which they hate, so there was no reason for them to stay. But the Draziri had never forgotten them. Over the years, the Draziri developed their religion right along the lines of the typical religions of early emerging civilizations: a creator god who sits in judgment and sends people to heaven or hell and they modeled this god on the image of the Hiru, a beautiful being who was a legend. The religion grew into a planetwide theocracy."

"Then the Draziri developed space flight and stumbled on the Hiru," I guessed. "Which proved that their religion was a lie. There was no creator god. There was just an alien species."

"If that fact became public, their entire social structure would have collapsed," Tony said.

"And the Draziri priests wanted to keep their power."

"That too. They destroyed the planet before the general population could learn that the Hiru existed and then declared a holy extermination of all Hiru. At first, the Hiru didn't understand why, then when they did finally figure it out, some committed suicide to show the Draziri who they were killing. When they succeeded, the temple guards would destroy everyone who witnessed the Hiru's true form and then blame the deaths on the Hiru. People do horrible things in the name of keeping things just the way they are."

"Where did you take Mrak?"

"There is a little planet in the corner of the galaxy," he said. "Its sun is dying."

"I thought suns took billions of years to die."

"Not this one. It and the entire star system are slowly transitioning out of our dimension. The change has killed most of the biosphere and now the planet has entered the in-between stage, where it exists neither in our space-time nor in the new one. It's a ghost of a planet. I left him there. He no longer needs to eat or to breathe. He can't kill himself. All he can do is exist alone among the barren rocks on the shore of an empty ocean, watching the sun grow dimmer every day."

I shivered. "How long..."

"Not too long. Maybe another twenty years or so. A mind can only take so much."

"What then? Will he just sit in the dark forever?"

"No. I will get him before the sun dies and end it. If he goes mad before then, I'll end it sooner. Imprisoning a mad creature would be cruel."

And that's why seeing an ad-hal was never a good thing. I had to change the subject.

"Do you know anything about Sebastien North?"

He shook his head. "But I do know something about Michael."

The memory of Michael's corruption-ravaged body flickered before me. "What?"

"He was an ad-hal," Tony said quietly.

I took a step back. "Michael?"

He nodded.

"The corruption took him, killed him, and when it's fled his body, it focused on you."

"I know," he said. "Michael isn't the only ad-hal who disappeared in the past several years. Something is hunting us."

The ad-hal served as our protectors. Without them, we would be defenseless.

"This is for you." Tony handed me a small card. "I was going to wait until tomorrow, but since we started talking, let's do this now."

I opened the card. Three words in black ink. *You are summoned.* The Assembly was summoning me. My actions would be scrutinized. I would have to answer hard questions.

"Don't worry," Tony said. "The rallying point is at my father's inn. I'll be there to testify. You can bring Sean, too. You'll need to introduce him to the Assembly."

"Um…"

"You know you have to do it sooner or later," Tony said. "It will be okay, Dina. You're not the only innkeeper to survive the death of an inn, but you joined a very exclusive club today. We'll talk more in the morning."

"Yes, in the morning." I forced a smile. "Today is Christmas Eve for us. I served some very old wine."

Tony rubbed his hands. "Then I'm going to help myself."

"You totally should."

He hurried to the tables.

I turned and walked away. I had two hours before the feast. I needed to take a shower and think.

❧ ❧ ❧

I had just finished my shower when my magic told me Sean was coming up the stairs. I wrapped a towel around myself and opened the door. He was holding a bottle of wine and a tray with some delicious-looking pastries.

He saw me, in a towel, with wet hair on my shoulders. A wolf looked at me from inside his eyes, a wild wolf, hungry, feral, scarred, and every inch mine.

"Hi," he said.

"Hi."

"Can I come in?"

"Yes."

He stepped inside and set the platter and wine on the bed. A quick dash of anticipation mixed with anxiety rushed through me.

"I put my house on the market," he said.

"When?"

"Three days ago."

I was still lost three days ago. He sold his house while I was still out, not knowing if I would come back.

"I have an offer. I accepted it."

"What if I hadn't come out of it?"

"I knew you would," he said.

"How?"

"You don't give up. And..." He raised his hand and touched my cheek. His rough fingers grazed my skin, caressing. The breath caught in my throat. "You wouldn't leave me."

We stood next to each other. Suddenly I was very aware that I was wearing nothing but a towel. The wolf was looking at me through Sean's eyes, so close, if I reached out, I could touch him.

"This is the part where I should probably do that thing Arland does," Sean said quietly. "Where he announces that he isn't a poet, but a humble awkward soldier, and then composes a sonnet on the spot."

"But you come from the planet of warrior poets. It shouldn't be a challenge for you."

"So I'm told." His amber eyes shone, catching the light of the lamp. His gaze snagged on my lips. He was thinking of kissing me. The realization sent electric shivers through me. I bit my lip. His breathing quickened.

"About that sonnet," he said.

"Yes?" It felt like my whole life depended on what he would say next.

"I love you."

That was all I wanted to hear. I didn't even know until now how much I wanted him to say these words to me. He'd said it before, when I was under, but it was different then. Now it was everything.

"I'll never leave you," Sean said. "If you want to stay an innkeeper, I will be one with you. If you want to do something else, I will do that with you. Whatever comes next, I'll be there, because I want you more than anything I've ever wanted. That's it. That's all I've got."

I took a step and closed the distance between us. His strong arms closed around me. He bent down and kissed me. He'd kissed me before, but those times paled before this one. He didn't just touch his lips to mine. He drank me in, seducing, compelling, conquering my mouth. It was an full-out assault, all or nothing. He was offering himself to me and he wanted to know if I was his. I melted into it. I had never wanted anything more.

His hands tightened around me. A shiver ran down my back. His fingers slipped into my hair. I put my arms around him, trying to get closer to the heat of his body. He made a low masculine noise that drove me wild. I fumbled with his T-shirt. He pulled it off, revealing a hard chest corded with muscle, and then he caught me into his arms. My towel slid to my hips. My cold nipples pressed against the heated wall of his chest. I felt so hot, like I was on fire. His hands roamed my body. He made that noise again, that hungry male noise that made me lose my head.

My towel slipped to the floor. He let me go for a breath and then he was naked. We stared at each other in the moonlight slipping through the small window of my bedroom. The silver light slid over him, playing on his broad shoulders, his powerful chest, the ridges of his stomach, and lower, where his hard length made it obvious just how much he wanted me. His eyes glowed like liquid amber, heated from within by intense need. There was no softness in him, just dangerous, lethal strength. He was my wolf, half in the light, half in the shadow. I loved him so much.

I opened my arms. He came to me and swept me off my feet. I kissed his lips, his stubbled jaw, his neck... He dipped his head and nuzzled my neck, his tongue hitting just the right sensitive spot. The burst of pleasure dragged a moan out of me. We landed on the bed. The platter with wine went flying and the inn caught the bottle before it shattered. His mouth slid lower... His tongue grazed my nipple, painting heat over it, the sensation so intense, my whole body tightened in response. An insistent, impatient ache built between my legs. I wanted him to make love to me. The anticipation was killing me. I sank my fingers into his hair and wrapped my legs around him.

"Do you need me to slow down?" he asked, his voice a ragged growl.

"No, I need you to speed up."

"I can do that."

He looked into my eyes and thrust inside me, into the liquid heat. Pleasure swept through me and I cried out, thrusting my hips up to better meet him. He kissed me and thrust again, straight into the center of my ache, turning it into bliss. He moved inside me in a smooth rhythm, each thrust stoking the fire until I couldn't stand it anymore. My body shuddered and waves of pure pleasure swept through me. His body tensed, clenched, and I felt him empty himself inside me with a hoarse groan.

⚜ ⚜ ⚜

I lay my head on Sean's chest and rubbed my foot along his leg. He was smiling in the moonlight. It felt so good to lay next to him. Like nothing in the galaxy could hurt me. So that's what happiness felt like. I'd almost forgotten.

"Should we get dressed?" he asked, sliding his thumb along my shoulder.

"It's our inn. They'll wait for us."

They would wait, but others wouldn't. I raised my head and looked at him.

"What is it?"

"The Assembly summoned us."

"Are we in trouble?" He grinned at me.

"Yes."

He pulled me closer, his arm around me.

"I don't want tomorrow to come," I whispered.

"Why?"

"All the problems will come back tomorrow. The Assembly, the ad-hal, the corruption..." I was so happy right now. I wanted it to last a little longer. Just a few more hours.

"You won't have to deal with your problems alone," he said.

I hugged him tighter.

"We'll look for your parents together," he said.

I kissed him. A light sparked in his eyes. He pulled me on top of him. His mouth closed on mine—

Beast scratched at the door.

"Aunt Dina!" Helen called. "Mom said..."

I collapsed on Sean's chest, face down.

"...to tell you that you should wrap around your private time because Orro's head will explode."

A quick patter of feet announced her running down the hallway. Beast whined at the door, putting extra sadness into her crying just in case I failed to notice it.

Sean patted my back.

I rolled off him. He kissed me again and we got up off the bed.

"One thing," Sean said. "I'm not wearing a robe."

"My father wore a robe. All innkeepers wear robes."

"Not going to happen."

"Sean Evans, don't you start with me."

He bared his teeth at me and bit the air, clicking them.

Tonight was the feast, tomorrow would bring problems, but it didn't matter. Sean was right.

No matter what the universe threw at me, I wouldn't have to face it alone.

The Ripper of Souls jumped on the empty bed and regarded us with his witchy cat eyes. Great. We'd had an audience all along. It was probably absurd to be scandalized by a cat, but I was still embarrassed.

Sean frowned. "Where did you get this cat?"

"He was trapped in a glass box in a PetSmart."

"Did you notice he has a collar?"

"I noticed. I thought about taking it off, but he seemed to like it, so I let him have it. This is my first time owning a cat and I don't want to damage our relationship."

Sean grabbed Olasard and held him up.

"I don't think you should manhandle him like that. I've just gotten to the point where he comes when I call him and lets me pet him."

"Lights," Sean said.

The electric lamps snapped on. Gertrude Hunt had obeyed him. Huh.

He held the cat out to me, parting the fur with his fingers to expose the collar. A small metal plaque embedded in the blue nylon caught the light. Two letters, engraved in elaborate cursive, shone on the plaque.

S.N.

Sebastien North?

THE END

The Undying King Excerpt

His people once called him Cededa the Fair, then Cededa the Butcher, and then they called him no more.

Imogen couldn't help but gawk. Her attacker was the effigy's living twin, only far more painful to behold. The terrible beauty, trapped in marble, was no artist trick but a true reflection of the man standing before her, his malevolence increased tenfold by a piercing gaze that pinned her in place.

Flaxen hair fell past wide shoulders and framed a stern, pallid face. Clad in an indigo tunic and trousers overlaid by a tarnished chainmail hauberk, pauldrons and vambraces, he was heavily armed and armored. A short sword and hand axe were strapped at his narrow waist, and he casually cradled the hook-back glaive whose blade had lightly kissed her neck. Judging by the manner of his dress, he'd not come to talk but to do battle.

Imogen wanted to bow beneath the weight of his scrutiny. He may not be *her* king, but he was still a king if his resemblance to the effigy was anything to judge by. And not only the king but one possessing the title of The Butcher.

Her back teeth clacked together in a rising chatter as he shifted his stance, and those peculiar eyes narrowed even more. So light a blue they almost faded into the surrounding whites, his eyes reminded her of the blind Blessed—those whose milky gaze saw into the past and the future but never what was before them. Unlike them, Cededa took in the here and now with a predatory gaze. He was as strange and beautifully eerie as the city he guarded. And just as extraordinary. If he'd been human once, he wasn't now.

⚜ ⚜ ⚜

Click to continue reading THE UNDYING KING.

⚜ ⚜ ⚜

About Grace Draven

Grace Draven is the award-winning and *USA Today* bestselling author of RADIANCE and MASTER OF CROWS. In a last ditch effort to avoid doing laundry, she took up writing fantasy romance and hasn't looked back since. Laundry has now been assigned to the kids.

Grace currently lives in Texas with her husband, three kids and a big doofus dog that fancies himself her muse.

Please visit her website gracedraven.com to discover more.

Discover More By Ilona Andrews

Kate Daniels Series
Magic Bites
Magic Burns
Magic Strikes
Magic Mourns
Magic Bleeds
Magic Dreams
Magic Slays
Gunmetal Magic
Magic Gifts
Magic Rises
Magic Breaks
Magic Steals
Magic Shifts
Magic Stars
Magic Binds
Small Magics (compilation of short stories)

Hidden Legacy Series
The Hidden Legacy Series is being rereleased in 2017.)
Burn for Me (rerelease 3/17)
White Hot (rerelease 6/17)
Wildfire (coming 8/17)

The Edge Series
On the Edge
Bayou Moon
Fate's Edge
Steel's Edge

The Innkeeper Series
Clean Sweep
Sweep in Peace
One Fell Sweep

About the Author

"Ilona Andrews" is the pseudonym for a husband-and-wife writing team. Ilona is a native-born Russian and Gordon is a former communications sergeant in the U.S. Army. Contrary to popular belief, Gordon was never an intelligence officer with a license to kill, and Ilona was never the mysterious Russian spy who seduced him. They met in college, in English Composition 101, where Ilona got a better grade. (Gordon is still sore about that.)

Gordon and Ilona currently reside in Texas with their two children and many dogs and cats.

They have co-authored several *New York Times* and *USA Today* bestselling series. They are currently working on urban fantasy of Kate Daniels, the paranormal romance of Hidden Legacy, and their independently published series, Innkeeper Chronicles.

You can read more about their work on their website: http://www.ilona-andrews.com

Printed in Great Britain
by Amazon